Prologue

Kent, England
August 1795

IT ALL STARTED WITH A DARE. Samuel Brooks sat beneath Lord Bolton's desk with his knees pulled into his chest, arms tightly wrapped around them, desperately attempting to make himself as small as possible. If Lord Bolton had discovered him five minutes earlier, perhaps the man wouldn't have been upset with him. But now that Lord and Lady Bolton had launched into a vicious row, Samuel desperately wanted to disappear. He pulled his knees in tighter, holding his breath as he listened.

"How could you?" Lady Bolton asked. She spoke loudly; her husband had closed the study door behind them when they first entered so no one else would hear—no one else except Samuel, out of sight underneath the man's desk. "And with Sarah Rowe, too! She is practically a child, barely out of her leading strings. Have you no respect for me at all?"

Although he couldn't see him, Samuel was sure Lord Bolton was glaring at his wife the same way his father often looked at his mother. "How could I?" Lord Bolton echoed incredulously. He laughed slightly. "An easy question, Charlotte, with an obvious answer. At least Miss Rowe lets me into her bed!"

Lady Bolton groaned. Samuel thought he heard her sit down on the settee across from the desk. He inhaled sharply, moving his hand to cover his mouth. There was a small space between the floor and the desk. If Lady Bolton's eyes drifted downward, she might notice him there if she looked closely enough. He tried to stay very still.

"When are you in Linfield long enough to take advantage of such pleasures?" Lady Bolton asked. "I never let you in my bed because you are never here. You spend half your year in London!"

Lord Bolton gave an annoyed huff. "What would you have me do? Relinquish my seat in the House of Lords?"

"Of course not!" Lady Bolton exclaimed. "But you could at least give up your mistress and make an effort to spend more time here with your wife and children. You may not realize it, but when you are not here, they do miss you. *I* miss you."

There was a brief silence. "Do not bring Charles and Rosamund into this."

"How can I not?" Lady Bolton sniffed. "They are your children, and you would rather gad about with an eighteen-year-old chit than spend time with either of them—or *me* for that matter."

Samuel frowned. Lady Bolton sounded like she was on the verge of tears. He wanted to crawl out from under the desk and comfort her—like he often did for his mother in uncomfortable and tense moments like these—but he feared Lord Bolton's reaction if he showed himself now.

2

LADY AUGUST

BECKY MICHAELS

Mildred Press

For my mom

If Lord Bolton were anything like his father, Samuel would be in for an awful thrashing after overhearing all *that*. His parents had similar conversations back home at Dover Street—loud and angry, with the same wild accusations over and over again, often ending with his mother crying. Unfortunately, Dover Street was much smaller than Linfield Hall, and there were fewer places to hide and not listen, so Samuel received many thrashings as a result, for he was always overhearing things he shouldn't. He shuddered only thinking about the beatings. He often wished he could stay at Linfield long after the summer, but now he wasn't so sure.

The conversation between Lord and Lady Bolton continued for a few more minutes until Lord Bolton finally left the room, slamming the door behind him. Lady Bolton began to sob soon afterward, and Samuel debated what to do next. He eventually resolved to stay hidden beneath the desk where it was safe until she left.

Samuel remained quiet for a few moments, listening to Lady Bolton cry, feeling as though he might soon start crying himself when he felt a tickle in his throat. He tried to silence himself, but it was too late. He let out a small cough. Lady Bolton stopped crying right away.

"W-who is there?" she asked, her voice cracking as she spoke.

Samuel shut his eyes tightly, fearing what would come next. He heard Lady Bolton stand up, her emerald-colored skirts swishing around her feet as she walked from the settee to behind the desk. She pulled out Lord Bolton's leather chair, then bent at the waist, meeting Samuel's frightful gaze with one of her own.

"Samuel?" she asked, her look softening.

To Samuel's relief, she sounded more confused than angry. He offered her a sheepish glance, then crawled out from underneath the desk. Standing in front of Lady Bolton, he

slowly looked up at her, an obvious timidness to his movement. Her eyes were as red from crying as her hair, and she
held a crumpled silk handkerchief in her hand. She tilted her
head to the side, mouth slightly open as she regarded the
young boy in front of her.

"Have you been here all this time?" she asked.

Samuel looked down again, then slowly nodded.

"Oh, Samuel," she breathed. She knelt, making herself the
same height as him before reaching out to hold him gently by
his shoulders. "What were you doing in Lord Bolton's study
in the first place?"

Although Samuel was eight and didn't like to cry—his
father explicitly forbade it—he found himself bursting into
tears at the question. "R-Robert dared me to take one of L-
Lord Bolton's bottles of brandy. I am s-so sorry, Lady B-
Bolton. I promise I didn't hear anything. I swear!"

"Oh, dear," Lady Bolton said, taking Samuel by the hand
before standing up. She led him to the settee where they
could sit together. "Do not cry, Samuel. I am not angry."

"You aren't?" Samuel asked, hiccupping.

He watched, bewildered, as Lady Bolton dabbed his
tearstained cheeks with a dry patch of her handkerchief. She
smiled at him, and Samuel slowly stopped crying. He remembered why he loved coming to Linfield every summer, even if
it meant playing with Charles's annoying neighbor Robert
from time to time. Linfield was a peaceful respite from his
own home's harshness back on Dover Street in London. Even
his younger sister, Lucy, seemed happier at Linfield, riding
ponies or playing dolls with Rosamund, Lady Bolton's
daughter.

"No," she replied with a sigh before shooting a pointed
look at him. "Although I do wish you had not overheard all of
that. In the future, Samuel, if you ever find yourself in a
similar situation, you should make yourself known."

"You're right, Lady Bolton," Samuel said, sniffing and nodding. "I didn't mean to eavesdrop. I was only afraid of what you and Lord Bolton might do if you discovered me."

"Afraid?" Lady Bolton asked, furrowing her brow. She studied him carefully. "Whatever for?"

Samuel looked down, frowning. "Bad things happen when adults argue." He shyly glanced up at Lady Bolton, who studied him closely, her eyes filled with concern. "For instance, when my parents argue, I take Lucy to the attic. Mama says it's best to hide whenever Father's in one of his moods."

As he spoke, Lady Bolton began chewing her bottom lip as if she were thinking very carefully. "Do your parents often argue, Samuel?" she finally asked, speaking slowly. When he hesitated in answering, she swiftly added, "You can be honest with me."

Still, Samuel found himself unable to answer. He wasn't sure why. Lady Bolton sighed.

"Fine. If you don't wish to speak to me, then we must come to some sort of agreement if I'm to let you leave this study." Samuel's eyes widened, but Lady Bolton remained calm and spoke very softly. "If you promise not to tell Charles and Rosamund what you heard today, I will let you take one of Lord Bolton's bottles of brandy. And if you ever want to speak to me about your parents, I promise not to tell anyone, either."

His eyes still wide, Samuel watched as Lady Bolton stood up and moved to the sideboard where Lord Bolton kept an array of liquor bottles and glassware. She reached for a mostly empty bottle and brought it back to where Samuel sat on the settee.

"I am afraid motherly duty only allows me to help you so much," Lady Bolton said as she handed the bottle to him. Samuel inspected the inch of amber-colored liquid swirling at the bottom of the bottle, then looked back at Lady Bolton.

"What do you think of Robert?" she asked suddenly, moving to the window behind the settee. She crossed her arms, looking across Linfield's massive lawn toward the patch of trees in the distance, where his friends were playing in the old forester's lodge.

Lady Bolton looked back at Samuel, who was peering at her over the back of the settee. He shrugged. He didn't particularly care for Robert, but Charles and Charles's cousin, Edward, seemed to enjoy his company.

"I never realized a child of eight could be such a brute," she said, coming back around to the front of the settee and sitting beside Samuel once more. Samuel wasn't familiar with the word, but it did sound like the right way to describe Robert. "Lord Bolton is already trying to arrange a match between him and Rosamund."

"A match?" Samuel echoed.

"Ah—he speaks. A match means marriage, my dear. An arranged marriage seems rather primeval in this day and age, though."

Samuel made a face of disgust, causing Lady Bolton to laugh. Samuel ignored her.

Robert and Rosamund? He couldn't imagine them being husband and wife; Robert was five years older than Rosamund! And Samuel was sure he *was* a brute like Lady Bolton said—whatever that meant.

Although most eight-year-old boys didn't dream of marriage, Samuel already abhorred the idea. His parents always seemed so unhappy, and now he realized Lord and Lady Bolton were no different. Were all marriages so disastrous?

"Well," Lady Bolton said with a sigh, "I suppose all that is not your concern." She eyed the bottle of brandy that Samuel now held, then looked back at him. She waved her hands. "Run along now. And do make sure no one sees you with that." He moved to get up, but Lady Bolton stopped him, placing a gentle hand on his forearm. She leaned in close, giving him a warning look. "And do not let Charles have any."

Samuel nodded, though he knew there was no chance of that. Charles tended to do whatever Robert did, even if it meant risking bodily harm. He recalled last year when Robert dared Charles to climb the tallest tree at Linfield. Halfway up, Charles slipped and fell. The result? A broken arm. The rest of the summer was spent inside the nursery, having tea parties with Lucy, Rosamund, and Rosamund's numerous dolls.

Truthfully, it was one of the best summers of Samuel's life, and if he were honest, he thought he might prefer Rosamund's dolls to Robert.

Bottle of brandy in hand, Samuel left the study, dashing through Linfield's halls and out the front doors before making his way across the estate's massive green lawn toward the forest at its edge. The sun hung high in the sky, beating down on Samuel, his face and neck tanned from what had been a dry and hot summer. When he reached the trail that led into the forest, he found himself thankful for the shade from the trees towering above him.

The lodge, long abandoned by the earl for more profitable pursuits across other parts of the estate, sat on the side of a small hill five minutes down the trail. Samuel slowed when he reached it, carefully climbing the rocky path that led to the lodge's front porch. He gave the special knock at the door, then listened. He heard the other boys whispering inside, a shuffle of movement, then the unlatching of the lock. Charles was the one who opened the door, just a crack at first. His eyes drifted down toward the bottle of brandy in Samuel's hand. When their eyes met again, Charles was smiling.

"You did it," he said, pulling open the door all the way. He turned back to the other boys. Robert and Edward were sitting on a blanket spread out on the floor between the unlit hearth and a dusty old settee.

"He did it," Charles repeated, walking back toward the boys and sitting on the floor with them. Samuel stepped into the lodge, joining the others after latching the front door behind him. He glanced at Robert, who looked unimpressed.

"Took you long enough," Robert said with a scowl. He leaned across the blanket, snatching the almost empty bottle of brandy from Samuel's hands. "Was this the best you could do?"

Samuel glanced at Charles and Edward, who sat at his sides. Robert seemed to tower over them, even when they were sitting. His size was intimidating, but Samuel still met Robert's critical gaze directly.

"Yes," he replied, not daring to mention the scene with Lord and Lady Bolton in the study or that Lady Bolton chose a bottle that was nearly empty on purpose. His eyes nervously shifted from Robert to Charles and then Edward, who gave him an encouraging look. With bright red hair that rivaled his aunt's, Edward had been on the receiving end of one of Robert's ridiculous dares on more than one occasion himself.

Samuel turned back to Robert, swallowing. "That was all I could find."

Robert rolled his eyes at Samuel's response, taking the bottle's cork between his fingers and thumb and yanking it free. He took a swig, then offered the rest to Charles. Samuel held out his hand in protest. "Wait!" he exclaimed.

Charles turned and looked at him, confused. Lady Bolton's face flashed in Samuel's mind. He saw her blue eyes, swollen from crying. *Do not let Charles have any.*

Samuel blinked. Robert's face came into focus once more, and he was looking at Samuel as if he were mad. "Are you sure we should be drinking it?" Samuel asked, his words rushed yet apprehensive at the same time.

"Why else would I dare you to go get it?" Robert asked, grinning as if Samuel was a prize idiot. Charles remained quiet, staring at the bottle in Robert's outstretched hand. Samuel decided he would have to appeal to his friend directly.

"Your mother wouldn't want—" He was interrupted by Robert, who began guffawing as if Samuel were a court jester. Samuel did his best to ignore him, Charles's gaze meeting his. "Your mother would be furious if she found us drinking your father's brandy."

Charles's brow knitted, and there was a sharp twist in Samuel's gut. Even without him saying anything, Samuel already knew his friend would take Robert's side on this.

"Why would we want you to steal it if we didn't mean to drink it?" Charles asked. He started to laugh, turning back to Robert and taking the liquor bottle from him. "My friend Brooks is a strange one, isn't he?"

Samuel watched as Charles brought the bottle to his lips. Without thinking, Samuel abruptly reached forward and pushed the bottle from his hands. It fell to the ground and shattered, the amber liquid spilling onto the blanket, staining it. The boys sat in silence, staring at the broken glass. One by one, they turned and looked at Samuel.

"What the hell, Brooks?"

"For God's sake, Brooks!"

"What were you thinking?"

Samuel's heart started to race. He wasn't sure *what* he was thinking. Samuel didn't want Charles to drink the brandy—he knew that much—probably because he didn't want to disappoint Lady Bolton after the kindness she showed him earlier. Not to mention brandy always made his father angry and irritable, and Samuel already wondered if it would have the same effect on Charles. But how could he tell them that? They would call him all sorts of names, especially Robert.

In the end, Samuel stood up and ran out of the lodge instead of answering, the sound of Robert's laughter following him to Linfield Hall. When he reached the safety of the empty nursery on the second floor, he walked to the window, where he could see Charles and the others coming from the forest across the lawn. Robert split off from Charles and Edward, probably returning to his family's home, Sedgewick Park. Samuel turned away, frowning.

He walked toward his bed, falling upon the soft bedclothes with a loud sigh and squeezing his eyes tightly shut. *Idiot,* he thought.

Samuel turned over on his back, nestling himself back into the pillows at the head of the bed. He looked out the window, an oppressive feeling of loneliness developing in his chest. Birds chirped outside as the sun began its afternoon descent in the sky.

Hearing giggling coming from the hall, he blinked, propping himself on his forearms so he could see who was coming. It was Lucy, who was dragging Edward behind her. Despite the dragging, he was smiling; cousin Edward was always better at humoring Lucy and Rosamund than Charles.

"Samuel! Samuel!" Lucy exclaimed, rushing toward her older brother. "We are playing hide and seek. Will you play with us?"

He hesitated, glancing at Edward. Would Charles even want him there after what happened?

"Pleeease," Lucy begged. She looked up at him, pouting, her dark brown eyes like two round saucers. Even Edward encouraged him now.

"Come on, Brooks," he said. "I know you're upset about what happened with Robert this afternoon, but try to forget it, won't you? Besides, I'm not sure I can stand to listen to your little sister whine for much longer."

Lucy gasped, spinning around to face Edward. She crossed her arms across her chest, mustering all the precociousness the three-year-old could manage. "Excuse you!" she shouted.

Edward laughed, and so did Samuel despite himself. "All right," Samuel said, standing up and placing a hand on little Lucy's shoulder. "I'll join you. Who shall hide first?"

She excitedly turned and looked at her older brother, her dark brown curls swaying, tied back with a pink ribbon at the top of her head.

"Hooray!" she yelled, grabbing Edward by the arm once more, guiding him out of the nursery as she seemingly forgot all about his earlier rudeness. "Edward and I will hide first! Samuel, you stay here and count."

Samuel nodded. He turned around, closed his eyes, and began to count, all the while doing his best to forget the day's earlier unpleasantness, not knowing such unhappy memories would haunt him for many years to come.

Chapter One

Hampshire, England
August 1813

AUGUST SUMMER LAID IN BED, pretending to sleep. The room she shared with her friend Jane was dark and quiet, the light of the moon blocked out by a thick curtain covering the window. August listened carefully, waiting for Jane's soft snoring to begin. Then she would know it was safe.

Minutes that felt like hours passed. August rolled over on her side, facing Jane and slowly opening her eyes. The girl's mouth was slightly open against her pillow, and a mass of brown hair draped over part of her face. Was she asleep? August couldn't tell.

Quietly, August propped herself up with her forearm, peering over at her friend, watching for any sudden movements, but Jane remained still underneath the bedclothes except for the steady rise and fall of her chest. She must have been asleep.

Now was the time to move, yet a pang of guilt rocked August's stomach, holding her to the mattress beneath her. She hadn't told Jane her plans for that evening, yet August couldn't quite say why not. She knew she didn't have to fret over any kind of judgment from Jane, though her friend might have offered an apprehensive objection or two if she knew the truth of what August was about to do.

August slowly lifted her bedclothes, sitting up and swinging her feet over the edge of the bed, placing them on the cold floor. She tiptoed across the room toward the armoire, where she quickly changed out of her nightgown and into a day dress. The dress was a simple cut, yet still the best one in her wardrobe. She ran her hands over the soft muslin fabric, wondering what Henry would think.

Henry. Just the thought of him made her smile. The handsome young curate would be expecting her at his cottage any moment now.

As she reached to close the doors of the armoire, August heard rustling coming from the direction of Jane's bed. August froze. Slowly, she turned and glanced at Jane, who sat up in bed with her arms crossed. Jane regarded her friend with a confused look.

"What are you doing?" Jane asked, paying no mind to how loudly she spoke.

August crept toward the edge of Jane's bed, bringing a finger to her mouth and hushing her as she did. Jane regarded her with an unapologetic look, but when August didn't answer right away, she repeated her question, this time more softly. August sat down on the bed, closing her eyes and sighing. When she finally admitted her treachery, she spoke softly, looking down at her hands.

"You're going to have to speak up, August," Jane said, exasperated.

August sighed again, turning to face her friend directly.

She was sure her face was a dreadful shade of red. "I am going to meet Henry."

"*What?*"

Jane shouted more than asked the single-word question. Eyes wide, August hushed her again, this time slapping her palm over her friend's mouth for good measure. Jane said something else, the words muffled against August's hand.

"You have to be quiet," August urged, her words coming out like a cat's hiss. She glanced toward the closed door of their bedroom, then back at Jane. "Mrs. Thorpe will hear us."

When Jane finally nodded in agreement, August removed her hand. The two girls stared at each other for a moment.

"Have you lost your mind?" Jane finally asked, her voice still much too loud. August cringed before glancing at the door again. If Mrs. Thorpe, their headmistress, discovered her out of bed, she would be in all sorts of trouble, but at least August was leaving the next day.

"No, I have not lost my mind," August replied as calmly as she could, turning back toward Jane.

"He will ruin you!"

August snorted. "Janey, you speak of me as if I'm some sort of fine lady. Today, I am an orphan. Tomorrow, I will be a governess for a merchant family. What is there to ruin? I am a nobody. If I were somebody, perhaps—"

"What if you get with child?" Jane asked.

Her friend's voice was a horrified whisper. August fell silent, a thoughtful expression passing over her face. Of course, any intelligent female would consider such things before jumping in headfirst to what she was planning, and indeed she had. Henry had promised there were precautions he could take to prevent an event like that from happening, as he probably wanted one of her babes even less than her.

"You don't have to worry about that," August replied, the sort of headstrong response that only eighteen-year-old girls knew how to give. But Jane was three years younger, and although she was August's best friend, she was nowhere near as audacious. Tonight, Jane seemed to have found her nerve.

"*I* am not worried, but perhaps *you* should be!" she argued.

August sighed. What could she say to convince her? August shot Jane a pleading look as she searched for the right words. "When I leave for Portsmouth tomorrow, I will become a governess," August finally said. "You and I both know there aren't many chances for romance as a governess. Meeting Henry tonight could be my last chance to do something like this. My *only* chance."

Jane's face showed signs of softening—August knew Jane loved Mrs. Radcliffe's novels as much as she, after all—but she still ended up shaking her head. "What is romantic about sneaking out in the middle of the night for a tryst?"

August rolled her eyes at her young friend's naivety. "This is not about *romance*, Jane. This is about carnal pleasure, something you are much too young to understand."

August recalled her fear the first time Henry touched her and then the first time that touch lingered a little too long. But then that fear was replaced by curiosity and passion. She was always the first girl at Hardbury to volunteer whenever the parish vicar asked Mrs. Thorpe for help with one of his charitable projects—making baskets, knitting gloves and scarfs. Whatever it was, August always jumped at the chance to see Henry Fitzgerald, the curate.

Soon they would be alone. In his *cottage*. August's stomach fluttered from a combination of nervousness and excitement.

Meanwhile, Jane looked disgusted. "Do you honestly care so little for your virtue that you will give it to someone who will allow you to leave the next day with no promise of ever seeing you again?"

"Yes," August snapped, glaring at her friend before quickly turning away. She nervously wrung her hands in her lap, then laughed a little in an attempt to lighten the mood. "Honestly, Jane, you are beginning to sound puritanical."

Little did Jane know, August had considered such questions for the past year, ever since her flirtation with Henry began. August always knew such a flirtation would lead nowhere, but she never moved to end the budding attachment, despite Jane's constant chiding over the matter.

August took a more practical approach to the situation. Henry was the third son of a viscount, destined to become a vicar and perhaps even a rector after that. They both knew any relationship between them would be fleeting. He would marry a gently bred lady, and August would go on and become a governess. And not just any governess, a governess to a *merchant family*. She had already accepted her fate, even if Jane was having trouble doing the same.

"Who cares for a woman's virtue but her future husband?" August opined—a bad habit of hers, according to Mrs. Thorpe. Girls, especially orphans destined to become governesses, were not supposed to have opinions. "And what chances do I have of ever meeting such a man? I am an orphan, a soon-to-be governess. I have no one to recommend me but Mrs. Thorpe and Mr. Brooks. Whoever he is."

Mrs. Thorpe called Mr. Brooks her benefactor, but August only met him once. He was the one who paid her bills and determined her allowance ever since she arrived at Hardbury School for Girls at age six. August could not recall life before Hardbury, but she suspected she was a nameless babe left on the steps of an orphanage in the middle of the night. The matron there probably named her for the month and season she was born as some sort of a cruel joke, as if being an orphan wasn't already unpleasant enough.

Why Mr. Brooks chose to pluck August from that orphanage, where she lived in total obscurity, was a great mystery. Was he her father or a more distant relation? Or perhaps no relation at all? But such questions were not what August and Jane were discussing.

"Henry could propose if he wanted to," Jane mumbled.

August scoffed at the idea. "I don't blame Henry for not wanting to propose to me. He is the third son of a viscount, only three-and-twenty, with his whole life ahead of him. He could have anyone he wants. If I were him, I wouldn't propose to me either."

Jane pursed her lips. "I don't think you're giving yourself enough credit," she said, somewhat begrudgingly. "Any man would be lucky to have you as his wife."

August looked at Jane sideways. "You are only saying that because you are my friend."

"Perhaps," she said with a slight giggle. Even August couldn't hold back her smile. "And because I'm your friend, I won't stop you if you must go."

August grinned even more broadly, then reached for Jane's hand across the bed. She took it and squeezed. "Thank you, Janey."

"What should I do if Mrs. Thorpe checks in on us?" Jane asked, folding her knees into her chest and wrapping her arms around them as August moved to stand up and put on her boots. She shrugged, moving toward the window. After pulling back the curtain, she began to open it.

"Feign innocence, of course. Say you have no idea where I went! Someone could have kidnapped me in the middle of the night for all you know—you sleep so deeply, after all. There's no reason for you to get into trouble as well as me, especially when you still have three more years here."

With that, August lifted one of her legs over the windowsill, easily maneuvering herself onto the grass below, thankful their bedroom was on Hardbury's ground floor. Before she shut the window once more, she peeked her head around the window frame to look at Jane. "Try to get some sleep. I'll be back before morning."

"August," Jane said, scrambling toward the window from her bed. There was a pleading look in her eyes, but both Jane and August knew it was no use. When August Summer made her mind up about something, there was no persuading her otherwise. "Be careful. Please."

August laughed. She was always careful, wasn't she? "Good night, Jane."

A FEW HOURS LATER, August walked back down the dirt road that connected the school with Wilton, the closest village. The full moon illuminated the surrounding pastures, and she heard a cow moo in the distance. She picked some stray wild-flowers off the side of the road, picking at the petals as she considered the evening's events.

When she finally came into view of Hardbury, a large brick building that couldn't be missed—even in the dark—she quickened her pace. Jane would be worried, of course, and August was eager to speak to her. She hoped Mrs. Thorpe hadn't risen in the middle of the night to perform bed checks.

August had left their bedroom window slightly open when she left, and upon returning, she slipped her hands between it and the frame, pushing upwards. Using all her strength, she pulled herself up onto the ledge and slipped inside the room. After closing the window behind her, she turned toward Jane's prone figure beneath the bedclothes.

"Jane," August whispered, kneeling beside the bed. Her friend didn't stir, her face peaceful in her slumber. Meanwhile, August frowned. So much for being worried.

"*Jane*," August said again, this time more sharply—and with a firm poke to Jane's ribcage. The girl's eyes shot open, startled, but she sighed with relief when she saw August hovering over her.

"August," she said groggily. "You're back."

Jane sat up, watching as August moved to the armoire. She began to remove her day dress, silently switching into her nightgown. When she finished, August returned to her bed, burrowing beneath the bedclothes and then facing Jane.

"I am back," she said finally.

"What happened?" Jane asked, concerned, probably sensing the lack of enthusiasm in August's voice. After all, how could she be enthusiastic? The mystery of Henry Fitzgerald was over, and the reveal had not been as incredible as she hoped.

"Not much at all, actually," August said, furrowing her brow. She sat up in bed as Jane watched her with concerned eyes. "I mean, everything happened so quickly. There was some awkwardness, and then some discomfort, and then it was over. I thought I would understand all the poetry now—" she shook her head, eyes going wide "—but I still do not!"

Jane was quiet, and the two girls stared at each other for a long moment before Jane finally spoke. "Perhaps you were missing the key ingredient to achieving such understanding," she said thoughtfully.

"What do you mean?"

"You were missing *love*." The word was practically a sigh on Jane's lips. August groaned, rolling her eyes and falling back onto the bed, her head hitting the pillow.

"I suppose I shouldn't have wasted my time, then," she grumbled. Henry Fitzgerald was attractive, yes, but they never had much to talk about, nor was he a keen listener. He was much too self-absorbed for that. The idea of loving him was comical to her.

"I tried to warn you," Jane said. "If Mr. Fitzgerald truly loved you, he would have proposed by now."

August scoffed. "I do not want Henry's love or a proposal from him. The only answer I could ever give him would be no, for I do not love him, regardless of what happened tonight or how shocking that may be to you. But I suppose if you are right and I was missing that key ingredient, then perhaps I have not solved the mystery yet and never will."

A sadness grew inside her chest. It was unfair that some women grew up to be fine ladies who fell in love and married. The only future August knew was that of a mousy governess.

"What mystery is that?" Jane asked, interrupting August's thoughts.

"Sex and why some people lose their minds over it."

If the room wasn't dark, August might have seen her friend's face turn red. Instead, she only heard Jane sputter. "August! We shouldn't be discussing such things."

"Haven't we already, though in much less vulgar terms?"

Jane fell silent. August sometimes told her what Henry would do in their stolen moments over the past year. Frequently, she would describe the way he always left her wanting *more*. August believed tonight would be that *more*. Except tonight was much the same, even when it shouldn't have been.

"Do you know what he said to me tonight?" August asked, her head turning in Jane's direction once more. "He said he would marry me if I weren't a poor orphan. Well, mark my words, Jane. If I were a wealthy lady, I would not marry *him*— even if he were the last man in all of England."

Chapter Two

London, England
April 1816

SAMUEL BROOKS STOOD OUTSIDE ST. George's, holding an umbrella over himself and his mother. He shifted impatiently from foot to foot as his mother spoke to Mrs. Jennings and her daughter, afraid they all might catch a chill if Mrs. Brooks didn't let the poor women go soon. That or Miss Jennings might get the wrong idea about him, which he was sure was his mother's real intention behind making them stand out in the rain after church that morning.

Miss Jennings was a pretty girl—if one liked brown-haired, brown-eyed, slight things. But looks alone could not tempt Brooks into marriage, even as his mother's harassment over his perpetual bachelorhood became more severe with each passing year. He discreetly consulted his pocket watch for the time.

"Mother," Brooks said, interrupting something Mrs.

Brooks was saying about the weather, "perhaps we ought to let Mrs. and Miss Jennings be on their way. As you have pointed out, the rain has not been conducive for outdoor activities as of late. I believe that includes conversations on church steps."

His mother turned and smiled at him. If he were still a boy, perhaps he would have faltered at the forced expression, but his gaze remained stern. *I will not have you arranging a match between Miss Jennings and me,* he said with narrowed eyes.

Must you be as cold as the weather? His mother asked with a tilt of her head. When it became apparent that the answer was yes, Mrs. Brooks turned back to the other two women.

"I apologize, Mrs. Jennings," she said with a slight bow of the head. "I have kept you and your daughter in the rain for too long. Perhaps my son and I can call on you at Stratton Street sometime this week?"

Brooks stifled a groan.

"That would be wonderful!" Mrs. Jennings said with a smile, her eyes flitting from mother to son. Brooks didn't dare look at Miss Jennings, who was probably regarding him with one of those demure looks that a stupid man might find innocent. Fortunately for Brooks, he knew better.

After they went their separate ways and it was safe to speak freely, Brooks turned his head sharply toward his mother. "I hope you know I won't be joining you on that call. Unlike that girl's other suitors, I have actual work to do. Not to mention I'm not interested in Miss Jennings."

His mother's nostrils flared. They often did when she was displeased. She turned and glared at her son, her wrinkles in her forehead becoming more prominent. "Miss Jennings is a lovely girl," she said before turning away again and lifting her chin. "Perhaps you ought to give her a chance. She looks at you as if she adores you."

Brooks groaned. He loved his mother, but she had the

terrible habit of seeing the best in everyone—even those who didn't deserve it, like his late father. "Miss Jennings looks at any man who comes in her direct vicinity with adoration," Brooks said. "How can she not? She is on the wrong side of five-and-twenty, and her father was a rascal who did nothing to protect her and her poor mother in the event of his death."

His mother turned to him, her eyes widening and mouth falling open. "My!" she exclaimed. "I had no idea I raised you to be so arrogant! Mrs. Jennings and her daughter have certainly fallen on hard times, but that's no reason for us to turn up our noses at them."

Brooks huffed, shaking his head. "I am not *arrogant*. I am only pointing out that Miss Jennings wouldn't have looked at me twice last year when there was still the promise of a dowry in exchange for marrying her, and I was nothing but a mere solicitor working for her father."

"You do not give yourself enough credit," his mother murmured with a frown. "You may not be a gentleman by birth, but you are by nature, and your business is more successful than some of these estates belonging to aristocrats. You could be quite the eligible bachelor if you only went out and socialized more like your father did."

"Are you asking me to be more like my father?" Brooks asked, shooting a pointed look at his mother.

Mrs. Brooks offered a sheepish look in response. "No, but—"

"I apologize, Mother, but I have no desire to marry. And I think you and I would both agree that it's for the best that I have a demeanor opposite of my father."

They walked on in silence for a good five minutes before his mother began nagging him again. "But don't you ever grow lonely?" she asked.

He sighed. "Why would I? You always provide such ample conversation."

Mrs. Brooks glared at her son. "You know what I mean."

"Do I?" He dared his mother to say what she meant with only a pair of playful eyes and a slight smile. She flushed and looked the other way with a huff.

"Do not make me explain myself any further!"

Brooks chuckled. "I appreciate your concern, Mother, but the kind of loneliness you describe is easily cured in a man— and it only costs five shillings and a trip to Covent Garden."

"Samuel!" his mother sputtered. He winked at her, which only horrified her more. "Well, I do hope you take precautions like your father always did. I suppose the apple does not fall far from the tree."

That made him flinch. "Stop comparing me to father," he said to her through gritted teeth. She regarded him with an unapologetic look. He sighed again. "You know I only said those things to irritate you. I am far too busy to be some sort of drunken rogue."

When his father died two years ago, Brooks inherited his law practice—and all the work. But even before then, Brooks was much more conscientious than many of the young men his age at Oxford. While they drank, he studied. He didn't particularly like the way he—or others—became when they were drunk.

As for women? He couldn't recall the last time he laid with one. Finding and retaining a mistress seemed like too much work, and marriage was just out of the question. Even taking a hack to Covent Garden at the end of a long workday seemed like a hassle.

Willfully celibate would be the way Brooks described himself. To be sure, he was more than happy that way, not to mention confident that no woman could ever tempt him. And even if such a woman suddenly materialized in his life, his opinions on marriage would never change, and their relationship would be doomed—that much he was sure.

When they arrived back at their home on Dover Street after church, their butler Jenkins was pacing the entrance hall. He approached Brooks before the solicitor could even remove his hat, handing him a letter sealed with melted wax. Brooks recognized the Finch family crest immediately. He tore it open, his mother still hovering behind him. His face fell as he scanned the short missive.

"What is it?" Mrs. Brooks asked, voice full of concern.

"A letter from Charles," her son replied, refolding the letter and placing it in his breast pocket as he glanced at his mother. "Lord Bolton is not well. They don't believe he has much longer, and he has commanded me to come at once. I'm afraid I must go."

James Finch, the Earl of Bolton, was a friend of his late father, not to mention a client. When his father died, Brooks took up the mantle of being Bolton's solicitor himself.

"Shall I come with you?" his mother asked, furrowing her brow. "Lady Bolton might require comforting. We could hire a post chaise."

Brooks did not answer right away, too busy wondering why Lord Bolton would ask for him of all people on his deathbed. Brooks was the executor of his will, so he assumed it had something to do with that. For some reason, his mind drifted to that secret daughter of his. If he meant to include her in the document, Brooks hoped he did so quietly. Lady Bolton would be devastated if she knew the truth.

"Lady Bolton has Rosamund," Brooks finally said, pushing that secret—the one only he, his dead father, and Bolton knew—from his mind. "I will send for you if you are required. Perhaps it's only a false alarm."

Brooks left right away, hiring a post chaise as his mother recommended. He always did prefer private carriages to the stage or mail coaches when he was required to travel for work, as long carriage rides made him dreadfully ill. Stuffy coaches only made it worse. Still, his head started to ache almost immediately upon departure, and he grew increasingly nauseous as the carriage left London. Brooks was thankful that Linfield Hall was only thirty miles away.

Linfield should have conjured happy memories in his mind, ones of youthful summers long gone, filled with fresh air and exercise. But his relationship with Charles had soured over the years, their interests diverging at Oxford when Charles started preferring drinking and gambling above everything.

The hour was late when Brooks finally arrived at the country house in Kent. The butler showed him into the entry hall, a gaudy testament to the earl's power, with its massive crystal chandelier and clusters of portraits hanging on the crimson walls. A few moments later, Charles came down the main staircase—a marble monstrosity—and greeted him.

Charles looked worse for wear, with dark circles under his eyes and sunken cheeks. His hair was not the immaculate coiffure Brooks remembered whenever they ran into each other in London. His dark curls went off in every which direction, as if he had repeatedly been running his hands through them that evening. When he approached, the distinct smell of liquor followed him. Brooks gave a swift bow regardless.

"Must you always do that?" Charles asked with a grin, extending his hand.

"Are you still the son of an earl as well as my client?" Brooks asked, taking and shaking it.

"Yes."

"Then I'm afraid I must always do that."

Charles sighed, looking at Brooks disapprovingly. But Brooks did not falter, preferring to maintain the distance he had built up between him and his old friend. Anything Charles touched tended to turn to ruin, and Brooks wanted to avoid that, preferring the quiet solitude he found in adult-hood to the messiness of his childhood.

"Is he upstairs?" Brooks asked, glancing toward the stair-case. *He*, of course, being Lord Bolton. Charles nodded and waved Brooks upstairs, and together they climbed it to the second floor.

"The doctor told us he did not have much time left when he came for my father's daily appointment this morning, though he seems to be doing better now," Charles said. "This disease has been a fickle beast. Some days I think he might make a full recovery, but others..."

Charles shook his head and pursed his lips, and Brooks wondered what it was like to be close to one's father. Charles may have been the worst sort of degenerate, but he did love his father, just as the earl loved his son. Brooks, on the other hand, could only muster up such tender feelings for his mother.

"My mother and sister are visiting with him now," Charles continued, regaining the formality in his tone by clearing his throat. Charles never did like appearing weak, though Brooks felt he knew the truth behind his character, having known him so long. Charles was as weak-minded and self-conscious as most men, though the soon-to-be earl would never admit it.

"They had the servants prepare a room for you," he added.

"Thank you," Brooks said, "though I do wonder why your father wanted to see me so suddenly. Did he give any explana-tion? I have brought the will—"

"Do not mention the will to my mother," Charles said as they turned off the staircase and moved onto the second-floor landing, his voice suddenly sharp. They were nervous as well, then. Brooks dreaded what awaited him at the end of the hall.

Charles took a breath, relaxing his stern gaze. He slowly smiled at Brooks, laughing slightly in what appeared to be a desperate attempt to remain calm. "She was fretting about it all morning but would not say why." He stopped for a moment, turning and looking at Brooks, whose heart pounded. "She acts as if some great secret is about to be revealed. Do you suspect the same?"

Brooks thought of the school payments he arranged for the secret daughter and the argument he once witnessed between Lord and Lady Bolton in the study. Perhaps she already knew the result of her husband's infidelity. "I suspect nothing," Brooks said with a shrug.

Charles studied him for a moment, his gaze discerning as they searched one another's eyes, then continued down the hall. If Lord Bolton revealed any secrets that evening, Brooks would not allow himself to become a scapegoat. A solicitor had a duty to keep his client's secrets. Brooks had first discovered the existence of Bolton's bastard under his father's apprenticeship when his father ordered him to find the girl employment as a governess on behalf of Bolton. He couldn't have very well told Charles about her without causing a rift in the family.

When Brooks and Charles reached Lord Bolton's bedroom, they found him in bed, his wife sitting on one side and daughter on the other. "Brooks!" Rosamund exclaimed, pushing her chair back and rising to greet the solicitor.

Unlike Charles, Brooks maintained an easy friendship with Rosamund. If it weren't for her blonde hair, she would be a mirror image of her mother, both of them being tall with long, graceful necks and high cheekbones. Meanwhile, Lady Bolton's hair remained the same vivid red as it was twenty years ago. She rose, still wearing her silk dinner gown, floating across the room to offer Brooks her hand. He took it, and their eyes met. He wondered if they were both thinking

BECKY MICHAELS

about that day in the study. Lady Bolton had always looked out for Brooks, but had he done the same for her? A pang of guilt hit him, and he nearly flinched.

"How is he?" Brooks asked after he regained his nerve, eyes drifting toward the shriveled husk of a man lying underneath velvet bedclothes. The man appeared to have aged at least nine years instead of nine months since Brooks saw him last, and he had only been sick for a third of that. Brooks could hear his haggard breathing from across the room.

"Not well," Lady Bolton said.

Bolton's sunken eyes searched wildly while his body remained prostrate in bed. "Is that Samuel?" he asked, his voice hoarse. Brooks went to his side, where their eyes could finally meet.

"It is," he said.

"Leave us," Bolton said, mustering all the authority an aristocratic man as physically weak as him possibly could. Brooks turned to the man's family, finding three pairs of uncertain eyes staring at him. He tried to offer them a reassuring smile.

"We'll be fine," he said, nodding slightly. He watched each of them go, Lady Bolton lingering to offer Brooks a sad smile before finally leaving. She might as well have put a dagger through his heart if they shared the same suspicions.

"Sit," the earl said.

Brooks took Rosamund's old spot beside the massive four-poster bed. "What is it, my lord? Charles asked me to come straight away, and I did."

Though he appeared weak and fragile, Bolton attempted a smile. "You are a good boy, Samuel. Your father was always much too hard on you."

The younger man's jaw tightened, an involuntary reaction to any mention of his father. "I don't think you summoned me to Kent to speak about my father," Brooks said sharply. "What do you want, Lord Bolton?"

"Being bedridden gives a man much time to think, Samuel," Bolton said, an unmistakable sadness in his voice while his gaze became distant. "I have been thinking of my daughter. Not Rosamund, but August." Brooks frowned, and the two men stared at each other in silence. "I know you know about her. Your father told me he had you find her employment as a governess when she turned eighteen, but I think I could have done more for her."

So it was as Brooks suspected. He sat back in his chair, exhaling deeply. "You paid for her schooling. Isn't that enough?" Bolton scoffed, but Brooks continued. "You said it yourself. She has employment. She does not need you anymore." He shook his head, hoping he could talk Bolton out of this. "What more could you do for her?"

Bolton shook his head. "More than that," he stubbornly reiterated. "I wish to bring her here—to Linfield. I have never seen the girl for myself, and I would like to change that before I die. I fear I will not be able to rest in peace otherwise."

Brooks stared at the earl for a long moment. "And what of your family?" he asked, his voice rising with his anger. He thought of Lady Bolton, of the hurt she would feel at the revelation that her husband had fathered a child with another woman. Bolton made a dismissive sound.

"Plenty of men like me have bastards," he practically spat. "I may be dying, but I am still the Earl of Bolton. My wife and children will accept her if I tell them to."

Brooks couldn't help but raise a skeptical brow. Bolton would not be able to order his family to do his bidding much longer. "And what about when you are gone? Will they still accept her then?"

Bolton grew red in the face. "You will make them! As executor of my will, you will make them!"

He launched into a violent coughing fit. Brooks stood, procuring a handkerchief from his pocket and handing it to the earl. He took it and covered his mouth, coughing, staining the fabric with specks of bright red blood.

Brooks sighed. "I'm afraid it is not in my power to do such a thing."

Bolton ran his eyes over Brooks. "But it is in mine. I will leave her something to make them think twice before besmirching her. The ton does love a surprise heiress. She will have no problem finding a husband at the right price, especially if my son supports her in town."

Brooks fell silent, knowing the earl had it all wrong. The girl would be out of place in town, with a mother who wasn't hers and two siblings who knew nothing of her, but it appeared he had no sway over the man's decision. "How much do you intend to leave her?" he finally asked.

"Twelve thousand pounds."

His eyes widened. "Have you lost your mind?" he practically shouted. "That is the same as Rosamund's dowry."

"Equal sums for both Finch girls," Bolton said, his tone resolute. "And you will leave tonight to fetch her for me. The doctor says I do not have much time left."

Brooks opened his mouth to protest again. "Lord Bolton—"

"I will pay you handsomely, of course."

The young solicitor pursed his lips. He never was one to turn down a client, especially when money was involved. "Fine. But you will tell your family about her before I return. I mean no disrespect, my lord, but I refuse to be the one who breaks your wife's heart with such news."

Chapter Three

Portsmouth, England
April 1816

"Miss Summer. There is a man here to see you."

August looked from her book to find Mr. Dunn's housekeeper, Mrs. Howe, standing in the classroom doorway. Her two charges gasped. "A man?" Sophie, age eight, echoed.

"What sort of man?" Charlotte, age thirteen, asked in an equally curious tone.

August shot a warning look at the girls, who sat at a table in the middle of the room taking a French exam. Still, they looked from the housekeeper to their governess with wide, excited eyes. Although they were five years apart, they almost looked like twins due to their similar features: curly brown hair, round cheeks, and dark eyes—not to mention their matching mischievous smiles.

"Finish your exam, girls," August said, rising from her desk in front of the chalkboard. She smoothed the front of her dress. "When I return, I expect you both to be done." She walked toward the doorway, pausing in front of Mrs. Howe. August turned back to the girls, narrowing her eyes. "And do not even try to cheat. You know I will find out."

The girls giggled as August followed Mrs. Howe out into the hall. August quickly closed the classroom door behind them.

"A man?" she asked, eyes wide. Who could it be? August knew only one man—Henry Fitzgerald, the parish curate from Wilton—but she hadn't heard from him since she left Hardbury School for Girls. In one of her more recent letters, Jane mentioned that Henry was now the vicar in Wilton, making him even further above her station than before. What would he want with her now?

"He said his name was Mr. Brooks," Mrs. Howe explained.

August's eyes widened. Her mysterious benefactor was here? In Portsmouth? "Mr. Brooks? Truly?"

Mrs. Howe nodded. August followed the housekeeper down the hall in somewhat of a daze. Out of all the people to visit her, she did not expect Mr. Brooks. August and her benefactor had not corresponded since he wrote to ensure her happiness with her placement with the Dunns almost three years ago. She had assured him that the position was suitable enough and hadn't heard from him since.

Upon entering the drawing room, she expected to find someone with graying hair and wrinkles, just like the man who took her from the orphanage to Hardbury all those years ago. She saw a young man standing by the window instead, his side profile coming into view as she turned the corner into the room. August nearly froze at the entrance, surprised.

"Mr. Brooks," Mrs. Howe said. The man called Brooks turned and faced them. He was tall with fair, curly hair that was slightly mussed as if he had just been sleeping. An expensive-looking but slightly wrinkled tan overcoat with a brown collar covered his broad shoulders. Dried mud stuck to the bottom of his black boots.

August was sure the confusion was visible on her face. He could not be the Brooks who took her from the orphanage to Hardbury all those years ago. This Brooks was much too young! He could not be older than thirty, with blue eyes, a broad nose, full lips, and a cleft in his chin.

"This is Miss Summer," Mrs. Howe said, gesturing toward August, who smiled despite her nervousness. Brooks remained stone-faced.

"Thank you, Mrs. Howe," he said, nodding slightly at the older woman. "May Miss Summer and I have a moment alone?"

Mrs. Howe nodded and turned to leave. She stopped beside August, leaning over and whispering in her ear. "I will give you fifteen minutes."

August bit back a grin watching the older woman leave. If only Mrs. Howe knew how much could happen in fifteen minutes! When she glanced at Brooks again, she decided she did not think her mysterious benefactor, who somehow discovered the fountain of youth, was there to defile her. He looked far too severe for that.

After Mrs. Howe left, August and Brooks stood staring at each other for a long moment before she finally shook herself out of her reverie and gestured toward the pair of settees in front of the hearth. "Shall we sit down, Mr. Brooks?"

Brooks nodded, and the two sat across from each other, the warm fire crackling beside them. "You must be wondering why I'm here," Brooks said.

"Yes, I am," August admitted. She studied his face carefully, looking for signs of wrinkles, but there were hardly any. "Not to mention the Brooks I remember must be twice your age by now. You can't be the one who took me from the orphanage in London to Hardbury in Hampshire all those years ago."

The Brooks in front of her seemed to pale. "You must be thinking of my father," he muttered, fidgeting slightly as he spoke. "Before I was Lord Bolton's solicitor, my father was. He died two years ago, and I inherited his law practice."

August frowned at him. "I am so sorry for your loss, sir. He seemed like a wonderful man when I met him—but who is Lord Bolton?"

"The Earl of Bolton is your father," Brooks replied. August's heart dropped into her stomach. "Unfortunately, he is dying, which is why I am here."

Brooks paused, waiting for August to say something. She blinked, not quite believing what she was hearing. Was she dreaming? Was her father truly an earl? "Miss Summer?" Brooks asked.

August shook her head, swallowing. "I'm sorry, sir. I'm afraid I'm confused. Has he given you a message or something for me? Is that why you're here?"

"Not quite. The earl would like you to come to Linfield Hall, his country estate in Kent. His last wish was that he meets you before he dies, and I'm afraid we must leave at once if we are to make it in time."

August started to laugh, but when she saw Brooks's narrowed eyes and pursed lips, she faltered. "Oh. You're serious."

She swallowed again. But she was a nobody, not an earl's daughter! August always thought her parents were dead. Why else would she have ended up in an orphanage as a babe? Was the earl the one who asked the elder Mr. Brooks to take her to Hardbury?

"I'm afraid so, Miss Summer. My post chaise is waiting outside. Please pack your things at once. We must make haste."

August grew pale. She thought of the girls and Mr. Dunn, who only employed a governess because his wife died almost three years ago. He could not care for them by himself, not when he was always working. "I must speak to my employer first," August said, shaking her head.

"Why?" Brooks asked, furrowing his brow.

August stared back at him, puzzled. "Because he is my employer, and I do not wish to leave him shorthanded with the girls."

"The girls?"

August was beginning to think Brooks was quite thick-headed. "Yes, Mr. Brooks. *The girls*. My two charges, Charlotte and Sophie. You realize I'm a governess, don't you? I cannot just desert them, especially not to see a father that hasn't shown any interest in me until he began knocking on death's door. But do not worry, Mr. Brooks. Mr. Dunn is a kind employee and will surely grant me some leave to visit him."

Perhaps August ought to have been more polite, but what could she do? She could not drop everything to see a father who once deserted her just because he was an earl. Where had he been all her life before now? He could have visited her while she was at school, which she assumed he paid for, but he did not. So why should *she* drop everything and show up at his side now when he suddenly needed her? Besides, August had responsibilities now. Charlotte and Sophie needed her as much as he did, if not more.

Meanwhile, Brooks began to laugh. "What is so funny?" August asked, glaring at him.

"I do not think you understand, Miss Summer," Brooks replied, still chuckling. "But I suppose that's my fault for leaving out the best part. Your father means to leave you twelve thousand pounds when he dies."

August felt faint. *Twelve thousand pounds?*

"You will never work another day in your life."

BROOKS WAS weary from traveling when the housekeeper opened the door of Mr. Dunn's home on High Street in Portsmouth. He would have liked to speak to Miss Summer's employer before requesting an audience, but the housekeeper said the merchant wasn't home, and Brooks had no time to waste. He was sure Lord Bolton would haunt him if he did not return to Linfield Hall before his death, his daughter in tow, and the journey back to Kent would be long.

The girl was as Brooks expected—at first. She froze when she saw him, appearing slight and timid behind the older housekeeper's wiry frame. But when she smiled, he realized right away that this girl was a beauty. Her long-sleeved dress, though modest and unadorned, still somehow highlighted her ample bosom. Rosebud-like lips and fair-colored tendrils of hair softened and framed her angular face. When Brooks recalled his governess from childhood, he pictured a severe looking woman with spectacles. August was anything but that, and it made him gravely uncomfortable.

"W-what?" the young governess sputtered now, the color draining from her face. "T-twelve thousand pounds?"

Brooks nodded. The room fell quiet except for the fire crackling beside them. He waited for August to say something else, but she only stared down at her lap, mouth slightly open in shock.

"But why?" August asked, looking back up at him, a confused expression on her face. He couldn't blame her for being confused, but they didn't have much time for him to explain her father's state of mind when Brooks left Linfield.

He sighed. "Does it matter? If twelve thousand pounds cannot motivate you to pack your bags, I'm not sure what will."

The girl crossed her arms defiantly, perhaps rightfully so. He *was* acting rude, but *she* was trying his patience. "I do not believe you. You are some sort of miscreant, attempting to lure young governesses away with you while their employers are out of the house. Well, I will not fall for it."

Brooks raised his brow, wondering if his appearance after traveling for so long was awful enough to make her think he was some sort of reprobate. She remained still, with her arms still crossed across her chest.

"You are a stubborn one, aren't you?" he muttered, reaching into his coat to procure the addendum to Lord Bolton's will. He had the earl sign it for him before he had left. Brooks held out the piece of paper, and August reached over to snatch it from him. She quickly unfolded it, scanning its contents a few times before looking back up at Brooks.

"Well, I suppose it looks real."

"It is real, Miss Summer," Brooks replied, reaching to take the piece of paper back from her. He neatly folded it and placed it back inside his coat pocket.

"But the girls," August suddenly said, her eyes frantically searching his. "Who will be their governess? I cannot leave them."

Brooks furrowed his brow. Was the woman mad? She could not possibly be that attached to her charges. "Surely Mr. Dunn can find a replacement."

August shook her head, chewing her bottom lip as she did. It was full and plump, her bottom lip. Brooks forced himself not to look at it.

Willfully celibate, he reminded himself, though perhaps he ought to go to Covent Garden more often if a mere governess could have such an effect on him. His instant attraction to her couldn't have been healthy. Reminding himself that she was Charles's half sister did little to temper it. Her stubbornness, though, was beginning to annoy him.

"Yes," she said, "but the girls are very special to me, and their father works far too much and won't be able to care for them if I leave. I would hate for them to feel abandoned. I must find my replacement before I go. Perhaps you could help me by purchasing an advertisement in the local paper, or—"

"We do not have time for this," Brooks said through gritted teeth, becoming annoyed. "Your father—"

"Is on the verge of dying, yes, I understand," August snapped. Brooks blinked, taken aback. No, this governess was not the mousy girl he had expected. "But I have been Charlotte and Sophie's teacher, mother, and playmate for the past two and a half years. I will not abandon them for a man that abandoned me. Not even if that man is the Earl of Bolton."

Brooks's face softened. He never expected the governess to reject her father's wishes since they were about to make her very, very rich, but perhaps he should have. He never went to see his father on his deathbed, either, even when the man asked for him. He didn't even shed a tear at the funeral. Why wouldn't a woman feel the same way about a father who was never there for her either?

"Is Mr. Dunn truly so incapable without you?" he asked, sighing. "What about the housekeeper?"

August hesitated. "He is not incapable, only absent," she finally answered. "And Mrs. Howe is too busy for the girls." She shook her head. "I'm afraid I cannot go quite yet."

"But—"

"Mr. Dunn will not return home until after dinner tonight. I will speak to him about putting an advertisement for my replacement in the local paper at once."

Brooks opened his mouth to protest again, worried he would find himself trapped in Portsmouth for the next week. "Miss Summer—"

Suddenly, the drawing room door swung open, and two

little girls barged in, running toward August, shouting her name. "Miss Summer! Miss Summer!"

The youngest one climbed on her lap while the older one sat down beside her. They did not bother looking at Brooks.

"Girls!" August exclaimed. "I told you to finish your French exam! What are you doing downstairs? The gentleman and I—"

"Is it true you are an earl's daughter, Miss Summer?" the older girl asked, bouncing up and down on the cushion next to hers.

"Does that mean you are a lady?" the younger girl asked as well, her legs dangling off August's lap. Brooks grew uncomfortable watching the scene. He fiddled with his cravat, the room's fire suddenly feeling much warmer than before. The two girls reminded him of Lucy.

"I am an earl's daughter, yes, but I'm not sure that makes me a lady, Sophie," August replied. Brooks noticed she had an easy way with children right away, one that he lacked. "Now, are you going to be polite and allow me to introduce the two of you to our guest?"

The two girls glanced at Brooks, then scrambled to stand. They stood with their shoulders thrown back and their chins pointed toward the ceiling as if they were fine ladies.

"Girls," August said. She gestured toward him, smiling. He felt awkward sitting there, all three sets of eyes on him. "This is Mr. Brooks. He is my father's solicitor." August then waved her hand at her two charges, though her playful blue eyes remained fixated on him. "Mr. Brooks, may I present Miss Charlotte Dunn—" the eldest girl curtsied "—and Miss Sophia Dunn."

The youngest girl followed her sister's example, albeit more awkwardly, then smiled broadly at Brooks. Some of her teeth were missing, a somehow endearing feature on young children, though quite horrifying on anyone else. "You can call me Sophie," she said, giggling.

Brooks glanced at August, who stared at him hopefully. He was aware they were wasting time, but he stood up anyway. The girls gasped as he offered a swift bow. "Good day, Miss Dunn, Miss Sophie."

"He is very tall," Charlotte said, turning toward her governess.

August's eyes met his, and he noticed her cheeks turning pink. She quickly looked away, refocusing her attention on the girls, voice growing stern. "Now, girls, I have important business to discuss with Mr. Brooks. Please return to the classroom and wait for me there."

"You should go, you know," Charlotte said matter-of-factly, unmoved despite her governess's request.

August furrowed her brow. "What do you mean?"

"I reckon twelve thousand pounds almost makes you almost as wealthy as Papa."

August gasped. "Miss Charlotte Dunn! Were you eaves-dropping outside the drawing room door?"

Charlotte grew silent, looking toward the ground sheep-ishly, then back up at her governess. "Maybe," was all she said at first. August sighed.

"Are you going to leave us, Miss Summer?" Sophie asked.

Brooks noticed the little girl's dark eyes were beginning to brim with tears. He shifted uncomfortably, watching as August moved from the settee onto her knees in front of Charlotte and Sophie. Her eyes were level with Sophie's, and she looked from one girl to the other. "I will not go until I find you a new governess—I promise."

Brooks cleared his throat in protest, and August turned back and glared at him. Did this woman not understand what he meant when he said her father was dying? The earl would not be alive by the time they found a new governess. Charlotte glanced at Brooks, then back at August.

"But you should go with Mr. Brooks and see your father before he dies," she admitted sadly. "You are a lady now, not a governess."

The two girls turned away, and although August reached for them, they slipped out of her reach, heading toward the door of the drawing room with their heads hanging low and their arms swaying at their sides. They both threw a few long glances over their shoulders, frowning at their governess as well as him.

It was quite the production. Brooks nearly laughed. When they were finally gone, August rose, turning toward Brooks. Her hands formed little fists at her side. "You upset them," she said with a glare.

Brooks shrugged. "They are children. Everything upsets children. Surely they will recover."

August scoffed, looking him up and down. He narrowed his eyes at her, waiting for some sort of harsh judgment. "I suppose a man like you did not experience any hardship as a child," she said. "The loss of a mother is hard for any young girl. They are fragile!"

His face fell while she spoke, becoming a contemptuous glare. "You should be careful with such assumptions about my childhood, Miss Summer," he warned, his voice low, though she remained unmoved. "If you will not leave with me now, I will wait until Mr. Dunn returns. Perhaps he will be able to talk some sense into you. I would hate to see your father disinherit you again when he discovers you would rather remain a governess for a few more weeks than meet him before he dies."

"Let him," August said defiantly, lifting her chin toward the ceiling. "I have done quite well without his money for the past few years."

"Have you?" Brooks asked, looking her up and down, studying her unassuming clothes and the rest of her appearance. Chalk dust covered her hands.

"I have," she replied, glaring at him. "If you insist upon waiting, you can stay here in the drawing room."

"Fine," Brooks said, sitting back down with a loud thump. August remained standing, staring down at him. She glanced at the empty table between the two settees in front of the fire.

"I will have Mrs. Howe bring you a tray of tea and sandwiches," August said without looking at him. He regarded her carefully as she stared at the table. She turned toward him. "I hope you do not mind waiting a while. Mr. Dunn usually doesn't return home until after dinner."

Brooks glared at her back as she left the room. When she was gone, he pulled out his pocket watch, checking the time. It wasn't even noon. He sighed, closing his eyes and tilting his head until it was touching the back of the settee. Brooks would charge Lord Bolton extra for this—even if he were dead by the time they returned to Linfield.

Chapter Four

THEIR PRODUCTIVE SCHOOL day was over. The girls were far too distracted for any more lessons, no matter how exciting August tried to make them, not to mention August was distracted herself. How could she teach knowing Mr. Brooks was only a floor below them, waiting to whisk her away to some grand country house in Kent.

He had surprised her that morning, and not just with his sudden appearance and youthful good looks. Brooks surprised her when he played along with the girls, bowing to them, just as he surprised her with his careless attitude toward them when they were upset. He was a man of contradictions, this Mr. Brooks. She wondered what made him that way and what his secrets were. He seemed to grow offended when she accused him of not understanding the girls' plight, but why?

She couldn't be sure. Brooks was stubborn and determined—that much August knew. Three hours had passed when Mrs. Howe came upstairs to the classroom to report that her father's solicitor was still there.

August bit her lower lip. She hoped Mr. Dunn wouldn't stay at the office too late that night. Her employer would talk some sense into Mr. Brooks. August could not possibly leave until he found her replacement, and Mr. Dunn would agree. The girls needed her.

But when Mrs. Howe reported the news to the classroom, Charlotte groaned. "You should just go with him, Miss Summer. Mrs. Howe and I can tell Father what happened."

"He is very handsome, Miss Summer," Sophie added, nodding as if she had met plenty of handsome men and Brooks was the best one, all despite being only eight. "He will not wait forever, you know."

August's eyes widened, looking from Charlotte to Sophie. "Handsome? What do you two know of handsome men? And what does Mr. Brooks's attractiveness even signify? He is my father's solicitor—that's all."

"So you admit it," Charlotte said, a sly grin playing at her lips. "You think Mr. Brooks is attractive."

"Miss Charlotte Dunn!" August exclaimed, causing the two girls to giggle. August glared at them.

"Shall I set a place for him at the dinner table?" Mrs. Howe asked after the girls had quieted. August turned to the housekeeper. She hadn't even thought about dinner. It would be rude not to offer him something, especially if he insisted on waiting until Mr. Dunn came home that night.

"Oh, this is ridiculous!" August exclaimed, quickly standing up, pushing her chair behind her, its legs loudly sliding across the wooden floor. "We will call on Mr. Dunn at his office and be finished with this whole ordeal right away. Will you watch the children?"

"I want to go see Papa at his office!" Sophie exclaimed before Mrs. Howe could answer.

"Me too!" Charlotte added.

Mrs. Howe sighed, putting her hands on her hips as she regarded the two girls, who had already jumped from the table where they did their schoolwork, ready to leave. "I will watch them."

Charlotte and Sophie's shoulders simultaneously drooped. The older girl turned toward August. "But Miss Summer!" she whined.

"You must wait here, Charlotte. You too, Sophie. I'm afraid this is business for grown-ups." August headed toward the classroom door. "Behave for Mrs. Howe. I'll be back soon."

BROOKS SAT in the drawing room for what felt like an eternity. There was nothing more to do than sit there and drink lukewarm tea. He had already finished all the small finger sandwiches that the housekeeper brought up to him. Brooks ate them more out of boredom than hunger, though the little pieces of cucumber, cream, and bread were delightful.

He hardly stopped to eat or rest since leaving Linfield. He wanted to arrive in Portsmouth as soon as possible, paying extra to switch teams and postboys as frequently as he could. But now, the earl would be dead by the time they reached Linfield if the governess did not let go of her ridiculous need to find her replacement. His journey would be for naught.

But he supposed that didn't bother her, and perhaps rightfully so. Why should she show any care toward a dying father who abandoned her? And why should she care if he traveled all the way here in a carriage that made him sick? He glanced at his pocket watch to find it was early afternoon. Perhaps he should ring the bell and request a book or a newspaper to help pass the time.

Instead, he heard someone coming down the stairs, then watched the drawing room door swing open. August stood before him, a tattered red cloak fastened around her neck. A straw bonnet covered her blonde curls. Brooks quickly rose from where he sat, the gentlemanly thing to do whenever a lady entered the room. August watched him suspiciously for a moment, then cleared her throat.

"I have decided I should take you to Mr. Dunn's office," she said. "We can settle this business there."

"Very well," Brooks replied, hiding a smile. He predicted they would depart Portsmouth within the hour. Mr. Dunn would understand the urgency of the earl's request, even if August stubbornly did not. Brooks followed her outside, replacing his hat on top of his head. The postboy jumped down from the front of the yellow carriage.

"Where to, sir?" he asked.

Brooks glanced at August, who looked from the postboy to him. She studied him carefully, as if she was trying to discern if she would be safe alone in the carriage with him. He wanted to tell her she would have no choice very soon, but August turned to face the postboy. "We will walk, thank you. It's not too far."

She took off without him. Luckily, it was easy catching up with her, his long strides covering twice as much distance as hers. When he was beside her again, she looked at him out of the corner of her eye. "Isn't it inappropriate in your world for a gentleman and a lady to walk alone together?" she asked.

"My world?" he echoed incredulously.

"Yes," she replied, gesturing toward his coat and boots. "Your world where everyone dresses in fine things and knows earls. The exact opposite of Portsmouth."

Brooks chuckled. "I am a solicitor, and you are a governess. We are hardly a gentleman and a lady."

"You dress and act like a gentleman," August pointed out.

Brooks nodded slightly. "Yes, well, my clients are gentlemen. I must convince them to trust me with their sensitive legal issues somehow."

"Sensitive legal issues?" August asked, knitting her brow

together. The sun was bright that day, illuminating her alabaster skin. Brooks wondered if she knew how she seemed to sparkle in the daylight or if he was the only one who noticed.

"Yes—such as dropping everything to fetch a client's illegitimate daughter because her father decided she should have twelve thousand pounds."

She turned away, blushing. "I suppose you think I'm very foolish for not going with you right away. You think I should do whatever my father wants because he deigned to leave me such a sum."

Brooks didn't reply. She should know the answer was yes. "Well, there is more to life than money," she continued. "I value love and family over money. Don't you?"

He looked at her, opening his mouth to speak, but he wasn't quite sure what to say. Brooks wasn't sure he valued any of those things. "I'm in Portsmouth on an errand for my employer to fetch a stubborn governess that happens to be his daughter," he eventually said through gritted teeth. "With that knowledge alone, surely you must know I value money above all else."

She made a sound of annoyance before walking on in silence. Looking around, Brooks wasn't quite sure what kept her tied to this place, for being the hired help for two young girls was not the same as having love or a family. He had never been to Portsmouth before, but as they moved away from the residential area where the Dunns resided, he became less and less impressed with the place. The streets were dirty and crowded with unruly sailors, and the air reeked of saltwater and fish.

A stranger plowed into August's shoulder, knocking her backward. Brooks gently held her by the waist, steadying her, but his touch seemed worse than a stranger's to her. She quickly maneuvered out of his grip and moved onward, leaving him to trail behind her. Irritated, he looked over her head down the busy street, hoping they would be at Mr. Dunn's office soon.

"Here we are," she finally said, stopping in front of a brick building and opening the door. Brooks followed her inside, finding a man in his thirties sitting at a desk. He looked up from his papers, his spectacles nearly falling off his nose when he did.

"Miss Summer!" he exclaimed, surprised, rising from behind the desk. "What are you doing here? Are the girls all right?"

"Quite all right, Mr. Wilson," August replied, smiling. The man sighed with relief. "The girls aren't the reason for my visit."

She glanced behind her at Brooks, whose gaze remained fixated on Mr. Wilson. He had the beginnings of a paunch and was balding slightly. The man didn't even seem to notice Brooks standing behind August, too busy admiring the young girl despite the wedding ring on his left hand. Brooks didn't know why, but the observation made him bristle.

"Mr. Brooks traveled very far—from Kent, actually—for an urgent audience with Mr. Dunn," August explained, turning back to Mr. Wilson. The man, who must have been Dunn's secretary, finally tore his eyes away from August long enough to look at Brooks. "I agreed to show him the way to his office."

Mr. Wilson narrowed his eyes at Brooks suspiciously. Brooks ignored him, gesturing toward the door in the back of the room with Mr. Dunn's name on it. "May I?" he asked.

But it was a pointless question. Before the man could answer, Brooks impatiently went around August and walked toward Mr. Dunn's office door. Mr. Wilson tried to stop him, but Brooks pulled the door open anyway, stepping inside. The man he could only assume to be Mr. Dunn looked up from his desk.

August somehow slid inside the room, standing in between the two men. "I'm so sorry, Mr. Dunn!" she exclaimed. August gestured toward Brooks, who studied her employer carefully. He was an attractive man in his early forties. Unlike his secretary, he had a full head of hair, a fine set of teeth, and what appeared to be a firm chest and stomach underneath his vest and shirt.

"August!" he said, rising from his desk, looking from his governess to Brooks to his secretary behind them. "What are you doing here? Are the girls all right?"

"The girls are fine," August said quickly. She turned back to Mr. Wilson. "If you could give us a moment, please."

She ushered the secretary, who was reluctant to go, out of the small office and closed the door, leaving August, Brooks, and Mr. Dunn alone. As he looked at the merchant, Brooks's suspicions began to grow.

Love. Family. That's what August said she valued. Had something untoward developed between the governess and her employer? Something that kept August here rather than coming with him to meet her father? Suddenly, things started to make much more sense.

Well, if he had to be the one to put an end to it, he would. Brooks removed his hat. "I apologize for barging into your office like this, Mr. Dunn," he said, bowing slightly. "I'm afraid the matter is urgent."

"Urgent?" Mr. Dunn echoed incredulously, sitting back down behind his desk. He glanced at August. "Who is this man? What is he talking about?"

Brooks responded before August could answer, taking a seat in one of the chairs in front of Mr. Dunn's desk. "I am Samuel Brooks. You may recall I was the one who answered your advertisement for a governess, recommending Miss Summer as a suitable candidate."

Mr. Dunn nodded, watching August as she sat down beside Brooks. "Yes, I remember now. You were that solicitor from London. What are you doing here in Portsmouth?"

Brooks explained everything—that August was the Earl of Bolton's daughter, that the man's only wish was to meet her before he died, and that August would inherit a large sum of money once he did.

"A large sum of money?" Mr. Dunn asked, looking from Brooks to August.

Brooks stiffened. He hadn't said the exact amount because he didn't want the merchant getting any ideas. August's father wanted her out in London society, where she could make a more appropriate match. A widower merchant with two daughters from Portsmouth was far from a suitable husband for a twenty-year-old lady with twelve thousand pounds, no matter what sort of seductive spell this devious man cast on her.

"That's right," August replied. "My father wishes to leave me twelve thousand pounds."

"Twelve thousand pounds?" Mr. Dunn practically shouted. He looked from August to Brooks with wide eyes. "Is this true?"

Hesitantly, Brooks nodded. Mr. Dunn exhaled deeply, leaning back in his chair and folding his hands over his stomach. He stared at some indeterminate object on the ceiling.

"I told Miss Summer we must leave at once to make it back to Kent before her father dies," Brooks said. He glanced at August, who narrowed her eyes at him in a defiant matter, almost daring him to continue. He turned back to Mr. Dunn. "But she says she will not leave until you find her replacement. Please, you must talk some sense into her. I'm afraid if she defies the earl, he will disinherit her as quickly as he decided to leave her twelve thousand pounds."

Mr. Dunn tilted his head as he looked at August, appearing confused. Brooks smiled happily. "I cannot leave until I know the girls are in capable hands," she explained quietly, turning pale.

"Ridiculous," her employer said at once. "Mrs. Howe and I are more than capable. I'm sure we can more than manage while we search for a new governess."

"But Mr. Dunn—"

"Mr. Brooks is right, August," he said, this time standing up. Brooks bristled at the mention of Miss Summer's Christian name. He looked from the governess to her employer, who was gathering his things as if to leave. "You have been given a great gift. You must not waste it or risk angering your father."

August remained unmoved as Brooks rose from his seat, readying himself to quit the office like Mr. Dunn was. "I will take the afternoon to see you off. Do the girls know?"

August nodded slightly.

"Good," Mr. Dunn said with a single, firm nod. He paused for a moment, appearing as if he were thinking deeply. "They will be upset, of course, but you will write them, won't you? They will like that."

August looked up at her employer, mouth slightly open. Then, she nodded. "Of course, Mr. Dunn."

Brooks extended his gloved hand toward August. She looked at it, then at his face to glare at him. She stood up without his help, swiftly moving toward the door and opening it, leaving Brooks and Mr. Dunn by themselves.

"You will look after her, won't you?" Mr. Dunn asked. Brooks turned to him, perplexed, not sure what he meant. He only wished to bring her to Linfield and leave her there for the earl and Charles to handle. "Kent is a long way, I mean, and my girls adore her. They will be waiting for her letter declaring her safe arrival."

Brooks nodded, his lips pursed, still slightly suspicious of the relationship between the merchant and his governess, though Mr. Dunn seemed to release her from her position quite willingly. He was probably only imagining things.

"Of course, Mr. Dunn," Brooks said. He gestured toward the open office door. "Shall we?"

Chapter Five

AUGUST WALKED BACK toward High Street with Brooks and Mr. Dunn in a sort of daze. She didn't know why she thought Mr. Dunn would want her to stay on as long as possible. August was just another employee to him, easily replaced. Brooks must have thought she was so foolish!

When August first arrived at High Street almost three years ago, she didn't know what to expect, but after living in an orphanage and then Hardbury, she knew the only thing to do was try and make the best of whatever situation presented itself to her. She never had a real family, but she was always happy to make one with the people who surrounded her.

At Hardbury, Jane was like a little sister, and Mrs. Thorpe was like a mother. In Portsmouth, her two young charges became like sisters too, and Mrs. Howe was as beloved as an aunt would be. As for Mr. Dunn, he was the closest thing she ever had to a father figure, despite his long hours at the office, but he seemed eager to be rid of her now.

She glanced at Mr. Brooks, who walked beside her, a smug look on his face. She glared at him without him knowing. He couldn't possibly understand what it was like to be sent around from place to place with no real home or family, all at the whim of some earl she never met.

In the end, her things were packed into a small trunk and placed on the back of Mr. Brooks's post chaise. Mr. Dunn, Mrs. Howe, Charlotte, and Sophie stood in a line in front of the house. She looked up at its white façade, admiring it. She remembered how regal it first appeared to her upon arriving in Portsmouth. It would probably pale in comparison to Linfield Hall.

August approached the girls first, kneeling on the sidewalk to make herself eye level with them. They said their goodbyes, and August hugged them one by one, then both at the same time, squeezing them very tightly. Sophie openly cried while Charlotte did her best to appear stoic.

"I will send you both a letter as soon as I'm settled," August said. She had grown accustomed to sending letters to her make-believe family members. Jane received one once a week, Mrs. Thorpe once a month.

"Can we come to visit you?" Sophie asked hopefully.

August smiled at her. "Maybe when you're older," she said, standing up again. She turned to Mrs. Howe next, who she embraced, then to Mr. Dunn. "Thank you for everything, Mr. Dunn."

The man nodded. "I wish you nothing but the best." He glanced at his two daughters, then back at August. "Do not worry about us. We will be fine."

They would be fine without her, wouldn't they? August sadly smiled, took a deep breath, then turned away, letting Brooks help her into the carriage. He climbed in after her, taking the seat opposite of her. The carriage lurched forward very suddenly, and she nearly fell forward into his lap. "Sorry," she murmured, embarrassed as she straightened herself and smoothed out her wrinkled skirts.

Brooks didn't say anything, silently removing his hat and

placing it on the seat beside him. He ran his fingers through his already disheveled hair, and that was when she noticed the dark circles under his eyes. He must have been traveling for a long time, and she might have felt bad for him if she didn't find him so annoying.

They rode on in silence for what felt like a good half hour before Brooks finally cleared his throat. "Would you mind it terribly if I sat next to you?" he asked, pointing toward the empty seat beside her. She had slid against the wall of the carriage, content to look out the window and say nothing until they arrived in Linfield. Now, she glanced at the empty seat beside her, then back at Brooks, narrowing her gaze at him.

"Why?" she asked.

Brooks sighed. "Let me reassure you there's nothing untoward about my request. It's just that I get dreadfully ill when I ride in a carriage facing backward. I know it's not polite to talk about bodily functions in front of ladies, but I'm afraid I will throw up on your skirts if I do not change directions."

August's eyes widened. "Oh, dear! By all means, then!" She gestured to the empty seat beside her. "I wish you would have said something earlier."

She supposed he did look a bit paler than usual, and a thin layer of sweat had developed across his forehead. As he moved to sit beside her, he let out a deep breath, and she instinctively reached for a handkerchief inside her reticule. August leaned over and started dabbing his brow, causing him to recoil. She did the same. They stared at each other like two barn cats, unsure if they had just come across a friend or a foe.

"I apologize," August said quickly, turning away and stuffing her handkerchief back inside her reticule. She slid back toward the wall of the carriage, as far away from Brooks as possible. "Working as a governess, taking care of others becomes second nature very quickly."

"Funny," he murmured. "I do not remember my governess caring so much about me."

August rolled her eyes. Before she left Hardbury, Mrs. Thorpe warned her that some charges never took to their governesses. Some would play mean pranks, and she wondered then if Brooks was that sort of child. As for Charlotte and Sophie, they loved August immediately. She had always been thankful for that.

"Perhaps you can help nurse your father," Brooks suggested. The mention of the earl's illness piqued August's curiosity. She turned toward Brooks.

"What is wrong with him?" August asked.

"Some sort of wasting disease," Brooks replied with a frown. "He's been sick these past three months."

"Oh," she said. It took the earl three months to decide he wanted to see his illegitimate daughter? "I wonder why he did not send for me earlier. His change of heart seems so sudden."

Brooks snorted and rolled his eyes. "That's an understatement," he muttered. August stared at him, demanding further explanation with her eyes alone. Brooks sighed.

"Your father told me his sudden illness gave him much time to think. My guess is a man like that, once so powerful and strong, starts to feel his health rapidly decline and begins wondering what he did to deserve such a fate. Perhaps he believes it to be some sort of cosmic reckoning for how he did nothing more but send you to school, and now he wishes to make amends, believing it may save his soul."

"A cosmic reckoning?" August asked, arching her brow.

He shrugged as if he wasn't sure what he meant either. "The man feels guilty now that he's dying. That's the only explanation I have for his absurd behavior."

Something suddenly dawned on her. "You do not like the earl," August said simply.

"He is my client," Brooks replied, his tone sharp.

"Yes, but you disagree with what he's doing," she said, shaking her head. "Giving his bastard daughter an invitation to his country house and twelve thousand pounds." She laughed slightly. "What *could* he be thinking?"

Brooks did not try to deny it, and the two travelers fell silent. August turned to look out the window. She watched the sun lift over the horizon, painting the trees and fields gold. She couldn't remember the last time she had been in the country. The dirt road and the yellow fields of wheat they passed reminded her of the walk from Hardbury to Wilton.

August resolved to remain quiet for the rest of the journey, not wishing to speak to Brooks, who seemed to shift uncomfortably beside her very frequently. Every so often, he would even rub his temple as if in pain. It must have been his illness. The man did not look well. "Do you always fall ill during carriage rides?" she asked, unable to remain silent any longer after another half hour passed.

"Yes," he said. The body of the carriage jostled as its wheels went over a large rock, and he groaned. "I do not know how anyone can stand it."

August bit her lip. Perhaps a distraction was in order, something to take his mind off how terrible he was feeling. She did not wish to speak to Brooks, but she did have questions for him.

"Do I have any siblings?" August asked suddenly. Brooks turned to her, his brow knit together in confusion. She grinned at him sheepishly. "I have been wondering for a while now, so I thought I would ask."

Slowly, Brooks nodded. "You have an older brother, Charles, who will become the earl once your father passes. He is eight-and-twenty. And you have an older sister, Rosamund, as well. She is three-and-twenty."

"Only a few years older than me," August murmured to herself. She was not the praying sort, but if she were, she might have dropped to her knees and prayed at that very moment, if only for her sister to like her. She had make-believe sisters all her life—girls at the orphanage, Jane, the Dunn girls—but now she would have a real one!

"What's that?" Brooks asked suddenly, and August realized he had been staring at her as if concerned for her well-being.

"What's what?" she asked, pinching her brows together as he regarded her as if she were mad. He waved his hand in circles at her face. She leaned away from him, offended.

"That dreamy look in your eyes," he said impatiently. "What are you thinking? I'm afraid I must squash any hopes and dreams before they take flight. It's for your own good."

Hopes and dreams? August squinted at him. What could he mean? She shook her head. "I was only thinking about how wonderful it would be to have a sister. What is Rosamund like?"

August thought she heard Brooks stifle a groan. "No," he said.

She raised her brow. "No?"

"No," he said again, this time with an added shake of the head. She stared at him until he elaborated. "You must assume everyone except your father will hate you."

August frowned. He must have been joking. "You can't be serious."

Brooks only shrugged in response, and August fell silent as a result. A few moments passed, and she wrung her hands in her lap, staring at them. "Do my siblings truly hate me?" she finally dared to ask, turning back toward Brooks. "Or are you just saying that to make me nervous?"

Brooks ground his teeth together. August patiently waited for a response. "Truthfully, I do not know how your siblings feel," he finally said. "Your father had not yet told them when he ordered me to fetch you for him. He promised he would tell them before we returned."

"Oh," August said, her face falling. Panic set into her chest. "Then they are just becoming used to the idea of me. They will be shocked, especially when they discover how much money he has left me. I will be nothing but a wicked usurper to them, encroaching on their home while their beloved father dies."

"No," Brooks said, reaching for August's hand, taking it into his own. She looked at their intertwined fingers, then back at him, confused. Thankfully, her shocked expression did not discourage him, and he still held on to her hand.

"I have known Rosamund my entire life," he said, gazing up at August reassuringly. Her breathing hitched. "She is a good sort of girl, kind to everyone. If she is shocked, she won't be for long. I'm sure you will be fast friends."

August smiled at the soothing words. Even if they might not be true, they were undoubtedly comforting. "And what of my brother, Charles?" she asked.

Brooks suddenly took his hand back, leaning away from her. She clenched and unclenched her hand, trying to rid herself of the phantom feel of him. He shook his head, clearly not noticing the effect he had on her. "That I'm not quite so sure," he said. "Your brother has a taste for vice."

"Vice?" August asked, looking confused.

"Yes—drinking, gambling, whoring. You know the sort."

August nodded her head once. "Ah," she said, thinking of Henry for some reason. "A rakehell."

Brooks laughed. "Something like that," he said with an easy smile that made her stomach flip. "I'm surprised you know such a word."

August grinned at him. He must have thought she was some sort of innocent. "I think you would be surprised by many things about me, Mr. Brooks," she said.

His smile started to fade, and then he quickly looked away, back toward the window. Meanwhile, August felt proud of her ability to unnerve him. But then Brooks turned to her once more, a severe look on his face. August's confidence faltered.

"Your father's wife, Lady Bolton, will be at Linfield Hall as well," he said. "I would not expect much of a welcome from her, but I would also ask that you do not judge her too harshly. She is a kind woman who will be coming to terms with your father's betrayal. I'm sure she will learn to accept your connection both to her husband and her children, though, with some time and perhaps Rosamund's help."

August nodded at him, chewing her lower lip. "I would not blame her if she didn't," she said softly.

"But she will," he said with a sense of determination. August watched as Brooks turned to look out the window again, a thoughtful look on his face. "I have known Lady Bolton for a very long time. My father was Bolton's solicitor before me, but their relationship was not just one of business. They were best friends. So I spent every summer at Linfield, pretending to be a much wealthier lad than I was, playing with Charles and his neighbor and cousin. Lady Bolton always looked out for me."

"She sounds lovely," August said, turning to look out the window and arching her brow. How strange for Brooks to be Lady Bolton's champion, she thought.

With neither of them interested in having any further conversation, August reached into her reticule, pulling out a novel she had brought with her to pass the time. She had barely started reading when Brooks cleared his throat, causing August to look up at him. "What is it?"

"Is that *The Mysteries of Udolpho*?"

"Yes," she said, somewhat defensively, knowing how some people felt about Miss Radcliffe. "Why? Do you wish to tell me that novels will turn my mind to mush like Mr. Dunn and Mrs. Thorpe so often did?"

"I find nothing wrong with enjoying a good novel," he said, surprising her. A solicitor enjoying a leisurely pursuit such as reading a novel? How odd. "I would read one myself right now, but it would only make my illness worse."

"Ah," she said. She considered Brooks's plight for a moment, then sighed, staring down at the pages of *Udolpho*. "I could read aloud to you if you would like."

Brooks looked at her as if she said something terrible, and it took her a moment to realize why. Reading Miss Radcliffe aloud to the opposite sex would not be appropriate behavior in polite society.

"I'm sorry—that's inappropriate," she said, shaking her head, sure her cheeks were turning a dreadful shade of red. She looked down at the book in her lap. She nearly muttered that perhaps she ought to have brought the Bible instead. "There are so many new rules I will have to become accustomed to, aren't there? I do hope someone hires some sort of teacher."

Thankfully, Brooks ignored her babbling. "I would love for you to read to me."

"You would?" she asked, looking up at him, eyes widening.

He nodded. "Traveling becomes rather dull when all you can do is look out the carriage window, counting the minutes between now and the next stopping place. I will not tell anyone if you don't."

She grinned at him. "Very well, Mr. Brooks," she said with a nod. "Shall I start at the beginning?"

They continued like that for the rest of the afternoon, August reading and Brooks listening. It was heartening to find someone who enjoyed what she did, but she tried to remind herself it would not last. Nothing in her life ever did. Brooks would return to London once he delivered her to Linfield Hall, leaving her care to her family—as he should, of course.

He had already done more than enough for her father by fetching her, and he must want to return to his regular life sooner rather than later. She wondered if he would forget about her or if she might see him in London if her family ever went there.

He had mentioned, of course, that he spent summers at Linfield as a boy. She was curious if he did the same now, but with the way he spoke about Charles, she assumed they were no longer close enough for him to visit with any frequency. Except, it seemed, on matters of business, which August had to remind herself she was.

No amount of Miss Radcliffe could change that, even if her stories were somewhat scandalous. She must not get carried away, she told herself. After all, people did have a way of disappointing her time and time again.

Chapter Six

❧

DESPITE THEIR INAUSPICIOUS FIRST MEETING, Brooks found himself relaxing around August, but perhaps it was only his aching head muddling his typically more prudent behavior. What else could have driven him to sit beside her or reach for her hand? Worst of all, he agreed to let her read *Udolpho* to him.

Of all the terrible things to do in close quarters with a woman, he had asked her to read *Udolpho* to him! He might as well have asked her to strip naked. Miss Radcliffe's words did nothing but inflame his physical attraction toward her. As she read to him, he found his eyes drifting from her perfect lips to her full bosom and then back toward her lowered eyelashes.

Brooks attempted to calm himself by reminding himself his lust must be one-sided, for what could this bright-eyed chit know of sexual desire except for what she read in novels? He had his concerns about August and Mr. Dunn, but after watching her depart his house in Portsmouth, Brooks no longer suspected anything.

August only cried for her two charges, and she did not

seem like the type of woman to have a scandalous affair with her employer. She told him herself that she valued love and family above all else. August probably yearned for nothing but love and marriage like any young girl he could find at Almack's. But love and marriage were not what Brooks was thinking about as he admired August's figure, even when he was sure she was not interested in him at all.

Instead, Brooks seemed to annoy August on more than one occasion since they met, and she would probably be happy when he returned to London as soon as he delivered her to her father. Night had fallen, and the carriage was dark now. August had ceased reading and leaned her head against the side of the carriage, closing her eyes.

The next posting inn would be soon, and Brooks recalled Mr. Dunn's warning to look after her. Usually, he would have no qualms traveling through the night, switching postboys and horses at every stop, barely resting or eating himself. But it could be dangerous traveling at night, and August looked tired.

Would it be any more dangerous, he wondered, sleeping down the hall from her at an inn, completely unchaperoned? He imagined this was how all ill-advised matches began, especially for men who claimed to want never-ending bachelorhood. A budding attraction would eventually explode when just the right girl was near such a man, his reckless actions forcing him to marry her long before they even knew each other.

Brooks reminded himself that he would leave her soon, returning to his regular life as a bachelor. He would forget his strange fascination with this girl and remember all the reasons why he had no desire to marry.

Willfully celibate, Brooks told himself. He would not fall victim to this girl or anyone else. When they reached the next posting inn, the carriage's sudden stop outside shook her awake, and she regarded Brooks with half-shut eyes.

"Are we here?" she asked, seemingly still half asleep.

He sighed, looking outside the window of the carriage, toward the posting inn. The brick building seemed clean enough from the outside. A lantern hung over the red door, illuminating a black sign with white lettering that said *The Talbot Inn.*

"Not quite," he said. "We have another day of traveling ahead of us. I would go on through the night if it were just me, but I wouldn't want any highwaymen to attack the carriage with you inside."

Wide awake now, she glared at him. "Do you think I wouldn't be able to defend myself like you could?"

Brooks chuckled slightly. She probably could, given the opportunity. "Or perhaps I only value your life more than mine. We can have supper and rest here tonight."

"But what about my father? Didn't you say we were in a hurry?"

Brooks raised his brow. "So now you are eager to see him? We will leave at dawn if it so pleases you, but we will sleep here tonight."

"Oh, all right," she said with a huff.

He helped her out of the carriage and guided her toward the inn. The innkeeper came out from around the bar, where a few patrons sat enjoying their pints. "May I help you, sir?" the man asked Brooks.

He arranged for two rooms—one for him and his "sister," which caused August to raise her brow at him when he said it —and had the man bring them supper while they waited for the servants to prepare their lodging. They took their meal in the public dining room, which was empty except for them.

"Why did you tell the innkeeper that I was your sister?"

she asked in between bites of her dinner, a coy smile playing at her lips.

"I thought it would be easier to say that than explain the truth," Brooks said as he cut into his steak. If he had to suffer through someone's company at supper, the least he could do was enjoy the food.

"I suppose that makes sense," August said thoughtfully. "I have just realized, though, that you know everything about my family, but I know nothing about yours except that you are a solicitor like your father before you. What about your mother? Is she still alive?"

Brooks nodded. "Yes, she's still alive. I even live with her, unfortunately."

August looked as if she was trying not to smile. "Unfortunately?" she echoed. "What a terrible thing to say! Do your wife and mother not get along? That can be the only explanation." Brooks put his knife and fork down as he started to laugh. August glared at him. "What?"

He shook his head, picking up his knife and fork again. "That is a very sly way of asking me whether or not I am married," he said.

She flushed. "Many men don't wear rings, so I couldn't be sure. Let me be more direct, then, if that's what you prefer. Mr. Brooks, are you married?"

He shook his head. "No, I am not. The only Mrs. Brooks in my life is my mother, and her insistence on changing that is the only reason why living with her is unfortunate."

She looked at him as if she didn't quite understand, but why would she? She had not witnessed his parents' marriage fall to shambles as he had. "Don't you have any desire to take a wife?" August asked.

"None at all," he said, shaking his head.

"Because you prefer to be a bachelor?"

She said *bachelor* as if she meant *rake* instead, but not all single men were poorly behaved oafs like Charles. He shook his head. "I prefer quiet solitude."

She laughed at that. "Then I suppose a wife wouldn't do. But what about children? Surely they are worth giving up some of your solitude."

Children were part of the reason he would never marry. The idea of him becoming a father was comical when he had lived with such poor examples his entire life. He didn't know the first thing about fatherhood. "I have no desire for children," he said simply.

"I think I should like having my own family," she replied with a dreamy sigh.

He very nearly rolled his eyes. But why not humor the girl's dream? "Would you?" he asked with just the slightest hint of mockery.

She nodded, ignoring it. "I suppose when one grows up without one, it's all you dream about for quite some time. I had long given up hope before you arrived."

Holding his fork still, he looked up from his plate, eyes narrowing at her as he thought of all the ways he could have misconstrued her words. She must have realized them as well, for she flushed suddenly, then reached for her drink. "I only mean a man might be interested enough to marry me and have children with me now that I have money," she quickly said, averting her gaze from his.

"Were they uninterested before?" he asked—a stupid, prying question. But he *was* curious if there was a man from her past. Perhaps there was one who rejected her due to her lack of funds or connections.

But she would not admit to anything. Her blush only deepened, and she shook her head much too wildly to be convincing. "There were none to be interested *or* uninterested."

"Well, I do hope you'll be discerning of London men," he said, arching his brow at her.

"London men?" she asked, confused. "I thought I was going to Linfield Hall in Kent, not London."

"You will go to London eventually," Brooks explained. "Your father wishes you to be out in society. You will have a season like any other young lady your age."

"But that's a terrible idea! I do not know the first thing about polite society. I would think people in my father's social circles would look down on people like the Dunns—and I was their governess before all this!"

"You will have to learn how to impress them enough to make them forget all that, then." He paused a moment, watching August consider his words. "It's what your father wants, and if you desire a family, going to London and finding a husband is a good place to start."

August reluctantly nodded. A brief moment of silence passed. "You said I should be discerning of London men. Why?"

Brooks shrugged. "I am only trying to manage your expectations. You *do* have money now, and there will be plenty of charming men after it."

"Like you?" He nearly dropped his fork, and she laughed. "Oh, I am only teasing."

Still, he shook his head. "I will never marry. Unlike you, I find the idea of family vastly overrated."

She did not respond at first, only carefully watched him. The way she looked at him made him uncomfortable. She regarded him as if she could see the real reason behind his aversion to marriage and family. As if she could see his disappointment and fear. But rather than call him out for his lies, she only nodded, smiled, and dipped her head to take another drink so he could more easily admire her eyelashes.

Her eyelashes. Brooks nearly rolled his eyes at his own

ridiculousness. Instead, he put down his fork and dabbed his mouth with his napkin.

"Are you finished?" he asked. "Our rooms should be ready now. I would like to depart early tomorrow morning, so you ought to rest while you can."

She nodded at him. The innkeeper led them upstairs, showing them to their rooms which were across from each other. All that separated them was two doors and a narrow hall. After the innkeeper left, they stood in their respective doorways, looking at each other. The glow of the fire from August's room illuminated her from behind, creating a halo of light around her.

For a moment, he thought he might be losing his mind. "Good night," he quickly said before he did anything foolish, firmly shutting the door behind him. He leaned against it when he was alone again, closing his eyes and sighing.

BROOKS AND AUGUST left early the following morning. They traveled all day again, and Brooks did his best to control his errant desires. When August asked if he would like her to read aloud to him, the answer was a resolute no, though that meant his head ached all day with little to distract him from the pain.

Although August tried not to act offended, she barely spoke to him afterward. Dinner was awkward, and Brooks was thankful to be so close to Linfield that they would arrive early tomorrow morning.

Although the large brick house had failed to impress him for many years, August looked at Linfield Hall with awe when it finally came into view. She gasped as soon as she saw it through the carriage window, and when she looked back at him, her eyes were as wide as an owl's. "I have never seen such a large house!" she exclaimed.

Charles was there to greet them as soon as they stepped out of the carriage, and Brooks was pleased to find his appearance had improved since he last saw him. With it only being mid-morning, his valet must have just dressed him. But instead of his typical relaxed demeanor, Charles stood like a soldier about to go to war. When the two weary travelers approached him, he regarded August as if she smelled and Brooks as if he was a traitor.

All was as Brooks expected.

"Have we made it on time?" Brooks asked.

Charles nodded once. "Yes," he said without feeling. "He is still alive."

Brooks gestured toward August, and Charles regarded her with an air of both superiority and disinterest. Suddenly, Brooks dreaded leaving her there. He cleared his throat. "Allow me to introduce your half sister, Charles." The once crisp morning air suddenly felt thick and oppressive. "August, this your brother, Charles."

August attempted something that looked like a curtsey, while Charles offered only a slight bow of the head. Brooks could feel his friend's displeasure radiating from every gesture and look he gave him or August. "I trust your journey was pleasant, and father's solicitor acted as a fine enough escort," Charles said to August.

She nodded. "Indeed, sir, on both accounts. I am so happy to meet you finally."

Brooks felt his temper flare when her brother could only nod in response. There was no happiness on his end, and they all knew it. "I will take you to see Father, then," Charles said, turning on his heel and walking toward the house, the gravel crunching beneath his boots. August was the first to go after him, Brooks following in disbelief a short time afterward.

"Where are your mother and sister?" Brooks asked as they followed Charles up the stairs. Usually, he could hear their chatter from the morning room at this time of day as they ate their breakfast, but the house was silent. The footmen, meanwhile, seemed to cower whenever Charles walked past them.

"They spent the night at Sedgewick Park," Charles asked.

Sedgewick Park was the neighboring estate that belonged to Robert Kendall, now known as the Duke of Rutley ever since his father died ten years ago. Charles and Rutley remained friends into adulthood, enjoying the same types of debauchery even after the duke became engaged to Rosamund. Rutley and his treatment of Rosamund was another reason Charles and Brooks grew apart.

"Do they normally do that?" Brooks asked, furrowing his brow. It didn't make sense that they would leave when Lord Bolton was so ill.

Charles shrugged. "From time to time. I think they grow tired of my company on occasion." Brooks could guess what that meant. Charles must have drunk himself into a stupor after his father revealed his secret. He hoped Rosamund and Lady Bolton were all right, especially since he did not think of Rutley any more highly than Charles. "None of us were sure when you would be back, though my father finally revealed the reason behind your abrupt departure yesterday morning."

"Only yesterday morning?" Brooks asked, annoyed. He did not dare look at August to see her reaction. Meanwhile, Charles nodded.

"We were all shocked, as you can imagine," he said. "Naturally, I poured myself a drink to relax, and my mother and sister left soon after that."

Brooks and August exchanged a look as they reached the second-floor landing. He had mentioned vice, hadn't he? She turned away, and he frowned, wondering what she was thinking.

They followed Charles further down the hall, and Brooks

could hear coughing coming from the direction of Bolton's room. When Charles opened the door and ushered them inside, the earl was in the same position as when Brooks had left him.

"Brooks?" he asked. "Is that you? Have you brought August?"

"I have," Brooks responded without looking at him, his eyes fixated on August, who stood in front of him. Her fingers trembled at her side, and he watched as she clenched and unclenched her fists. He turned and looked at Charles, who remained motionless by the door.

Sighing, Brooks stepped forward, looping his arm under August's. She looked up at him, her brow creased and mouth slightly open from surprise. He offered his best reassuring nod, and she turned forward again, her face no calmer than before, but she allowed him to bring her to her father's bedside anyway.

"Oh!" Lord Bolton exclaimed, the thin skin around his sunken eyes crinkling as he smiled. "She is beautiful! Is she not beautiful, Brooks?"

Brooks did not answer, only tried to smile while letting go of August and slowly backing away, rejoining Charles by the door. They watched from afar as the young woman took a seat beside the bed and exchanged pleasantries with her father. Charles turned to Brooks, whose eyes remained fixed on August.

"I must speak to you alone," Charles said, dipping his head slightly, his words demanding but quiet. Brooks reluctantly met his gaze.

"Should we leave her here alone with him? What if—"

"We shall give you your privacy," Charles announced to his father and sister, interrupting the quiet protestations of his friend. Brooks glared at him, but August seemed unperturbed by their leaving, looking up at him and smiling. Brooks reluctantly followed his friend down to his father's study, and Charles immediately went to the sideboard, pouring himself a glass of brandy with a shaking hand.

"How long have you known about her?" he asked, not bothering to ask if Brooks wanted a drink. He moved behind the desk where Brooks once hid all those years ago. He took a swig of brandy and then slammed the crystal glass down on the desk, the remaining liquid threatening to spill over the rim of the glass and onto his father's papers.

Brooks sighed, placing a hand on his hip. "I believe it was almost three years ago. My father asked me to find a governess position for the earl's daughter. You can imagine my confusion when I thought he meant Rosamund until he explained that no, there was another one." The room fell silent, and Brooks and Charles stared at each other. Brooks eventually continued. "You must understand why I could not tell you. Your father was a client, and I was handling his private business."

This explanation did not suffice for Charles. "But I am your best friend, and that stranger is my sister. I deserved to know!"

Brooks scoffed. "Oh, Charles, you and I have not been best friends for a long time. Not since before we both went to Oxford."

Charles glared at him without speaking, angrily picking up his glass again and taking another drink. He finished the remainder of what he poured only a moment ago with one loud gulp, moving to the sideboard for more. Brooks groaned when he heard the pop of a cork.

"And this is why we have not been best friends for a long time," he complained. "You overreact. You drink. I had almost forgotten how tiring it all was! No wonder your mother and sister went to Sedgewick Park. I almost think I even prefer Rutley to you now."

Charles turned to look at Brooks, pointing at himself while waving his drink-carrying hand at Brooks, spilling some of the amber liquid onto the carpeted floor. "You think I am overreacting? My father just gave away part of my inheritance to that girl. Twelve thousand pounds! *Twelve thousand pounds!* Do you even understand how much money that is?"

As his former friend's voice became more and more shrill, Brooks involuntarily flinched as he recalled his father's drunken rages. Charles took a deep breath, shaking his head as he took a sip of his drink. "Don't you have any sway over him as a solicitor?" he asked, squinting at Brooks, who remained unmoving throughout Charles's entire outburst. "Couldn't you have talked him out of it? Surely you think he's acting foolish as well!"

Brooks sighed. The answer was yes, but August didn't deserve Charles's anger when it was their father's decision. "You should give your sister a chance," Brooks said. "I think you might find you actually like her, and I don't believe she means to cause you any more trouble than she already has."

Charles shook his head. "You do not understand," he said, his voice cracking as if he might cry. "I *need* that money he has given her."

"Charles—"

"I need it, Brooks!" he shouted, throwing his half-filled glass at the wood-paneled wall of his father's study. The glass shattered, amber liquid spilling onto the wall and floor. Crystal shards, large and small, lay scattered across the carpet.

"Have you lost your mind?" Brooks asked in horror.

Charles ran his hands through his hair. "There are certain debts that I promised to pay when I gained control of the estate's coffers. Now I am not sure I will have it all without mortgaging the estate."

"Debts to whom?" Brooks asked, furrowing his brow.

Charles appeared reluctant to answer before mumbling a response he couldn't hear. Brooks rolled his eyes. "For God's sake, Charles, you were shouting well enough before. Speak up!"

"The duke!" Charles exclaimed.

Brooks stared at him for a moment, not quite believing his ears. "As in the Duke of Rutley?"

"Do not look so surprised, Brooks. He was always the one accompanying me to every card room at every party and club. Neither one of us could ever say no to a game of cards, but he was always the lucky one. I was not." Charles sighed. "The man has covered my losses on more than one occasion, believing I would be able to pay him back once I controlled Linfield. He even agreed that Rosamund's dowry could go toward the total amount, but now she wants to end the engagement. I won't let her, though, no matter how much she complains."

"Rosamund doesn't want to marry Rutley anymore?" Brooks asked, furrowing his brow. Rosamund had wanted to marry Rutley since she was thirteen years old and decided he was the most handsome man she would ever know.

Charles nodded, placing his hands on his hips. "She has grown to be so spoiled and selfish. I hope my new sister isn't like that."

"Rosamund is spoiled and selfish?" Brooks echoed in disbelief. "Your family has lost a great deal of money due to *your* irresponsibility. How much do you owe the man?" Charles mumbled something again. Brooks groaned. "Speak up, Charles. This family will be entirely your responsibility any day now. How much is it?"

"Twenty thousand pounds!"

Brooks grew pale. No wonder Charles did not want August to have any of her inheritance. Unable to look at his friend any longer, he turned to leave.

"Where are you going?" Charles asked.

Brooks stopped. "I am going to check on your father and sister. I can think of nothing productive to say to you right now."

"Then you should know Father wishes for us to call her Lady August—as in Lady August Finch. What a joke! Our family will be the laughingstock of London this season."

Brooks did not respond, leaving Charles to drink alone in his study.

Chapter Seven

AUGUST HAD IMAGINED what it would be like to meet her parents for as long as she could remember. None of what she envisioned compared to sitting by Lord Bolton's side at Linfield Hall. She hadn't been lying when she told Brooks that her father's home was the largest house she had ever seen.

As for her father's bedchamber, she had never sat in such an impressive-looking room in all her life, and she felt smaller than ever beside the earl's massive canopy bed. Fine paintings hung on the walls in gilded frames, making her feel like such an outsider.

The earl was much smaller and frailer than she had expected, clearly the victim of a long illness. His body looked thin beneath the bedclothes, and he did not look like he belonged at Linfield any more than she did in such a weakened physical state. Her first instinct was to reach for his hand and hold it, wishing to give him some sort of physical anchor to this world.

He smiled at her when she did. "My sweet, kind girl," he said. His voice was as weak as he looked, so she listened carefully, moving her chair closer to him. "You are more beautiful than I ever imagined."

"Thank you, Lord Bolton, but you mustn't waste your words complimenting me," she replied, flushing, wondering if he was somewhat delirious. "Tell me how you feel. Is there anything I can do to help you?"

He patted her hand. "You have already helped me. I could not have rested peacefully without seeing you and saying goodbye."

Bolton coughed violently, bringing a handkerchief to his mouth with a shaking hand. August couldn't help but recoil from him, noticing the bloodstains on the small piece of fabric right away. She had seen this illness before. One of the girls at Hardbury died of it not so long before August left. She had been thankful she and Jane had remained untouched at the time.

"What a sorry state I am in," her father said once his coughing fit had subsided. She noticed the faintest twinkle in his blue eyes as he turned to look at her. "You must be wondering how this old man could be your father. I swear I was as spry as someone your age only three months ago."

August shook her head, frowning. "Oh, no, Lord Bolton— I am not wondering that at all. If anything, I am wondering why you have asked me to come here."

Her father's brow wrinkled. "Didn't Mr. Brooks tell you? I mean to leave you twelve thousand pounds when I die, which could be any day now by the looks of it."

"Do not say that," August murmured. She sighed, unsure of how to say what she was feeling without offending him. "But you did not have to bring me *here*, revealing my existence to your entire family, who I am sure will hate me."

Her father's eyes widened. "They will not!"

August hushed him. "A man in your condition should not be shouting," she said as kindly as she could. He glared at her, the twinkle in his eyes gone. So he had a temper. Perhaps that was where she got hers.

"Father," she continued more resolutely, "I will not delude myself into thinking I am more to you than what I am. I know you wish to ease your guilty conscience, but you could have told Mr. Brooks to write me a letter about your passing. You could have opened an account in my name without ever revealing who you were. Wouldn't that have been enough for you?" He made a sound of protest, but she continued anyway. "Instead, you have shocked your entire family—and for what? I would have been more than pleased to rent a set of rooms in Wilton to live out the rest of my days as an old spinster, with no one ever knowing how rich I was."

After Brooks grew tired of speaking to her the day prior, August had spent much of the carriage ride yesterday wondering what she would do once she saw her father. She finally decided that she must convince him to let her live a quiet life, away from her family and society. Regardless of her wealth, she would never be accepted.

"Wilton?" he echoed incredulously, and the thought occurred to her that he may not know where that was.

"The village closest to Hardbury, where you sent me to school." Her father still stared blankly at her. "In Hampshire."

Bolton huffed. "You do not belong in a country village," he said, uttering the last two words with disdain. "You should go to London and find a husband like all the other young girls your age."

August shook her head. She had no interest in the ballrooms of London, preferring the idea of a quiet, peaceful existence. "And who will be my chaperone? Your wife?"

"Of course!" the man exclaimed.

August couldn't believe her ears. He shouldn't expect such a thing from Lady Bolton, not after he only just revealed

August's existence to her, especially with August being a physical manifestation of his betrayal of their marriage.

"What about my real mother?" August asked suddenly. "I always thought you were both dead, but now that I know you are alive, perhaps she is as well. Is she?"

Bolton grew paler than he already was. "Forget your mother. She is no one important. Lady Bolton will be your mother now."

August furrowed her brow. "What do you mean she is no one important? Who is she?"

Before he could answer her, the door to his room swung open. "August," Brooks said from the doorway, watching her with a concerned look. Charles was nowhere to be found, and the solicitor gave a sidelong glance at the man in bed. "You should let your father rest. Lady Bolton and your sister will return from Sedgewick Park soon. We can wait for them in the drawing room."

Reluctantly, she said goodbye to her father and then stood up, following Brooks out into the hall. She spoke as soon as he closed the door behind them. "I was just about to find out who my mother is," she said, annoyed.

He stared at her for a moment, then shrugged. "She was most likely a courtesan that society has since forgotten. I could have told you that."

August's face fell as Brooks began walking down the hall toward the main staircase without her. She scampered to keep up with him. "If that's truly the case, then it supports my belief that none of this is a good idea. I have seen him, he has seen me, and now I should go. You will open an account for me when he dies, and I will use the money to live peacefully in Wilton."

"Wilton?" he asked incredulously.

She glared at him. Didn't these people know there were places in England other than London? "Yes, Wilton. The village near Hardbury, my old school. I could rent a set of rooms there and be near friends." She shook her head. "I do not wish for Lady Bolton to embarrass herself as my chaperone in London as my father wants."

Brooks stopped in the middle of the hall, looking at her curiously. "What about that family you wanted?" he asked. "I hardly doubt there are any eligible bachelors in Wilton."

August thought of Henry. No, she supposed Brooks was right. There were no eligible bachelors in Wilton. Her nostrils flared, and she continued down the hall. "Regardless of that, Wilton is the best place for me."

"I agree that it may be difficult to convince Lady Bolton to accept you," Brooks said, following her. "But allow me to speak to her before you resign yourself to a life of spinsterhood in Wilton. You are far too pretty and rich for that."

August flushed, avoiding his gaze. Was he flirting with her? She did not dare ask, too afraid of the answer one way or another. It didn't matter anyway, as Brooks would be leaving soon. "When do you return to London?" she asked.

He paused. "I thought I would stay until I was certain you were safe. Charles has not given me much faith in his ability to look after you."

August frowned. So they had quarreled, and that must have been why her brother was not with them as they entered Linfield's cavernous drawing room. A pink-and-cream carpet covered the floors, and they sat on chairs with golden feet. She admired the painting over the marble fireplace, a cherub surrounded by flowers. But then August glanced down at her dress, noticing the frayed hems at the sleeves and feeling embarrassed. When Lady Bolton and Rosamund entered the drawing room soon after them, August became even more uncomfortable.

"Perfect timing," Brooks muttered, standing up and smiling. August stood as well, turning to face her sister and her father's wife with a deep breath.

They were both tall women, each towering over August, though she didn't consider herself that short. Rosamund almost reminded her of herself, with her fair hair and angular features. August was relieved that she smiled unreservedly, grinning until her cheeks rounded and her eyes squinted.

Lady Bolton, meanwhile, stood as still as a sculpture, chin upturned as she regarded August. She couldn't have been older than fifty, her hair still a brilliant red piled on top of her head. August almost died of shame standing next to her father's beautiful wife in her outdated clothes.

Before Brooks could say anything, Rosamund approached August directly, taking her sister's hands into hers. August was sure her sister felt her tremble. "You must be August," her sister said anyway, smiling. Slowly, August nodded.

Rosamund squeezed her fingers slightly. "I am your sister, Rosamund. It is lovely to meet you finally. I have always wanted a sister." She turned back to her mother. "Isn't that right, Mama?"

"Indeed," Lady Bolton said, taking a seat in one of the armchairs with an irritated look on her face.

Rosamund turned back to August. "How was your journey?" she asked with the ease of an old friend. "I trust that Brooks has taken good care of you."

Her sister shot Brooks a playful look, and the three of them joined Lady Bolton in sitting, with Rosamund and August on one settee and Brooks in one of the chairs across from them. "It was not too terrible," August said, forcing a smile. A heaviness hung in the room as they all fell silent.

"Will you stay a few nights with us, Brooks?" Rosamund asked after a while. At least someone was brave enough to make conversation with Lady Bolton looking as wretched as she did. August tried to think of something thoughtful to say to the poor woman. "You must be tired from being in a carriage for so long. I know how ill they make you."

Brooks nodded. "I will stay a few nights, but then I must return to London. My mother must be worried about me by now."

"I already wrote to her," Lady Bolton drawled. "She is aware of the whole sad affair."

Lady Bolton and Brooks exchanged a look that August couldn't quite read. Another uncomfortable silence filled the room until Charles entered a few moments later. Brooks looked as if he was ready to pounce, carefully watching him.

"I see that everyone has met," her brother said, slurring his words while holding a glass of brandy. He haphazardly slumped into a chair beside Brooks, his long legs spreading in opposite directions. He looked at August. "My mother has not scared you off yet, has she?"

"Charles!" Rosamund exclaimed.

"Do you often find yourself drinking before noon, Charles?" Brooks asked.

August ignored them, answering her brother directly. "Lady Bolton has been nothing but kind." She offered a small smile in her direction, though the countess appeared unmoved. "You have all been nothing but kind, welcoming me into your home."

Charles looked unimpressed by such sentiments, while Rosamund reached out and patted her sister's hand, still smiling. She tried not to feel too much glee over such a simple gesture of comfort. August could still hear the voice of Brooks, telling her not to hope for too much.

"How was Sedgewick Park?" Charles asked. "Have you and Rutley made up after your most recent squabble? I won't have any more of this talk about you two not marrying this summer."

August raised her brow, turning toward Rosamund. Was

her sister engaged? That was something Brooks hadn't mentioned.

"My feelings have not changed," Rosamund said. She glanced at her mother, who nodded at her. Rosamund turned back to Charles. "I would like to break off the engagement."

Her brother's eyes turned dark. His head snapped toward his mother. "Are you condoning this?"

"Rosamund is free to marry whomever she wishes," the countess said, her voice unwavering despite the intensity of her son's gaze. "Her father and I have always agreed on that. If she does not wish to marry—"

"Father will be dead soon," Charles snapped, "and what will matter is my opinion, not yours."

Everyone in the room looked at him, equally horrified. August was beginning to realize her brother was a downright bounder, and she didn't blame Brooks for their growing apart. Charles and his behavior must have been to blame for any quarreling.

Her brother turned back to Rosamund, his face pinched with displeasure. "If you wish to keep your dowry, you will marry Rutley. I will hear no more talk of you breaking off the engagement."

Rosamund defiantly lifted her chin. "I do not need a dowry. I'm sure I can find someone who doesn't care— someone far better than Rutley."

Charles rose. "You will marry Rutley if you expect to continue living in this house!" he yelled. "I will turn you out of Linfield if you break your engagement."

"Charles!" Lady Bolton and Brooks cried in unison. August could only look upon the scene with wide eyes, suddenly realizing she was not the only issue this family faced.

Rosamund did not shout, only rose as well, her chin still defiantly high. She brought August with her, pulling her up by the wrist to stand beside her. August nearly yelped at the sudden movement.

"I will not entertain this conversation any longer," Rosamund said firmly, wrapping her arm around August's. "I am going to show August to her room. We will talk about this later—in private."

Rosamund turned on her heel before their brother could say anything else, practically dragging August with her. She looked back over her shoulder at Brooks, who was saying something to Lady Bolton. Soon they were back in the entry hall, heading up the marble staircase.

Rosamund eventually let go of August's arm, shooting her an apologetic look. "I'm sorry about that," she said, her voice suddenly demure again. "Sometimes Charles and I do not always see eye to eye."

August only nodded, afraid to say anything. She walked with Rosamund up the stairs in silence until they reached the third-floor landing. "I had the servants prepare a room for you down this hall," Rosamund said, leading the way.

The room was nowhere as large as her father's, but it was much more impressive than where she slept at Mr. Dunn's. Curtains made of red velvet hung from the bed's canopy, and a dressing table and a large wardrobe sat in the corner of the room. Her small trunk from Portsmouth rested at the foot of the massive bed; she supposed one of the servants had brought it upstairs when they first arrived.

"I'm afraid I don't have anything appropriate to wear for dinner this evening," August said sheepishly after seeing the trunk.

"No matter!" Rosamund said with a wave of her hand and a smile. She went to the side of the bed and tugged the bellpull. "I will have my maid bring in some of mine. She can take your measurements as well. I will send them to London for new clothes for you."

"Rosamund—"

"Or," her sister interjected, suddenly pacing the room, "we could leave for London tomorrow. We have already stayed here too long this spring, and I admit I am growing quite bored of the country."

August watched her sister curiously. She never thought she would feel sorry for someone like Rosamund—so pretty and wealthy, with a mother who loved her—but August found her mind changing. "You wouldn't want to leave your father, would you?"

Rosamund sighed, sitting down on August's bed. "No, I suppose I wouldn't. We will have to send the measurements, then."

August sat down beside her, putting a hand on Rosamund's shoulder. The older girl turned to her.

"I'm sure Charles will come around," August said, biting her lip. "And if he doesn't, Mr. Brooks tells me that Father is leaving me enough money that I could buy a house of my own. Nothing quite so spectacular as this, but you are more than welcome to live with me."

Tears sprung to Rosamund's eyes, and August smiled at her. "You know, I meant it when I said I always wanted a sister," Rosamund said. "I was not only trying to be polite."

"I believe you," August said, her grin broadening as her sister pulled her into a comforting embrace.

Chapter Eight

After August and Rosamund went upstairs, Brooks asked for a private audience with Lady Bolton in the garden. The day was warm enough, even if it was still April, and Brooks thought it was best if Charles was left to have his tantrum in the house by himself. The soon-to-be earl watched them go with a glare.

"I suppose you two are leaving to conspire against me," he grumbled before finishing his glass of brandy. Brooks looked at him with disgust.

"We are going for a walk in the garden," Lady Bolton said matter-of-factly. "You are welcome to join us, but I'm sure you would prefer to sit here and sulk and drink." She turned on her heel, her skirts swishing behind her.

"You have always liked him better than me," Charles said. Lady Bolton stopped, closing her eyes, her jaw tensing. "Ever since we were boys."

Lady Bolton sighed. She turned her head, looking at her son over her shoulder. "Don't be ridiculous, Charles."

Lady Bolton began walking again, Brooks at her tail. "How long has he been like this?" he asked when they were out of earshot of the drawing room. Lady Bolton turned and looked at him as if he were woefully ignorant.

"Hasn't he always been like this?" Lady Bolton asked, an underlying tone of exasperation in her voice. "Isn't that why you stopped coming to Linfield? You grew tired of my son's antics by the time you turned eighteen."

Brooks frowned. "Yes, but I have never seen him so unkind to you—or his sister. I understand he's under a lot of pressure, but—"

"Ah," Lady Bolton said with a nod of the head. "So he told you about his gambling debts, did he? Twenty thousand pounds! I can hardly believe it. I blame his father for always indulging him. He's turned into such a spoiled, selfish man, just like my husband."

They had reached the garden by then, a collection of gravel paths leading through hedges with flowers that had some weeks to go before finally blooming that year. Brooks could hear the faint sound of a fountain in the distance. He recalled summers where he happily played with Charles, when yes, his father did indulge him, but Lady Bolton did as well. Brooks thought his friend's jealousy was utterly unfounded. Lady Bolton did love her son, and any affection she held for Brooks sprung from pity over his sad home life.

"If you know about the debts," Brooks said, "then you must know Rutley is the man he owes."

Lady Bolton stopped suddenly. "What?"

"Surely he told you that," Brooks said, shocked. Lady Bolton shook her head a little, and Brooks sighed. "Rosamund's dowry is part of how Charles intends to pay him back."

Lady Bolton's eyes widened. "Did Charles say that?"

Brooks nodded. "So you see now why he's eager for Rosamund to marry him. I'm not sure how she will get out of it."

Lady Bolton frowned. "If only my husband hadn't given twelve thousand pounds to that... that bastard of his! Did you know he expects me to be her chaperone for a season in London?"

"Her name is August," Brooks said as patiently as he could. He understood Lady Bolton's hurt over the situation, but she must have known August needed the same kindness she showed him when he was younger. She was only an innocent girl, after all.

"Whatever her name is, I will not do it," she replied stubbornly.

"Lady Bolton—"

"I will hear no more of it, Brooks!" she exclaimed. Brooks nodded once, knowing when to stop pushing someone. Her temper seemed to subside, and she spoke again. "I have been thinking of sending her to my sister-in-law in London. You know Lady Ramsbury, don't you? She is a widow and a dowager duchess with no other real responsibilities at the moment. I can think of no one more suitable than her."

Brooks frowned. He knew the Dowager Duchess of Ramsbury. He was sure everyone in Mayfair did, especially the men—regardless of their age. There wasn't a word for a female rakehell, but Lady Ramsbury would be described as such if there was one. She had been a widow some ten-odd years, developing quite the reputation for herself in the process. Everyone seemed to turn a blind eye to her bad behavior, though, thanks to her title, wealth, and the fabulous parties she frequently hosted.

"I can think of no one worse for her," Brooks argued. "You know her reputation. August is young and unrefined. She needs someone to teach her the ways of this new world, and I can think of no one better than you and Rosamund. Could you not—"

"Please desist, Mr. Brooks," Lady Bolton snapped, stopping in the middle of the pathway. Brooks stood at attention. "I will not do it, and no one can make me—not even my husband—especially when he's finally dead."

Brooks watched her walk on ahead, sighing. He was disappointed for a moment, then wondered why he even cared. He had told himself that he would deliver August to Linfield, and that would be that.

Then why, he asked himself, did he worry so much for her future? Unable to arrive at an answer, he reluctantly continued his walk through the garden, listening to Lady Bolton as she commented on much more pleasant topics such as the scenery and weather.

AUGUST STOOD ALONE in the drawing room before dinner, wearing one of her sister's dinner dresses. The maids did their best to make it fit August's more petite frame, but the gown still felt slightly too big. Her sister's silk evening gloves fit wonderfully, though, and they were undoubtedly the best pair of gloves August had ever worn. She couldn't stop running her hands over them, all the way from her wrists to the crook of her elbow.

Charles invited the duke to dinner, which August could tell displeased Rosamund a great deal, though her older sister tried not to show it. Meanwhile, Lady Bolton seemed to have changed her tune about the man. She hovered close to Rutley in the drawing room, laughing at something he said, while Rosamund sat alone in front of the fire.

August could tell right away that Brooks did not like the duke. When he said something that made the countess laugh, he turned and rolled his eyes, probably thinking that no one was watching. August smiled to herself, finding his constant surliness somewhat endearing. Their eyes met from across the room, and Brooks approached her. They stood by the pianoforte in silence, surveying the scene in front of them.

"You did not tell me my sister had a fiancé," August finally said, looking from the handsome duke in the corner to Brooks beside her. The solicitor looked at her sheepishly.

"I suppose I forgot," he said, laughing slightly.

"You forgot?" August asked incredulously, raising her brow.

Brooks nodded. "They have been engaged for so long that sometimes I forget that they're not yet married. The wedding has been put off every year for one reason or another. Ironically enough, it's usually Rutley who is trying to cry off. I wonder what happened to make Rosamund do it this time."

August blinked as Brooks seemed to consider the answer. Eventually, he shrugged. "I suppose it doesn't matter. The family will delay it another year, using your father's death as an excuse. And then we'll do it all again next year, except with a different excuse."

August stared at him, then turned to the people in front of them. All the riches in the world, and they were still miserable. August did not understand. "Why is it so important to Charles that they marry?" she asked. "What power does the duke hold over him?"

She watched Brooks smile at her. "You're very clever, Lady August."

August cringed. "Oh, please do not call me Lady August. It feels so strange. The only ladies here are the countess and my sister."

"What shall I call you then?" he asked, raising his brow. "I cannot call you Miss Summer anymore."

"Just August, then," she said. He seemed to freeze, carefully watching her. "And what shall I call you, Mr. Brooks?"

"Just Brooks is fine," he replied, his voice cracking. He cleared his throat, and she tried not to smile. He seemed nervous, but she couldn't understand why. "I spoke to Lady Bolton today, by the way. I think you might have been right about her."

August bit back a smile. "What did you say?" she asked after no longer being able to stop a grin from spreading across her face. "Did you say you think I could have been right?"

"It's not ladylike to brag, you know," Brooks grumbled. "And making an enemy of Lady Bolton is no cause for smiling." He must have noticed August's anxious look because his face softened. "But do not worry. As the executor of your father's will, I will make sure you receive your twelve thousand pounds. And if your father's dying wish is that you be out in society, I will see to that too."

August stared at him. Why was he going through such pains to see her settled? Brooks could have left Linfield that day to return to London but didn't. So why did he linger?

"That's very kind of you, Brooks," she said, finally looking away from him. August was sure she must have been blushing.

"I am only doing my job," he said.

August looked back up at him, nodding. "Of course," she said, forcing a smile. "But it's kind, nonetheless. And I thank you for it."

Before he could say anything, August looked toward her sister, who remained seated alone in front of the fire. "I think I'll check in on my sister before dinner if you don't mind. She looks miserable. Excuse me."

She quickly walked away, reminding herself that developing any sort of attachment to Brooks was foolish. He did not want her that way, and August could think of plenty of reasons why, including one he didn't even know yet.

Chapter Nine

DINNER WAS MUCH LESS tempestuous than the family's last meeting in the drawing room. All were on their best behavior with the duke visiting, though Rosamund remained in a sullen state for most of the night. She barely spoke to anyone except August. Although he was wrong about Lady Bolton, Brooks was glad Rosamund had taken August under her wing.

Rutley was his usual charming self, appealing to everyone but Brooks and Rosamund. He had become even more irritating in adulthood, though in different ways compared to childhood. The duke always knew the right thing to say to charm the ladies, Lady Bolton included, and he was a handsome bastard—even Brooks could see that. The countess seemed to have all but forgotten Rosamund's wishes now that Rutley could make or mar the estate with the twenty thousand pounds that Charles owed him.

Even August seemed to like the duke, but that could have been because he acted interested in what she had to say—unlike Charles, who pretended that August didn't exist. If Brooks had to guess, Rutley was only acting kind to impress

Rosamund with his generosity toward her half sister, who seemed to like the girl more than anyone other than Brooks. Still, his feelings didn't matter in this situation, and they would surely fade into indifference.

When dinner had finished, Rutley had gone home, and the ladies had retired for the evening, only Charles and Brooks remained in the drawing room. Charles was very drunk, and Brooks observed him sadly.

"What happened to you, Charles?" he asked. Charles furrowed his brow as if he didn't understand the question.

"What happened to *you*, Brooks?" Charles slurred every word he spoke, causing Brooks to roll his eyes. His old friend took a swig of brandy, then wiped his wet lips with the back of his hand. "You used to be fun."

"You and I both know I was never nearly as fun as you and Rutley, even before my father died and I wasn't running the entire practice."

"Perhaps you could hire me to help you." Charles grinned mischievously. "You and I both know I need the money to pay for my father's bastard."

Brooks grimaced. "I wish you would not call her that."

"Does Brooks have a soft spot for my new little sister?" Charles teased.

Brooks felt his face go hot. Was he that obvious? He cleared his throat, eager to change the subject. "Speaking of little sisters, when will you tell Rosamund why you are insisting she marry Rutley? She will not bend to your will without a good reason."

Charles's expression soured, and he took another sip of brandy. "She will bend to my will with or without reason. I will be earl soon, and she will do as I say."

Brooks's face fell. "You truly are an awful older brother."

"How would you know? You no longer have a sister."

The vicious jab was like a knife to the side. If Brooks was

a violent man, he might have punched Charles, but he resisted. A swift blow to the jaw wouldn't change Charles, so Brooks rose from his chair instead.

"You must tell her. If you do not, I will." Charles stared up at him, silent but angry. Brooks bowed slightly. "Good night, my lord."

BY THE TIME Linfield's inhabitants rose the following day, Lord Bolton was dead. Rosamund was the only one who cried upon hearing the news. They gathered in the drawing room, waiting for the undertaker. The servants put out trays of tea, fresh fruit, and cakes in an attempt to calm the family's nerves.

Instead, Charles reached for the brandy while Lady Bolton paced the room, her concerned eyes intermittently falling on each of her children. August sat beside her sister and attempted to comfort her.

Meanwhile, Brooks sat at the desk, drawing up the necessary papers when a rich man died. Upon reviewing the ledgers, Brooks knew Linfield Hall would be in trouble if Charles didn't come up with twenty thousand pounds and pay off Rutley soon. He would have to sell something to protect Linfield, perhaps the dowager cottage or the family's house in town.

Brooks was considering what Charles could do when Rutley suddenly appeared in the doorway of the drawing room. Their eyes met, and Rutley smiled slightly at him. Then Charles noticed the duke from across the room.

"Your Grace!" he exclaimed, walking toward Rutley. "I appreciate you coming. My sister is inconsolable, and I thought your presence might comfort her."

Rosamund swiftly rose from where she sat, leaving a flabbergasted August behind. Her sister walked toward the two men. The features on Rosamund's face were pinched together in irritation, and Brooks and August exchanged similar looks of concern before turning back toward the scene.

"What are you doing here?" Rosamund asked in a low voice.

Her brother bristled at that. "Is that any way—"

Rutley silenced Charles with a look. He skulked back across the room toward his mother, leaving the couple alone.

"What are you doing here?" Rosamund repeated after her brother let them be. They spoke so softly now that Brooks was the only one who could hear them from the nearby desk.

Rutley raised his brow. "Your brother sent a servant over with the news. I thought you might need comforting."

Rosamund remained stone-faced despite Rutley's desperate look. Brooks found it entertaining to watch Rutley be the pleading party for once instead of Rosamund.

"I have my sister," Rosamund said, glancing back toward August. "I do not require any more comforting." An awkward pause lingered between them while Rutley struggled to find something to say. Rosamund cleared her throat. "Truthfully, I have been thinking, and—"

"Perhaps we should go somewhere more private to talk."

Rutley turned and looked at Brooks. His sharp gaze caused Brooks to turn away, back toward his papers. He waited to hear them leave, and when he was sure no one was watching, he quietly stood up from his desk, following them. Eavesdropping was generally frowned upon in polite society, but Brooks never did trust Rutley with Rosamund.

They had gone into the library, closing the door behind them. Brooks stood quietly in the hall, trying to listen. Luckily they spoke loudly and angrily enough that he heard them quite easily.

"I have been thinking very carefully about our last conversation," Rosamund said, her voice confident, "and I have decided I do not believe you."

"What?" Rutley said incredulously. There was a prolonged pause. "You do not believe what, exactly?"

"I do not believe you truly love me." A masculine groan pierced the room. "Even though you have finally said it, and I told you that was all I wanted."

"All right," Rutley said. Brooks imagined him crossing his arms as if he was about to bargain with another member of the House of Lords. "What can I do to make you believe me? What else can I possibly do to make up for the sins of my past? I cannot completely erase them, you know, as much as you might want me to do so."

Another pause. "I think that's the problem, Robert. I know you cannot erase them, and no number of promises or sweet words can make me trust you again. I thought you had changed when you proposed a few years ago, but when I found out... when I found out... the true reasons behind you constantly delaying the engagement and then the wedding..."

Her voice broke, and Brooks stiffened. She was crying. He didn't have to think too long as to why. Rutley had been unfaithful to her, and Rosamund had somehow found out. Perhaps that was why Lady Bolton had initially sided with Rosamund when she told Charles that she wanted to break off the engagement, especially when her husband's illegitimate daughter was sitting on her settee at the time.

"I have tried everything I can to earn your forgiveness," Rutley said, his words cold and angry. "What more can I do? You are acting ridiculous, Rosamund."

Brooks winced. Despite his limited experience with women, even he knew that was the wrong thing to say. But Rosamund hardly reacted. Perhaps she was used to it.

"I think it's best we call off the engagement," she said, sniffling. "We will only make each other miserable. After watching what's happened with my sister, I am now sure of it. I could not bear it if you had an affair while we were married, and I do not trust you enough to believe you wouldn't. So how could I marry you?"

The two fell silent. Brooks waited for Rutley's response when suddenly a hand touched his shoulder. He jumped, quickly turning to find August standing there, smiling up at him. "What are you doing?" she asked, her voice at full volume.

Brooks quickly wrapped his arm around her, leading her away from the door, afraid that Rutley or Rosamund might hear them. When they reached a safe distance, he stopped to scold her. "What did it look like I was doing?" he asked. "I was eavesdropping."

He turned, looking over his shoulder in the direction of the library. No one was following them, so he breathed a sigh of relief and turned back to August. "You should never sneak up on an eavesdropper."

She narrowed her gaze as she looked up at him, placing her hands on her hips. "Or perhaps you should never eavesdrop," she retorted. "Why did you follow them in the first place? I saw you leave the drawing room earlier when you thought no one noticed. You are lucky I did not tell on you when Lady Bolton and Charles asked where you were."

"What do they want? Is that why you came searching for me?"

She nodded. "I'm not entirely sure, but I watched them conspire in the corner of the drawing room after everyone left. It was very unkind to leave me alone with them."

"I'm sorry," Brooks muttered, then shook his head, touching his thumb and forefinger to his temple. After a moment, he dropped his hand, looking at August. "You said you saw them conspiring. What do you mean?"

August shrugged. "They were whispering furtively while

occasionally looking at me, thinking I wasn't noticing. I'm sure they were discussing how to rid themselves of me now that my father is gone. I think you should reconsider your position on me renting a set of rooms in Wilton."

But Brooks only thought of the Dowager Duchess of Ramsbury. He had yet to mention her aunt's existence to August, but he should have known the countess and Charles would send her to Lady Ramsbury as soon as possible. But how could Brooks convince them to let August stay? Lady Ramsbury was an entirely unsuitable chaperone.

"And why did they ask you to go fetch me?" he asked.

"Come with me to the study, and we will both find out."

Brooks nodded. As he walked with her, Brooks began thinking of ways to persuade them into letting August stay on at Linfield. Unfortunately, his ideas were limited. "Why do you look so alarmed?" August asked, her eyes searching his. "Is something bad about to happen?"

He quickly shook his head. "It's nothing," he replied, offering a reassuring smile.

Charles was sitting behind his desk when they arrived, looking quite pleased with himself. Lady Bolton stood by the window, her face like marble. Charles waved to the two seats in front of him. "Sit down, please," he said.

Brooks and August exchanged a look, then moved to sit in the two chairs across from Charles. Lady Bolton paced behind them while Charles spoke. "Now that Father's gone, Mother and I have come up with a solution for the little problem he has left us."

August shrank into her chair. Brooks did his best to remain calm, though he found himself wanting to lunge at Charles more and more. "What do you mean by that?" he asked.

"Father wanted August to have a season, but Mother will be in mourning for the next few months," Charles explained. "She cannot be her chaperone. We have been considering other options, and—"

"Why don't you wait a year?" Brooks interjected. He would reason with them, he thought. Once they saw August's charms—and she received some much-needed polish—they would be happy to chaperone her next year.

Charles furrowed his brow. "You haven't even finished listening to what I have to say," he said, annoyed. "We thought August could go and stay with her aunt, Lady Ramsbury."

Brooks gripped the arm of his seat. So it was as he suspected. He turned back to Lady Bolton, who gave a little shrug and paced on.

"Wouldn't you like to meet your aunt?" Charles asked August as if she were a little girl. She glanced at Brooks, her forehead wrinkled with confusion. Of course, she couldn't know Lady Ramsbury's reputation, so she would see no issue living with her in London. To her, Lady Ramsbury was likely just another relative to meet that was hopefully nicer than her brother.

Turning back to Charles, she smiled. "That sounds like a lovely idea. I would love to meet someone else who is related to me and maybe stay with them awhile."

"Wonderful!" her brother exclaimed, grinning and clapping his hands together as if nothing had ever pleased him more. August appeared excited as well.

"Are you sure Lady Ramsbury is the right chaperone for August's entrance into society?" Brooks asked before brother and sister squealed with too much glee. August gave him a confused look. "A girl only has her first season once, after all."

"Oh, come now, Brooks," Charles said with a smile. "My aunt isn't so bad. A bit eccentric, perhaps, but—"

"She has a terrible reputation," Brooks interrupted, not wanting to dance around the subject any longer. He looked over his shoulder at Lady Bolton. "August needs someone to guide her, not debauch her."

August raised her brows at him in the same defiant way she treated him the morning they first met. She turned back to her brother. "Well, I think she sounds lovely."

"What—"

"That's the spirit, August!" Charles exclaimed.

Brooks gritted his teeth together. "But—"

"I will write to her immediately."

"You!" a voice shouted from the doorway.

Brooks turned and looked, though he remained perplexed by August's response to his comment. Shouldn't a young lady *worry* about being debauched? But Rosamund stood in the study before he could say anything, pointing an accusatory finger at her brother. Rutley rushed in behind her, reaching for her waist. She batted his hand away.

"You have mortgaged my future!" Rosamund yelled. She charged at him with a very unladylike scream, but Rutley grabbed her around the waist, pulling her backward. She let out a loud sob, crumpling against his chest.

Charles stood up, his hands on his hips. "For God's sake, man!" he exclaimed. "Why would you tell her?"

"She tried to cry off!" Rutley shouted back. Rosamund still sobbed against his chest. "I thought I would tell her what was at stake."

Brooks clenched the arms of his chair. Rosamund pushed Rutley away, stumbling toward her mother. "Mama, did you know?" she asked.

Lady Bolton's eyes darted toward Brooks, and soon Rosamund was looking at him, a look of horror in her eyes. "Brooks?" she asked.

He shook his head. "I only found out—"

"You all knew!" she exclaimed, looking about the room wildly. She then gestured toward August. "You all knew except August!"

Rosamund dashed out of the room, the sounds of her cries echoing through Linfield Hall.

Chapter Ten

"I WILL TURN her out before I let her cry off, Rutley," Charles said to Rosamund's fiancé sometime after she left the room. "I doubt she would rather be homeless than marry you."

Rutley arched a single eyebrow. "A comforting thought," he said sarcastically. "I will return later this week, once tempers have cooled."

When August first saw Rutley at dinner the night before, she thought him very handsome. He was tall, with dark hair and eyes and a profile that resembled a Renaissance sculpture August once saw depicted in a book. Judging by looks alone, August wondered why Rosamund didn't want to marry him, but now she was beginning to understand. Tempers did not just *cool* after what had happened in the study.

As Rutley left the room, Lady Bolton moved to do the same. "I will go check on her," she said. "I'm sure I can think of a way—"

"No," Brooks said, standing up from his chair. August carefully watched him, waiting for him to say more. She was still annoyed over his comments about her aunt debauching her. He seemed to think she was this delicate flower, in desperate need of his or someone's protection. But how bad could her aunt's reputation be? She was a dowager duchess, after all.

"August should go," he said, looking down at her. August quickly turned toward Lady Bolton, who stood motionless in the doorway. "She is the only one of us with whom Rosamund isn't angry."

August supposed that made sense. But as far as she saw it, Rosamund's family had treated her very poorly, whether her brother would admit to it or not. August wasn't entirely sure what comfort the sister Rosamund had only known for one day would bring her, especially when August seemed to be the only one in the dark about what Rosamund *meant* when she said her brother had mortgaged her future.

After Lady Bolton reluctantly agreed with Brooks, August went upstairs like a nervous soldier marching into battle. Rosamund's room was on the second floor in the opposite wing from her father's. When she reached the landing, she tried not to think of his dead body down the hall. What would he say if he knew such a nasty argument had occurred between two of his children the day he died? He probably would have been so disappointed.

As for her, she was upset she didn't get to know him more —if only to get more information about her mother out of him. The woman's identity might become a mystery that her father took with him to the grave. When August reached Rosamund's door, she slowly raised her fist, knocking on it.

"Go away!" her sister immediately shouted back. "I do not wish to speak to anyone!"

"It's me," she called back. "August." When there was no response, she continued. "I have been asked to check in on you. They say I'm the only one with whom you aren't angry. I can't promise to be much comfort, seeing how we hardly know each other, but—"

The door swung open. Rosamund stood on the other side, her face blotchy and wet with tears. When she saw August, she let out a loud sob, then dashed back toward the bed, throwing herself upon it. August closed the door behind her, frowning. She sat down on the bed beside Rosamund, a crumpled heap beside her. Sighing, August wondered what to say. If she were in a similar position, what would comfort her? Perhaps she might not want to talk about it all. Maybe a distraction was in order.

"Your brother has ordered me to go and stay with Lady Ramsbury in London," she said suddenly.

Rosamund sniffed, turning to look at her sister. "What?" she asked, her eyes swollen from crying.

August smiled sadly at her. "I am to leave Linfield and go live with our aunt. I suppose if Charles thinks she would take in someone like me, she might also take in someone like you, even if you decide to go through with calling off your engagement. Since your brother said he would toss you out of the house if you did, I thought I would mention it in case that's what you wanted to do."

Rosamund seemed to consider this for a moment before loudly sighing. "Oh, August, I am not sure what to do!"

"I'm not sure what you should do either," August admitted. She only just met Rosamund, and she barely knew Rutley or their history as a couple. "But I also have no idea what you meant when you told our brother that he mortgaged your future."

Rosamund sat up, moving to sit beside August on the edge of the bed. "The duke told me that he paid off my brother's gambling debts," she explained, all the while sniffling. "If I do not marry him, my brother will owe him twenty thousand pounds instead of only eight. Do you see now? My brother will fall into financial ruin if I do not marry the duke."

August chewed her lip, considering this. She thought of her inheritance, the one that her father suddenly bequeathed her. That explained why Charles did not like her. It was not out of loyalty toward his mother. It was the fact that she had taken twelve thousand pounds from him—twelve thousand pounds he desperately needed.

"Or," August began, her mind spinning, eager to present an alternative to Rosamund, "we could forget all about Charles. I could give half my inheritance to you, and we could both go live with Lady Ramsbury."

Rosamund laughed. "That does sound like a marvelous idea, but I'm not sure I could forget Charles entirely. He is my brother. I do love him, and I do not wish to be turned out of the house." Looking around her sister's bedroom, August did not blame her. The entire house was magnificent. "Besides, does Lady Ramsbury know she's about to take two nieces under her wing?"

"I'm not sure she knows she's about to take one, let alone two," August admitted. Now they were both laughing. When they were through, Rosamund sighed again.

"You are a kind girl, August, but you should have your inheritance," she said with a sad smile. "That's what Papa wanted for you, and I think I want it for you as well. You may have told me about your life at Hardbury and Portsmouth without a single complaint, but I have already decided you deserve a much easier future. You mustn't worry about me."

"But—"

"You mustn't!"

August fell silent, looking at her hands resting in her lap. She felt as though she might cry, and she supposed this was why Brooks told her to be careful with her family. It was easy to get hurt when one cared too much. She felt it now after the emotional tumult of the past few days. She looked back up at Rosamund, tears in her eyes. "It will be hard not to worry about you."

"Oh, August." The two girls embraced, both crying. Rosamund buried her face in her sister's shoulder. "If I do end up getting married, you must come to Linfield this summer for the wedding."

"If your mother and Charles will allow it, I should like that very much."

"I will force them."

When they were through with the tears, Rosamund took a deep breath. "So," she began, backing away from their embrace to look August in the eyes, "you are to live with Lady Ramsbury. Are you prepared?"

August furrowed her brow. "What do you mean?" she asked. "Is it true that her reputation is terrible like Brooks said?"

Rosamund laughed. "My aunt has had a line of gentleman callers at her door ever since her husband died. The London papers love to report on their comings and goings from her home in Mayfair, which I suppose may make her seem rather scandalous to someone who doesn't know her."

August realized then why Brooks might not want her living at her aunt's. Men coming and going whenever they pleased? To a place where an unattached twenty-year-old girl lived? August was already entering society with multiple strikes against her, including one Brooks didn't even know. She was not the innocent that he thought she was, not so unaware of why her aunt might enjoy the attentions of so many gentlemen callers. She didn't know how much longer she could let him think she was a complete innocent.

"Nevertheless, she isn't so bad," Rosamund continued. "I think you will like her, and she'll make sure you receive your polish before taking you out in public." She paused a moment, a thoughtful look on her face. "Although... I hear she throws a lot of parties at her house on Park Street, so you may have to adapt quickly."

August was rather skilled at adapting quickly—at least she thought so. The orphanage, Hardbury, and Portsmouth. She had made many homes in her short twenty years. "I wish you were coming with me," August said woefully. "What if Lady Ramsbury wants nothing to do with me either?"

"I'm sure Charles will write her a very persuasive letter on the subject," Rosamund replied, squeezing August's hand reassuringly. "I also believe we will end up seeing each other before the summer."

August raised her brow. "What do you mean?"

"This mourning period will be over when Charles grows bored of the country, which will be much sooner than propriety demands," Rosamund said with a sigh. "The same goes for Mother, though she will dread facing the scandal your introduction to society will bring. Still, I wager we will see each other again in London within a month."

August smiled at her sister. "I should like that very much."

Rosamund's blue eyes twinkled. "So would I."

AUGUST RETURNED DOWNSTAIRS WITH ROSAMUND, where Lady Bolton was waiting in the drawing room. For a moment, August thought Lady Bolton might soften toward her after the thankful look she gave her while embracing Rosamund. But Lady Bolton wanted to talk to her daughter in private, so they went to the garden, leaving August behind in the drawing room.

Unable to sit still, she walked through the room, picking up and studying various trinkets on tabletops as she passed them. She picked up a miniature of her brother, staring at it and frowning. The likeness appeared surprisingly friendly, though August knew a much different story. Eventually, she heard someone come in, and she turned to find Brooks standing in the doorway. "I see Lady Bolton and Rosamund have already reconciled," he said with a slight smile.

"So it would seem," she said. August put down the miniature and walked toward the fire without saying anything. He joined her there, and they watched the flames crackle and pop at their feet.

"Do you think she will still try to cry off?" Brooks eventually asked.

August tilted her head at him, half smiling. "Perhaps not, especially now that *tempers have cooled*," she said. She imitated Rutley's baritone voice, causing Brooks to chuckle. "In all seriousness, I'm not quite sure. I can tell she does not want to marry him, but I think she understands the risks of calling off the engagement now. Rutley could ruin the whole family if he doesn't get his way."

"So you know the truth now?"

August raised her brow. "That my brother is not only an avid drinker but an avid gambler as well? Yes, I do."

Brooks nodded, looking back toward the fire. "I did try to warn you."

August wrung her hands in front of her. "I have been thinking," she said, taking a deep breath, "and I do not think I would like my inheritance if it means my sister must marry a man she hates. If my money would prevent Charles from being ruined by Rutley, then—"

"August," Brooks said, his voice low and full of warning as he shot her a sidelong glance before turning to face her. "We must rid you of this self-sacrificing behavior of yours. Do not bend to your brother's will because you think that will make him love you. Let me assure you that it will not. And then where will you be? Poor and obscure again. Charles is a selfish man who will run up his debts again as soon as you have paid them off for him."

She glared at him. "I do not care about my brother's love, but I do care about my sister's happiness. I'm sure you see no merit in sacrificing something of yours for someone you care about, but I do. I wonder if you care about anyone at all."

"If I did not care, I would not still be here."

They held each other's gaze for a long while in silence. August didn't know what to say. Did he mean he cared about her? Her heart pounded so loudly against her chest that she was sure Brooks could hear it.

"I am sorry for snapping at you," he finally muttered, turning back toward the fire. "I did not mean to speak in anger. I have only been thinking much of your future in the past forty-eight hours, and for some reason, I have decided I should like to see you happy."

August nearly stopped breathing. For some unspeakable reason, Brooks *did* care about her. She felt a flush rising toward her face, straight from her heart. She was thankful he did not turn and look at her, still fixated on the fire in front of them.

"You say you want a family," he said. "Go to London and find a husband to make one of your own. Aside from Rosamund, I'm sure your family here is useless to you."

Her face fell. She realized then that Brooks did not envision himself as that husband. Brooks was only a good man who wanted to see her settled in the world after plucking her from her relative comfort as a governess. He had no ulterior motives, only honorable intentions. He was bound to her for now by duty, but that could not last once she arrived at Lady Ramsbury's.

"And what of Lady Ramsbury?" she asked softly, wishing to change the subject.

"Your brother has sent her a pleading letter regarding your impending arrival in town," he said, turning toward her and frowning. "I thought we could leave for London today.

Charles has lent us his carriage. We will go to Dover Street first."

"Dover Street?"

"Where my mother and I live."

August's heartbeat quickened. "You will not take me straight to Lady Ramsbury's?" she asked, confused. She shook her head. They could not do that. "I should not like to impose on you for any longer than I must."

"You are not imposing," he said. His tone was firm, and August's stomach did a flip. "I should like to speak to Lady Ramsbury myself before bringing you to her. She must be up for the task first."

"And if she's not?" August asked, raising her brow at his protectiveness.

Brooks sighed, rubbing the back of his head. "I will have to think of something, then," he said. "It might be up to me to find you a husband."

The thought of that nearly made her laugh when she was already foolishly dreaming of becoming Mrs. Brooks herself. She reminded herself that she hardly knew the man, and what she did know of him tended to be grumpy and disagreeable.

"Why do I need a husband, anyway?" she asked. "Am I not wealthier than most men now? If my aunt rejects me, I would be more than happy to return to Wilton and live out the rest of my days in obscurity."

"You mention this place called Wilton frequently," Brooks suddenly observed. "You seem very eager to return there. Why?"

She bristled, not liking the suspicious look he was giving her. "I only thought I could save Charles and Lady Bolton the embarrassment of the ton discovering my existence."

"Well, that's not what your father wanted."

She groaned. "Why are we so preoccupied with what my father wanted? What about what I want?"

"I thought you wanted a husband and children," he argued, seeming exasperated.

"Yes, but if Lady Ramsbury rejects me—"

"I do not think she will reject you," Brooks said sharply, interrupting her. "I could deliver you to her house straight away, and she would probably accept you, believing your triumphant entrance into society might make for a fun project. It's *my* apprehension over her chaperoning you that forces me to demand an audience with her first."

They stared at each other for a moment, her eyes searching his. August did not know what to say, not understanding why Brooks should care so much about her.

"You should know my sister told me why you think Lady Ramsbury might not be the right chaperone for me," she finally said.

"Did she?" Brooks asked with a roll of his eyes.

August nodded. "She insinuated that my aunt takes lovers now that she's a widow. That perhaps her home might not be the best environment for a young girl of marrying age."

Now it was his turn to blush. "You and your sister should not be speaking of such things," he grumbled. "And what would the two of you know about lovers, anyway?"

August's temper flared, hating that he thought she was someone who needed his protection and shielding from the world after she had been taking care of herself for so long. "What do I know about lovers?" she asked, echoing his question back to him.

He nodded, taking a step closer to her. Their faces were close now, only mere inches apart. "Yes," he replied. His voice was soft, and her eyes drifted toward his lips. Her palms became sweaty. "What does Miss August Summer know of lovers?"

"Well, I have had one," she said without thinking. She immediately regretted it, seeing how Brooks looked at her with wide eyes and a slightly open mouth. She had rendered him speechless, and now she could think of nothing else to say either. She felt like dashing out of the room. Breathing became uncomfortable.

"Do not look so shocked," she said, stepping away from him, unable to stand so close to him any longer. Her voice became shrill. "I'm sure *you're* not a virgin either."

Stupid, stupid girl. Her mind told her to be quiet, yet she pressed forward anyway, seeing how she couldn't possibly take her words back now.

"So perhaps you ought to worry about *me* being up for the task before you start criticizing my aunt," she finally said, pushing past him, deciding she would prefer to die of mortification in the privacy of her room.

Chapter Eleven

THE CARRIAGE RIDE to London was awkward, or at least it was for Brooks. August sat in silence across from him, looking out the window, frowning for the entire journey. Brooks stole glances at her every so often, all the while wondering if she noticed. If she did, she didn't say anything, leaving Brooks to his own tormented thoughts. He could not understand why he cared so much, but he did, especially regarding August's earlier confession.

He would have liked to ask her more, but he wasn't sure if it was his right to ask at all. Did August give a man her innocence because she had thought he loved her? Because she thought he would marry her? Perhaps that was why she kept mentioning returning to Wilton, but why August wanted to return to a blackguard was beyond him.

For his part, Brooks would have liked to throttle the man. As a young female of marrying age, innocence was a precious commodity in the market that August was about to enter. Her lack of virginity would be another thing the ton could use against her if such information came to light. He wanted to tell her as much, but he wasn't sure how he could without sounding like an ass. He had done that enough around her already, so he decided to say nothing at all.

By the time they arrived at his home on Dover Street in Mayfair, the hour was late, and Brooks was exhausted. Gas lamps illuminated the street, and August stood upon the sidewalk looking up at the five-story brick townhouse in wonder. If she was impressed by his modest home, Brooks thought she might faint upon seeing her aunt's mansion on Park Street.

"This is your home?" she asked. She touched one of the white stone columns that held up the decorative balcony above the house's front stoop.

Brooks nodded as Jenkins, the butler, opened the door for them. "My office is on the first floor as well," he said, stepping inside and handing his hat and coat to Jenkins. "How are you, Jenkins?"

"Very well, sir," Jenkins replied, shooting a tentative look at August. "You have been away much longer than expected. You have clients looking for you."

Brooks did not want to think about clients right now. The hour was late, and he must get August settled, as well as tell his mother why she was here. "We will discuss it in the morning," he said.

Meanwhile, Brooks watched as August slid off her cloak and removed her bonnet, handing both to Jenkins, who still appeared confused. August stared up at the crystal chandelier hanging from the center of the foyer in awe.

"You do quite well for yourself," she said, her eyes meeting his. He half smiled at her despite himself, appreciating how impressed she was. Girls of the ton tended not to look twice at men who must work for their incomes.

Brooks turned back to his butler. "Jenkins, where is my mother?" he asked. "Has she already retired for the evening?"

Jenkins nodded. "Yes, sir, but only recently. Her maid just

returned belowstairs from her bedroom, so she may still be awake."

"Show Lady August to the drawing room and prepare one of the bedrooms for her," Brooks told Jenkins. He glanced at August, who stood in the doorway of the reception room that led to his office, peering into the darkness. She turned back to him upon hearing her name, clasping her hands behind her back and smiling.

Despite the long journey, she looked as beautiful as ever, especially under the glow of the candlelight. Her cheeks always seemed to have a healthy color to them, and her hair almost looked better in a slightly mussed state. Dover Street felt so small compared to Linfield, and suddenly Brooks felt very aware that they would be sleeping under the same roof with much fewer walls separating them.

"It will have to be Miss Lucy's room," Jenkins said, interrupting his thoughts, causing his head to snap in his direction. Brooks hadn't mentioned his sister, Lucy, to August, as he didn't like speaking about her. Judging by how August stepped closer to the two men—obviously so she could hear better—he would have to tell her about his younger sister soon.

"Aren't there any other options?" he asked softly, though he knew August would still undoubtedly hear him.

"Not unless you use your father's bedroom tonight, and Lady August uses your bedroom, and—"

"Never mind, Jenkins," Brooks said sharply, shaking his head. He had no desire to take his father's room then or ever, even if it was the largest in the house. "Preparing Lucy's room for Lady August would be the simplest solution. Lady August, if you'll excuse me."

He bowed slightly, then quickly headed up the stairs two steps at a time. He wasn't sure why he was bothering with formalities in front of Jenkins. The man had been in the family's service since Brooks was a boy, so nothing ever surprised him. Perhaps Brooks was the one who needed the formalities, especially when he knew the only thing that separated his room from Lucy's was a single wall.

His mother's bedroom was on the third floor, and Brooks knocked softly on its door. He heard his mother stir in bed on the other side. "Who is it?" she asked.

"Your son."

His mother granted him entrance straight away when she heard his voice. On the other side of the door, she was sitting in bed, wearing her nightcap. A book rested on her lap.

"Oh, thank goodness you are home!" she exclaimed, reaching out to him. He went to his mother, kissing her on the cheek.

"Hello, Mother," he said.

Mrs. Brooks searched her son's face with her eyes. The wrinkles on her visage always became more prominent when she was concerned about something. "I was worried sick after receiving Lady Bolton's letter," she said. "Has the girl been safely delivered to Linfield Hall?"

"I am afraid not," Brooks replied with a sigh, taking a seat at the end of his mother's bed, staring at the rose-colored walls instead of looking at his mother. The fire in the hearth cast a warm glow over the room.

She furrowed her brow. "What do you mean? What happened?"

"The girl," he said, turning to look at her, "is presently in our drawing room."

His mother's eyes widened. "What?"

Brooks nodded. "It's true. Lord Bolton passed away this morning."

"Oh, how awful!"

"Indeed," Brooks agreed bitterly. "His wish was for his daughter to not only have twelve thousand pounds but to be out in society, with Lady Bolton chaperoning her. Naturally, Lady Bolton took offense to this."

His mother sighed. "Yes, she said as much in the letter she sent me earlier this week, and I cannot say I blame her. But why is the girl here at Dover Street now?"

"With his father dead and no one to stop him, Charles has written to his aunt—"

"Lady Ramsbury?" his mother asked, gasping.

Brooks nodded again. "Charles has written to his aunt with the hopes that she will be the girl's guardian until she marries."

"And what does Lady Bolton say?"

"She came up with the idea herself," Brooks grumbled with a wave of the hand. "Neither of them has any interest in poor August, so she agreed to live with her aunt right away. Of course, she has no idea what sort of woman Lady Ramsbury is."

"Oh!" his mother nervously exclaimed. "Surely she cannot be a good influence for a young lady! I will write to Lady Bolton at once—"

"Do not waste your time," Brooks said with a sigh, running a hand through his hair. "Neither Lady Bolton nor Charles will budge. Rosamund is the only one who has accepted her, and now we are left to hope that Lady Ramsbury will as well."

His mother looked down at her book, nodding slightly. "So why didn't you take her to Park Street this evening?"

"I did not want to leave her on Lady Ramsbury's doorstep late at night without speaking to the woman first. Besides, who knows what the dowager duchess is doing at this hour or if she's even at home. You must understand that August is a twenty-year-old girl with twelve thousand pounds. She didn't attend finishing school like other marriageable girls she may meet at parties, and I will not see her fall victim to their cruelty if Lady Ramsbury cannot teach her their ways. She needs someone willing to protect her. Lady Ramsbury must understand..."

His voice trailed off as he suddenly noticed the strange way in which his mother was watching him while he spoke. Her expression was one of bewildered amusement, and he thought she might laugh at him at any moment. "Why are you looking at me that way?" he asked, annoyed.

His mother's half smile turned into a full grin. "I should like to meet this girl. I have never heard you so concerned for a female someone in your life—not since Lucy, and she was your sister."

Brooks huffed, rolled his eyes, and then stood up, heading toward the door. His mother was incorrigible. "Must you always be playing matchmaker?" he asked.

"I see it as my motherly duty to help you find someone you might love."

"If such an emotion even exists."

His mother angrily sighed and looked at her book, refusing to dignify such a comment with any other response.

"She will stay here tonight, and I will take her to Park Street tomorrow after I have had my audience with the dowager duchess," Brooks said. When his mother did not respond, he pursed his lips together, feeling guilty. "Why don't you have breakfast with her tomorrow?"

Mrs. Brooks finally looked at him, smiling. "Of course," she said, delighted. "I will entertain her for as long as you would like."

He nodded once. "Good. I will use the morning to catch up on my work and call on Lady Ramsbury sometime tomorrow afternoon. Once I settle everything with the dowager duchess, I will bring August to her before dinnertime."

"Why doesn't she stay here for dinner?" Mrs. Brooks

asked. "Or perhaps she ought to stay two nights instead of one. That will give Lady Ramsbury plenty of time to—"

Brooks shot his mother a warning look, effectively silencing her. They both knew she was grasping at straws now. "Good night, Mother."

He opened the door and left the room, unable to entertain any of her matchmaking ideas where August was concerned. Considering Brooks might actually like August, his mother's actions could be much more dangerous than forcing him into conversation with Miss Jennings after church. How quickly his mother had forgotten the poor girl when another female with twelve thousand pounds was staying under their roof.

The female in question was standing by one of the front bay windows when he went to the drawing room looking for her. She turned when she heard him enter, smiling at him. "How is your mother?" she asked.

"Fine," Brooks replied, still feeling annoyed by the dratted woman. There was nothing untoward or dishonorable about being concerned for August's well-being. Nevertheless, he kept a safe distance between himself and where she stood at the front window. She watched him curiously, probably noticing his discomfort.

If Brooks did not control his emotions, he would soon become no better than the assumed blackguard who took her innocence. He cleared his throat, urging himself to think no longer on such subjects. "You will have breakfast with her tomorrow morning. I will have work to catch up on after being away from town for so long, but I plan on calling on your aunt in the afternoon. If all goes according to plan, this will be the only night you stay with us."

August's smile seemed to fade, but she still nodded at him. "I understand. Will you take me to my room now? I am rather tired."

Brooks nodded, and he showed her to the fourth floor in silence. Reluctantly, he opened the door to Lucy's room and ushered August inside. The servants had lit the fireplace, the light of the fire bouncing against the walls.

August walked around the room while Brooks forced himself to accept that soon a stranger would be alone with Lucy's old possessions. He stood there and silently watched in fear, waiting for her to discover something much too personal and ask him a question about it. Eventually, he pointed to the bellpull by the bed. "Ring that if you should need anything."

"Yes, I know how a bellpull works," she replied with a smile, coming to stand in front of him, her hands clasped in front of her.

"Right," he said with a curt nod, feeling foolish. "I will leave you, then. Good night."

He was halfway out the door when August called his name. He immediately turned around, facing her. His eagerness made him feel all the more foolish. "What is it?" he asked much more sharply than he intended.

"I only wanted to apologize for what I said earlier." She did not look at him, but that didn't stop him from realizing her cheeks were flushed. He swallowed. Hard. "I shared something private that I shouldn't have, and I don't wish you to worry yourself over me any more than you already have, or—"

"It's already forgotten," he blurted, not because he *had* forgotten it, but because he did not wish to discuss it any longer, especially in the warmth of her bedroom.

"Very well," she said, seeming a bit taken aback by his sudden response but nodding anyway. She squared her shoulders as they both stared at each other. His discomfort grew until it was nearly unbearable. "Good night, then, Brooks."

"Good night, August."

Chapter Twelve

BROOKS SLEPT POORLY THAT NIGHT. After waking from a dream about August coming to his room in the middle of the night, he decided it would be impossible to close his eyes without thinking of her, so he rose at the crack of dawn and rang for Jenkins instead. The butler helped him bathe and dress, then provided him a list of appointments that he had missed while he was away.

In that way, Jenkins was much more than a butler. He helped Brooks with whatever he needed throughout the day, taking on the functions a valet or personal secretary would for a wealthier man. One must find economies where one could as a solicitor, despite how impressed August was by his perceived wealth. Truthfully, Brooks wouldn't have minded abandoning his Mayfair address to save money, but that would have been bad for business, and Brooks wasn't a complete fool. The ton depended on him as much as he relied on the high fees they were willing to pay.

"You will have to work on rescheduling these," Brooks said, reviewing the list Jenkins provided as the butler tied his cravat, annoyed he missed so many clients. "And I'm afraid you will have to do the same with my afternoon appointments as well. I will keep my morning ones, but I am to call on Lady Ramsbury at her Park Street mansion this afternoon."

"Shall I send a note ahead of time?" Jenkins asked.

Brooks sighed, nodding. "Tell her I'll be there at half past three."

"And what of Lady August?"

Brooks hoped Jenkins didn't notice the way he twitched at the mention of her name. "My mother agreed to occupy her for the day. Make sure you set an extra place for her in the dining room this morning. They will take their breakfast together."

"And you?"

Brooks looked at his butler, annoyed. "I will have my breakfast in my office as I always do."

Later that morning, he struggled to focus on his meetings and papers, too busy wondering what August and his mother were doing upstairs. He hoped they were getting along, but he didn't want his mother to encourage August to develop any sort of attachment to him. Brooks had already decided not to see any more of her after bringing her to Park Street. Of course, that should be easy enough since he avoided most social gatherings.

When he finally rose from his desk at three, he was eager to speak to the dowager duchess. The day was sunny, so Brooks decided to walk to Lady Ramsbury's home, which was less than a mile away, hoping the exercise would calm his rising nerves.

The dowager duchess lived in a mansion made of white stone, at least four times the size of his home on Dover Street. Lady Ramsbury's late husband had provided handsomely for his wife in his will. He left his title and country estate to his nephew, of course, but the London mansion was hers, along with a large sum of money that would keep her wealthy until her very last days on Earth. The woman was lucky; some widows, like his mother, Mrs. Jennings, and even Lady Bolton, received nothing, forced to depend on others' kindness.

Instead, the Dowager Duchess of Ramsbury continued to live a lavish life long after her husband died, surrounded by suitors as if she were a diamond of the first water and not an aging widow. Still, men frequently settled for her company in bed instead of an engagement, proving her looks were just as tempting as her riches. When Brooks arrived at half past three, he quickly discovered that he was not the only man Lady Ramsbury was entertaining that afternoon.

The dowager duchess sat at the grand pianoforte by the window, playing a song Brooks recognized to be one of Schubert's compositions. Her eyes were closed, and she seemed to feel each key with her entire body instead of merely pressing them. Music filled the room, and Brooks watched as the men —young and old, some he even knew to be married— appeared enraptured by her.

Truthfully, he thought them all rather pathetic. Everyone knew Lady Ramsbury would not marry again, not after her husband had been dead for fifteen years now. He wondered if she enjoyed toying with them, seeing as how not many women had the opportunity to make men bend to their every will without ever having to worry about depending on them.

When the song was over, Lady Ramsbury opened her eyes, and the entire room applauded. Even Brooks politely clapped, though he could not yell "Bravo!" like one of the gentlemen in the room did. He rolled his eyes, feeling downright embarrassed for the man, so clearly smitten with a woman who would never care about him the same way.

Lady Ramsbury rose from her seat at the pianoforte, her eyes meeting his before addressing the rest of the men. "I'm afraid we must end the concert early, gentlemen," she said, her words met with immediate groans from her audience. "I must have a private meeting with my solicitor, Mr. Brooks."

None of them had noticed him enter, but they all turned and looked at him now, their eyes like daggers. "It should not take long," he said, eager to assuage any fears before they turned into vicious rumors about him and Lady Ramsbury. "I'm sure Lady Ramsbury would be happy to continue playing for you in a half hour."

They all turned and looked at her.

"Of course," she agreed, though Brooks thought she sounded exhausted. Her reassurance that the concert would continue was enough to make them leave, each man bidding their private farewells to the dowager duchess before walking out of the room. As they passed Brooks, their glares did not escape his notice.

When they had all left, Lady Ramsbury sighed and smiled at him, sitting down in one of the armchairs and ringing the handbell on the table beside her. A footman entered, and she asked for a fresh tray of tea. After he left, she pointed to the settee beside her chair.

"Sit," she said. Brooks did as she asked, moving his mouth to speak once he was beside her, but she interrupted him before he could say a word. "Where is my niece?"

"She is at Dover Street. I wanted to speak to you before—"

But Lady Ramsbury didn't let him finish. "Why are you holding my niece hostage from me?"

Brooks did not feel nervous often, but now he faltered. The dowager duchess could be mighty intimidating when she wanted to be. "What? I am doing no such thing!"

"A courier delivered a missive from Charles yesterday," she said calmly, lifting her elegant chin as she regarded him with sharp hazel eyes. "He related the whole unfortunate story in his letter, pleading with me to be the girl's guardian until she married. He also told me my brother wanted her to be out in society."

She paused for a moment, still staring at Brooks. Her tone became irritated. "Did you think I would reject such a call to service? Is that why you brought her to your home on Dover Street instead of here? As far as I can tell from my nephew's letter, that was never part of the plan. I'm assuming you made that decision yourself."

Brooks matched her irritated tone with one of his own. "As I started to say earlier, I wanted to speak to you before I brought her here." He thought of the crowd of gentlemen that just filed out of her drawing room. "The scene I walked into this afternoon should be enough explanation as to why. We arrived late last night. How could I know what was occurring here at such an hour?"

She glared at him. The wrinkles on her forehead and the corners of her narrowing eyes were the only evidence that she was an aging woman. Meanwhile, Brooks prepared himself for a harsh retort. "You are worried what my adoring fans might do to her, yet you do not care at all what having her stay at your home will do to her reputation."

Brooks scoffed. "I am her father's solicitor, and I live with my mother. I do not like what you are insinuating."

"You also traveled alone with her for many hours, leaving me to wonder if she is compromised already, making her chances of a good match very slim."

"I have not compromised her," he said with a groan. He didn't mention what August told him in the drawing room at Linfield; that would be their secret. "What has made you all high and mighty? You know I am not some sort of scoundrel."

"But I suppose I am."

He sighed, and she watched him with a critical gaze. Brooks had not come here to argue with Lady Ramsbury. He had come there to ensure she would protect August—nothing more, nothing less.

"I only wanted to make sure you were up for the task before I delivered her here directly, especially after seeing her brother and Lady Bolton's behavior at Linfield," Brooks explained as calmly as he could. "Aside from Rosamund, she has not seen much affection from her family. She also knows very little of our world here in Mayfair. You must teach her before you take her to a party."

Lady Ramsbury scoffed. "I know that."

But Brooks still wasn't sure. "She needs someone to protect her and show her the ways of the ton. They may turn a blind eye to your behavior due to your title and wealth, but August is still the illegitimate child of an earl with no knowledge of who her mother is." Lady Ramsbury winced slightly. Brooks wasn't the only one who knew the risks of introducing someone like August into polite society. "Anyone might use that against her. I am sorry for doubting you, but I hope you can understand my concern and why I need to know you'll take this seriously."

"I think you'll take it seriously enough for the both of us," she drawled, looking at Brooks with a slight smile all of a sudden. "If I didn't know you any better, I would think you were in love with the girl. Your passionate concern for her well-being is evidence enough. Are you sure you don't want to marry her yourself?"

Brooks stiffened. "Certainly not. If I have your word that you will not lead her to ruin, I will bring her to you before dinnertime."

Lady Ramsbury studied him carefully, as if she was trying to discern something about him. He fidgeted in his seat, uncomfortable under her intense gaze. "Did you know I always wanted a child?" she finally asked.

He shook his head. How could he have? One did not

partake in such personal conversations with members of the ton. Everything was about appearances to these people. But she nodded, her gaze softening. "I have—always. Unfortunately, it's never been a possibility for me, which is probably why I never bothered remarrying."

They sat in silence as Brooks realized what she was saying. He very nearly apologized, but Lady Ramsbury cleared her throat and spoke in a resolute tone. "I will protect her. Whether she's legitimate or illegitimate, she's still my blood, as much as Rosamund and Charles are. I think having her here will give me a new sense of purpose, and truthfully, I could use a break from the gaggle of men that come here every afternoon."

Brooks raised his brow. "But your adoring fans—"

"Oh, be quiet," she said, though Brooks noticed a slight smile playing at her lips. "I am having a dinner party tonight. Why don't you and your mother come with August?"

Just as he was beginning to think Lady Ramsbury could handle a young girl's introduction into society, his heart fell into his stomach. "A dinner party?" he asked, shaking his head. "Tonight? It's much too soon."

"You cannot keep her to yourself forever, Mr. Brooks, as much as I can tell you would like to," she said. He tried to defend himself, but she continued before he could. "If you attempt to be sociable tonight for the girl's sake, perhaps I might consider you as one of her potential suitors."

"You misunderstand. I do not want to be August's suitor. I only want—"

"That's quite enough, Brooks," Lady Ramsbury said with a laugh as the footman returned with a tea tray. "You will give yourself away if you protest too much."

Brooks shot her a sullen stare. Meanwhile, the footman placed the tea tray on the small table beside the dowager duchess. "Shall I pour for you?" she asked.

"No," Brooks said, annoyed as he stood up. "I should return to Dover Street. This girl has taken me away from my business for much too long, so I shall be delighted to bring her here tonight, dinner party or not. After that, you will see no more of me, so do not worry about putting me on your list of potential suitors."

Lady Ramsbury seemed amused by his declarations, despite the stern look he gave her. Marrying August was the furthest thing from his mind, no matter what his mother or Lady Ramsbury said. He would attend the dinner party, ensure Lady Ramsbury was an appropriate guardian for August, and then return to his everyday life, washing his hands of the situation for good.

Chapter Thirteen

Earlier that morning, a maid woke August. She lifted her hands above her and stretched as the woman went to the front of the room, pulling open the curtains. Light poured in, and August squinted. How late had she slept?

"What time is it?" she asked the maid.

"Nine o'clock, my lady," the middle-aged woman replied. August's eyebrows shot up, feeling surprised. She could not remember the last time she slept so late. "The missus asked me to help you bathe and dress. You'll have breakfast with her at ten."

The missus must have been Mrs. Brooks. She was eager to meet Brooks's mother and happily got ready, hoping the woman was friendly. August would have liked to know who this mysterious Lucy was after she just slept in her bedroom, but Brooks was acting much too guarded last night to ask him. She hoped his mother would explain.

She had noticed a few things about the room that hinted a young girl once inhabited it. First, a collection of dolls sat along on top of one of the window seats overlooking the street below. Someone had turned them to face the window as if they were watching the people and carriages go down the road.

Next, there was a miniature in a heart-shaped frame on her bedside table. The likeness was a young man with red hair, a prominent nose, and sharp blue eyes. August wondered who he could be if not this mysterious Lucy's sweetheart. She would have liked to have known his name and what happened to him. Perhaps Lucy was with him now.

After being scrubbed clean, the maid opened the cherry-colored wardrobe and pulled out a lavender frock from inside. August held her hands up in protest. "I do not need to borrow any clothes," she said before gesturing toward her trunk at the foot of the bed. "I'm sure I have something clean to wear in there."

The maid stared at her, still holding the same lavender day dress. "The missus insisted. She said Miss Lucy's clothes would fit you perfectly."

"But she's never even seen me," August blurted.

The woman blinked, unperturbed. "I will make it work," she said, almost defensively.

August sighed. "Oh, very well."

The maid smiled, walking toward her with the dress, which was much nicer than anything August had ever owned. "Before you put that on me, could you tell me who Miss Lucy is?" she asked.

"The master's sister, of course," the maid replied, looking at August as if she were stupid.

"Right," August said, nodding. "I knew that."

Finally dressed, the maid escorted August to the dining room on the second floor. The room was modest compared to Linfield Hall, with a table that only sat eight instead of double that amount. Mrs. Brooks sat waiting for her at the end of the table, opposite the room's entrance. She looked up when she heard them enter, her face brightening when she saw August.

"There you are!" she said happily. Mrs. Brooks was a pretty woman in her late forties, and August immediately recognized her nose and chin as similar to her son's. Her hair and eyes, though, were much darker than the solicitor's. She gestured to the seat across from her. "Please, sit. I was hoping you would be down soon."

"I am so sorry if you have been waiting long," August said, walking quickly toward her seat at the table. A young man dressed in livery pulled it out for her, and she sat down. "I do not normally sleep so late, but I must have been tired. It has been a long few days of traveling."

Mrs. Brooks smiled kindly at her as two footmen served them breakfast. "I have not been waiting long," Mrs. Brooks reassured her. "We typically do not eat until ten here."

August looked around the room, wondering where Brooks was. "Does Mr. Brooks ever eat breakfast with you?" she asked.

"He will before we go to church on Sundays, but never in the middle of the week. He usually rises early to get some work done before his appointments that day, taking his breakfast in his study."

August nodded, unsurprised. "Although I haven't been acquainted with your son long, if there's one thing I have learned about him, it's that he takes his work very seriously—and that he much prefers being alone."

The older woman laughed. "Indeed, though I do hope he was not too much of a bore during your travels."

"No, of course not! He has been extremely helpful in guiding me through this..." August searched for the right word. "This situation over the past few days."

When the footmen finished serving them, August looked down at her plate to find generous portions of eggs and bacon, plus a slice of plum cake. "Oh, this looks wonderful!" she told Mrs. Brooks.

"I'll give your compliments to our cook," the older woman replied, smiling. For a moment, it was silent except for the clinking of utensils and plates. "Was your room last night satisfactory as well?"

August looked up, meeting Mrs. Brooks's gaze. Slowly, the younger woman put down her knife and fork and nodded, knowing this was her chance to ask about Lucy.

"Yes," she replied before gesturing toward the lavender dress that she wore. "It is very kind of you to let me stay in your daughter's room and wear one of her dresses. Hopefully, my aunt will agree to my brother's scheme and take me shopping soon. In the meantime, you'll have to thank Lucy for me the next time you write her."

The older woman's face fell. August's eyes immediately widened when she realized she had said something wrong. She glanced at the footmen, hoping for some sort of hint as to what it was, but they remained stone-faced. "Did my son not tell you?" Mrs. Brooks asked.

August shook her head wildly. "N-no."

The woman sighed. "My daughter Lucy passed away last year."

August watched as Mrs. Brooks looked down at her plate. "I'm so sorry, Mrs. Brooks. I had no idea."

Mrs. Brooks looked back up at her, the woman's kind smile returning. "Do not worry about it, my dear. I am not surprised Samuel did not say anything to you. He does not like to talk about it."

August furrowed her brow. "How did she die?" she asked.

Mrs. Brooks's kind smile started to fade, and August realized right away that she had been much too bold with her question. She shook her head. "I'm sorry. That is none of my business."

"A long illness took her, I'm afraid," Mrs. Brooks said, providing no more detail than that. August nodded, thinking of her father. How terrible that a young woman might die of the same thing before she even had the chance to live!

"I had a schoolmate who once passed away after a long illness. Even though she died young, I always took comfort in the fact that her soul must be in a much better place. I'm sure it's the same for your daughter."

Mrs. Brooks carefully watched her while she spoke. "She would have liked you," she said after a long moment.

August laughed slightly, unable to stop herself. "That's a very kind thing to say to someone you have just met. I'm sure I would have liked her as well."

"My son likes you, so I know she would have liked you." August's cheeks warmed. She looked down at her food, unable to think of any sort of response to such a statement. "Perhaps you and your aunt could come for dinner once you become settled."

August's heart fluttered. She thought she would not see Brooks again after she went to her aunt's. "If you and Mr. Brooks set a date, I most certainly will come."

Mrs. Brooks smiled. "I will happily see to that."

WHEN BROOKS RETURNED to Dover Street, Jenkins told him his mother and August were taking tea in the drawing room. As he handed his coat and hat to the butler, Brooks could hear their laughter from where he stood in the entry hall. When he entered the drawing room, they were so enamored with each other's company that neither of them noticed him until he cleared his throat.

"I see you have both made a new friend in one another," he sullenly observed, already worried what secrets his mother might have revealed to August.

"Brooks!" August exclaimed, appearing much more at ease than she had when he left her last night. "Indeed, your mother has been a wonderful hostess. I hope you have good news about my aunt, though I must confess I find myself much at ease here at Dover Street and wouldn't mind if I had to stay here another night or two."

Brooks sat down in one of the armchairs, trying not to glare at his mother, who seemed unperturbed by his lack of enthusiasm, probably as eager to make August her daughter-in-law as he was to remove her from his life. Things had gotten out of hand, but no more. August would go to Lady Ramsbury's, whether the wretched woman was hosting an untimely dinner party that night or not.

As for his mother, she would have to accept the fact that he was determined to remain single, regardless of what heiresses happened to walk into his life. Brooks never made exceptions to the various rules he had set for himself over the years.

"Your aunt would like you to come to Park Street straight away," he said.

August smiled broadly, her cheeks rounding as she did. "That's wonderful news!"

Brooks watched his mother try to hide her disappointment, and she frowned at him before forcing herself to grin back at August. He continued. "But there is to be a dinner party at Park Street tonight."

"A dinner party?" August echoed incredulously, interrupting him. Her excitement quickly faded, and her forehead wrinkled. Somehow he knew this news would make her nervous. Like him, August seemed to understand the realities of what her father wanted her to do. Going from the governess to member of the ton was no easy feat.

"Yes," Brooks replied. "She extended invitations to all three of us. I think she would like to prove to me that she can successfully guide August through a social gathering, though—"

"But I have nothing to wear!" August exclaimed, interrupting again.

He sighed. He knew August was unprepared for such an event, which was what he would have said had she not spoken over him. August's wardrobe was nothing more than a small collection of faded muslin gowns, barely nice enough for daytime. There was nothing appropriate for a dinner party in Mayfair. Perhaps August would refuse to go, and she would have to stay another night at Dover Street, as much as it would displease him.

"I am sure I can find something amongst Lucy's old things," his mother said, causing Brooks to stiffen. That was when he noticed the lavender day dress August was wearing couldn't possibly belong to her. His heartbeat quickened.

"That's very kind of you, Mrs. Brooks," August said before looking at him, frowning slightly. Brooks realized then that his mother must have told her who Lucy was, and now it was only a matter of time before she started asking him questions about his sister, ones he had no desire to answer. He should have known this would happen from the moment she took her first step into his home.

Brooks abruptly stood, unable to face August and his mother any longer. "Put her in whatever you want," he told his mother. "Just be ready to leave at half past six."

He left before they could say anything. He went to his room, where he shrugged off his jacket, discarding it on the ground. He tore off his cravat next, crumpling the fabric in his hand before throwing it on the floor as well.

Sitting on the bed, he reached to pick up his sister's miniature on his bedside table. He wondered what she would think of his present situation. Lucy would probably laugh at him and tell him he was acting ridiculous. If he liked the girl, he should just tell her. But how could he?

He put the miniature back down on the table, turning to face the wall. He did not believe in marriage for plenty of reasons. One girl could not change those reasons, no matter how he felt about her. He ran a hand through his hair, then shook his head. He needed to get a hold of himself.

Reaching for the bellpull, Brooks convinced himself whatever feelings he presently had would be fleeting. She would leave for her aunt's, he would forget about her, and his life would go back to normal. All he had to do was get through this dinner party, and then he would be done with her—temptation gone for good.

When Jenkins arrived, Brooks stood up. "Pour me a drink," he said. "Then help me dress for a dinner party at Lady Ramsbury's."

Jenkins raised his brows, seemingly out of surprise, but Brooks ignored him, anxious for his glass of brandy. Brooks snatched it from Jenkins as soon as he carried it within a foot of him. He quickly tossed the beverage back and handed it back to an openmouthed Jenkins.

"Another, sir?" he asked in a tremulous voice.

Brooks nodded, wiping his lips with the back of his hand. "Yes, Jenkins."

"YOU MUSTN'T LET him discourage you," Mrs. Brooks told August.

August stood in Lucy's old room. The wardrobe was open, and a collection of evening gowns had been laid in every direction across the bed. August looked at them all, each one prettier than the next.

"Lucy would *want* you to wear them," Mrs. Brooks added, forcing August back to the present. She turned to Mrs.

Brooks and the maid behind her and tried to smile. Mrs. Brooks gave an encouraging nod.

August looked back at the dresses on the bed, biting her lip. Although she certainly cared for Brooks's feelings on the matter, the dresses were beautiful, and why shouldn't she look nice meeting her aunt, the Dowager Duchess of Ramsbury, for the first time?

"Very well," she said, pulling a salmon-colored dinner dress from the pile of frocks. "I will wear this one."

Mrs. Brooks smiled at her. "Wonderful choice," she said before turning to her maid. "I will let you handle the rest."

Once August had been dressed and her hair done up, she took one last look at herself in the tall mirror in the corner of Lucy's room. She turned back to the maid, grinning slightly. "I hardly recognize myself."

Unlike Rosamund's dress from two nights ago, Lucy's gown fit her, showing off her shape. The salmon-colored fabric complimented her skin tone, and the maid had decorated her hair with gemstones, making her blonde hair sparkle. She wondered what Brooks would think.

When the maid left, August took a moment to breathe deeply. She was nervous, but she could not let the prospect of meeting her aunt scare her. August wasn't sure if she could handle any more rejection from her family after her brother shirked all responsibility.

August left her room and went downstairs, finding Brooks waiting by the front door in the round entry hall. He was facing away from her as she started to descend, but when he heard her, he turned and looked. She smiled nervously, and she thought she saw him clench his jaw.

"Lady August," he said, meeting her at the bottom of the stairs. She furrowed her brow. Did he sound different? "You look lovely."

"Have you been drinking?" she asked suspiciously, smelling brandy on him.

He laughed once, appearing much more relaxed than he usually did. "You only spent two days with Charles, yet now you know what a man smells like when he's been drinking. Your father would be proud."

She ignored his sarcastic comments, growing concerned. "Why have you been drinking? I hope I didn't upset you by wearing one of Lucy's dresses this afternoon. I tried to talk my way out of going to dinner so I didn't have to wear any more of her things, but your mother insisted."

Brooks stared at her for a long moment, not answering her question. She frowned, searching his face. "Brooks?"

"I do not like dinner parties," he finally explained. Still confused, August continued looking up at him. He sighed. "The brandy helps calm my nerves."

August started to nod. "I see," she said. Then, she grinned at him. "Perhaps I could have some as well, then. Out of the two of us, I have much more reason to be nervous."

"Is that so?" he asked, smiling despite himself. August nodded in response. "Well, I am happy to report you do not have anything to fret over. Your aunt is eager to meet you, and you look beautiful." August felt her cheeks grow hot as Brooks continued. "I'm sure the evening will be quite the success."

"Thank you," was all August could say. She was glad when Mrs. Brooks came downstairs because Brooks finally turned away, heading toward the front door. She always felt like she forgot how to breathe whenever he was near her.

"Come along now," he told the two women. "I have a hack waiting outside."

August followed, taking a deep breath just in case she might need it later.

Chapter Fourteen

AUGUST WAS SUCH a natural that Brooks hardly recognized her that night, even when he first saw her on the stairwell at his home on Dover Street. The girl was a real beauty, but he had known that from the morning he first saw her. Now he watched her talk to the two young men beside her at dinner with ease. She seemed to know exactly when to laugh at a joke or bat her eyelashes, capturing their attention as if that was what she was born to do.

Glancing at August's aunt at the head of the table, Brooks knew even the dowager duchess was impressed by her niece's easy way with the opposite sex, especially when the men at the table had been far above her station only a few days ago. Lady Ramsbury proudly watched her niece as she carried on like a seasoned member of the ton, triumphantly lifting her chin as she did.

On his part, the scene made Brooks want to drink even more than he already had at home. He reached for his port glass, finishing the remaining red liquid in one gulp. A footman moved over his shoulder, quickly refilling it, and Brooks did not bother trying to stop him, though he probably should have, being thoroughly foxed already. But if that was the case, what was the harm in another glass?

He looked around the dining room as he continued to drink. There were twenty of them there that evening—ten men and ten women. Brooks could tell from the various whispers and conversations he overheard that every man was interested in August, regardless of their marital status. The niece of an independently wealthy dowager duchess? The heiress to a recently deceased earl? Well, she must be rich—and maybe even richer once Lady Ramsbury died.

If they did not want her for themselves, they wanted her for their second or third sons. First sons were out of the question, seeing as they all assumed she must be illegitimate. The members of the ton had to draw the line somewhere, after all, so an heir for August was out of the question.

Meanwhile, the other young women in the room acted as if they hated her, wondering who this mysterious newcomer was. The young lady beside him that evening admitted as much after she caught him looking at August for at least the ninth time that evening. He wasn't sure the exact number, having lost count during the first course.

"She is not even that pretty," the woman beside him muttered under her breath.

Slowly, Brooks turned and looked at her. "Pardon me?"

She exhaled loudly and placed her fork on the table, and Brooks thought she might roll her eyes at him. "My dowry is six thousand pounds, but you and these men will not even look twice at me now that there is a larger prize to be won," she complained.

Brooks looked down at his plate, carving himself a bite-sized piece of goose. "Perhaps it's the mystery that enthralls them," he suggested.

Or perhaps they all think you are abominably rude.

The girl cast a sidelong glance at him. "Do you know

where the late Lord Bolton found her?" she asked furtively. "Aren't you the family's solicitor?"

He finished chewing, then gently put down his knife and fork, turning to face the irritating chit directly. "Yes, that's right. I am the family's solicitor, so I wonder what makes you think I will divulge any of their private information to you?"

She blushed furiously, turning away from him and saying no more. They both returned to eating their meals in silence while Brooks surreptitiously gazed at August from time to time.

After dinner was over, the ladies moved to the drawing room while the gentlemen remained at the dinner table, enjoying their brandy and passing around a tin box of snuff. Brooks skipped the snuff but took the brandy, quietly getting up and leaving the room when the subject of conversation turned to the women of the party. He dreaded what he might do if he heard them talk about August.

He wandered through the halls of Lady Ramsbury's Park Street mansion until he found the library, which he thought might provide a quiet reprieve from the evening's activities. He walked toward the fireplace, putting one hand on the marble mantel as he looked down into the fire, his body slightly bent at the waist. He held his glass of brandy at his stomach, occasionally bringing it to his lips, letting the beverage burn his throat until it was gone.

He stood there in silence for what felt like a long while until a cheerful female voice interrupted his solitude. "My!" the voice exclaimed. "What a wonderful room! I have never seen so many books!"

He grimaced, standing up straight and placing his empty glass on top of the mantel. He put his hands on his hips, looking around the room in question. Yes, the floor-to-ceiling bookshelves did seem to contain more books than he had ever seen in one place, but they could not keep his attention

—not now. His eyes eventually fell on the owner of the female voice. August stood looking at him from across the room, clasping her hands in front of herself and looking up at him as if he were somehow interesting.

He did not want her to look at him that way. Soon she would start asking all sorts of questions in an attempt to get to the core of him, to find out what made him "him." He was unsure if he knew the answer himself, and he would rather August not get to it first.

Knowing he was in danger of just that, he thought he should discourage her in some way. Perhaps make fun of how she looked at everything with such wide-eyed wonder. Instead, that feeling of tenderness he worried about before seemed to overtake his better senses.

"You ought to read them all," he said. "Tell me which one you like best. There are so many of them that I doubt you'll be able to choose where to start."

"I am not sure if I will have any time," she replied wistfully. "Your mother says I should be practicing the pianoforte every day in case someone asks me to perform at a dinner party once I'm officially out. Not to mention it sounds like my aunt has already contacted the best tutors in London to help me become more accomplished. You will be happy to hear that, of course."

"Why would you think that?" Brooks asked, furrowing his brow.

"I know you think my aunt might try to corrupt me, but I don't think she has that in mind at all. I think she only wants the best for me." She shook her head. "But that's not why I have come to find you. We are about to play charades, and my aunt suggested you be my partner for the evening. Won't you come to the drawing room with me?"

For a moment, Brooks stared at her, studying the curve of her neck, wondering what she would do if he placed a kiss there. He turned back toward the fire, alarmed by such feelings. "I am not sure I am quite up for it tonight."

August did not respond, nor did she leave. Instead, she came to stand beside him at the hearth. He looked up at the massive portrait of the late Duke of Ramsbury, framed in gold, hanging above them. He very nearly asked the man to give him strength. "I suppose we will not see each other again after this," he said, turning to August instead, hoping the words would bring him back to reality instead of his present hazy stupor.

"I suppose not," she said beside him, her voice quiet. He wondered if she was sad to be parting with him, but she had never given any indication she had grown attached to him. After all, she probably had a whole slew of men waiting to partner with her in a game of charades in the drawing room.

"Were you serious when you told me you had a lover?" he asked suddenly. The words came out abruptly, surprising him as much as her if her wide eyes were any indication. Her cheeks flushed.

"Y-yes."

They were silent for a moment. Brooks searched her face, wishing he could know what she was thinking. "And did you love the man?" he asked.

August did not answer right away. She continued to stare at him like an owl instead. "W-what?" she finally stammered.

"Did you love him?" he repeated, already dreading her answer. Love was not an emotion so easily forgotten, and if someone hurt her...

But she shook her head. "No," she said, her voice low. "It was over two years ago, just before I left Hardbury. I suppose I was curious." She laughed slightly. "Curious to a foolish extent, one might say."

"But were there any expectations—"

"None," August said, cutting him off before he could say

any more. "I thought I would be a governess for my entire life. As I said, I was curious and didn't want to die an old maid." She laughed harder this time. "All these books and poems about... about... Well, you know. I wanted to understand them."

"Do you understand them now?" August faltered, staring at him, her laughter and smile fading. "Do you?"

"Not really," she murmured, shaking her head and turning away from him. "If I'm honest, the event in question was quite disappointing."

Brooks sighed, maybe from relief, and they stood in silence for a moment. He took a step toward her, close enough so that he could take her cheek in the palm of his hand. He kept his thumb underneath her chin, pressing against it, tilting her head upward until his gaze captured hers. She sharply inhaled.

"Are you still curious?" he asked softly. August wildly searched his face, appearing confused. He took his free hand and gestured to the books lining the walls. "About what all the naughty books and poetry are about, I mean."

He was certain August nearly stopped breathing. "To a foolish extent," she finally managed to whisper. Her lips trembled, but not for long. Brooks brought his head down to hers, capturing her mouth with his.

AUGUST NEVER KNEW kisses had the power to make her light-headed. But when the solicitor's soft lips captured hers, she was thankful he grabbed her by the waist and pulled her toward him, for she was afraid she might faint at any moment. He leaned into her, their torsos molding together until she felt like he was part of her.

As they kissed, she felt a familiar heat stir in her core. She knew right away she wanted more than this, more than only frenzied kisses and roaming hands beside the heat of the fire. She would have liked Brooks to pick her up and carry her to the nearby settee made of red velvet, to kiss her in places that weren't just her lips. She wanted him to take his time with her, to show her what Henry couldn't. She wanted to feel him inside of her.

With her arms wrapped around his shoulders, her right hand was free to snake its way deftly up his back. August found the curls at the nape of his neck, gently playing with them with deft fingers. She felt him moan against her mouth, the vibration reaching the bottom of her stomach. There was no question that she wanted him, and he wanted her. But he pulled away, leaving her to look up at him with swollen lips and hooded eyes.

At some point, she became aware of a horrified look in his eyes. She blinked, shutting her mouth. Slowly, he stood up straight, her hands gripping his upper arms for balance as he brought her with him. He didn't have to say anything for her to know he regretted it. He had seen the lust in August's eyes and suddenly remembered the rules. And he didn't want to marry.

She wasn't sure which bothered her more—his remembering or the fact he didn't want to marry. August frowned at him.

"There you two are!"

August dropped her hands to her side, quickly turning to find her aunt standing in the doorway. If she had seen or noticed anything, she gave no indication. Meanwhile, August's heart pounded like a drum in her chest.

"Have you convinced Mr. Brooks to stop hiding and come play charades?" Lady Ramsbury asked. August's mouth was so dry that she felt incapable of speaking. She turned over her shoulder, giving Brooks a pleading look. He cleared his throat.

"I was just telling Lady August how tired I am, and we were saying our goodbyes," he said. The fire in August's stomach had slowly dissipated, leaving her with an uncomfortable emptiness inside her gut. Listening to Brooks speak to her aunt, she knew she must have suddenly become white as a ghost.

"Then you trust me with her care?" Lady Ramsbury asked, arching her brow as if she were skeptical.

"Of course," he replied with what appeared to be a forced smile. "It was foolish of me to doubt you. You are more than capable of introducing August to suitable young men to marry." The emptiness inside her twisted, and she very nearly winced in pain. Brooks turned to August, his expression unreadable. "Could you tell my mother I have gone home?"

Reluctantly, August nodded, then helplessly watched as Brooks swiftly left the room.

Chapter Fifteen

AUGUST'S AUNT noticed her pallor after the incident with Brooks right away. She walked toward her niece, who still stood in front of the fire. Lady Ramsbury reached out to hold her by the elbows. "Are you all right, dear?" she asked.

Realizing she couldn't tell her aunt what happened unless she wanted Brooks to be in terrible trouble, August cleared her throat, trying to regain her power of speech while thinking up some sort of excuse. "I am fine, Aunt. Just a bit offended, I suppose."

Lady Ramsbury offered her niece a pitying glance. "Oh, you mustn't let Brooks discourage you." August raised her brow, remembering that the man in question's mother had said the same thing. "No one's ever been able to catch his eye, and there are much more eligible men you should focus your attention on."

August looked down. She did not want to think of other men, especially not after what just happened. The gentlemen she sat next to at dinner were entertaining enough, but she kept stealing glances at Brooks throughout the evening whenever she could.

But she was acting ridiculous! She had only known the man for a few days. One kiss didn't mean anything, and she had the whole of Mayfair to meet. "You are right," August finally said, giving a firm nod.

"And if he is interested in you, surely he will call," her aunt drawled, wrapping her arm under her niece's and guiding her into the hall. August furrowed her brow. *Would* he call? She refused to hope, or at least she told herself she shouldn't after he had run from her like a child only a few moments earlier. She turned to her aunt, trying to recall the name of the gentleman who sat on her right side at dinner, hoping to distract herself.

"What was the name of the young man with the dark hair that sat beside me at dinner?" she asked.

"That was Lord Ridlington," her aunt replied as they walked down the hall together.

"He is very amusing." Her aunt looked at August with a raised brow, smiling slightly. August tried not to blush. She had not expressed interest in any man for a long time, not since she once told Jane stories about Henry. "Do you think he could be my partner this evening?"

"The marquess is usually my partner, but I suppose you could borrow him for the evening. I don't mind being only a spectator for tonight's game."

Usually her partner? August couldn't help but wonder if the marquess was one of her aunt's many lovers that Rosamund mentioned. August flushed, turning away from her aunt. "Oh, that's all right," she said with a slight shrug. "You are tonight's hostess! You have to play. I think I'll have fun watching."

Lady Ramsbury shook her head. "Being, as you said, tonight's hostess, I'm afraid I must insist you play. I must ensure all my guests have fun, and you will have plenty more playing than watching, especially with Lord Ridlington as your partner. He will be perfect for you."

But August grew suspicious. "Aunt, are you planning a match between the marquess and me? From the way you said he is usually your partner, I thought... well, I thought..." August searched for the right words. "Rosamund mentioned you developed quite a reputation after your husband died." Her voice dropped an octave, whispering furtively. "Is it true you have taken many lovers?"

Her aunt gasped. "Do you mean to tell me that my niece has been the one spreading that awful gossip about me?" she asked. August's face fell, then her aunt suddenly grinned. "I am only joking. Rosamund is completely right."

August stared at her aunt with wide eyes, her jaw very nearly on the floor. "And Lord Ridlington?" she managed to ask.

Lady Ramsbury winked, but they came upon the drawing room before August could ask any more. After regaining her composure, August scanned the room for Mrs. Brooks. "There she is," August said. "And she's with Lord Ridlington as well."

The two ladies walked toward the marquess and Mrs. Brooks, who shot August a concerned look. "Where is my son?" she asked.

"I'm afraid he left, Mrs. Brooks," August explained, frowning apologetically.

Mrs. Brooks looked from August to Lady Ramsbury then back to August. The older woman's nostrils flared. "Left?" she asked.

"He said he was tired," August explained, hoping that would be the end of it. There was no use trying to make sense of Brooks's actions. He would do whatever he wanted, and August would remain at this dinner party. She ought to make the best of it as she always did.

But then Lord Ridlington surprised her by laughing. August stared at him, waiting for him to regain his composure. "I'm afraid your man Brooks is not one for social engagements like these," he said when he was through laughing. "I'm surprised he even made it this long. A testament to your charm, Lady August."

"If I had any charm, I would not have been left partnerless for charades," August countered. She glanced at her aunt, waiting for the dowager duchess to say something. The older woman smiled.

"Ridlington, will you be Lady August's partner this time?" Lady Ramsbury and the marquess exchanged some sort of peculiar look that August didn't quite understand. She decided then and there that they were most certainly lovers. "She must play, and I don't mind only watching."

"I would love to be her partner," Ridlington said, turning to August and smiling, revealing two dimples, one on each cheek, as he did. Between his boyish grin and bluish-gray eyes, August was impressed her aunt was having relations with such a handsome man. After a rousing game of charades where Ridlington proved himself to be a more than capable partner, he and August sat on one of the settees in front of the fire together. The hour was late, and everyone had gone home except for him. Lady Ramsbury sat at the pianoforte, playing what sounded like some sort of experimental tune of her own.

"I hope you and your aunt come to my ball next month," Ridlington said softly. August glanced at her aunt, who she didn't think was listening. She turned back to the marquess.

"That depends on whether or not my aunt thinks I'll be ready to go to a ball in a month," she replied, smiling slightly. Ridlington clucked his tongue on the top of his mouth.

"You, Lady August Finch, would be ready to go to a ball tomorrow."

August fought back a blush. "That's very kind of you, my lord, and I'm sure my aunt and I would love to attend next month if she thinks I'll be ready like you do." She paused a moment, carefully considering her next words. "You said earlier that my solicitor Mr. Brooks is not one for social engagements. Does that include balls?"

He grinned. "I'm afraid so, but I'll send him and his mother invitations if you would like. You never know—he might surprise us all and show up."

Meanwhile, Lady Ramsbury rose from the pianoforte. August noticed that wherever her aunt went, the woman exuded regalness. She floated more than walked, looking as if she didn't have a care in the world—and why should she? A wealthy, independent woman with a man like Ridlington at her beck and call? August was beginning to think that her aunt was the most powerful woman in the universe.

"I believe it's time for my niece and I to retire, Ridlington," Lady Ramsbury said. August watched as the marquess and dowager duchess stared at each other, neither flinching despite the intensity of their gazes.

"Very well," Ridlington finally said, rising from the settee. August followed suit, and the marquess looked from her to Lady Ramsbury. "Shall I come round tomorrow afternoon?"

The dowager duchess shook her head. "I'm afraid there can be no more gentleman callers until August has had her official debut."

"Is that so?" Ridlington asked, his tone almost skeptical. He narrowed his eyes at Lady Ramsbury. "Then why the dinner party?"

"Why? Because that's how I planned it." The marquess and August exchanged confused looks. They turned back to the dowager duchess, awaiting further explanation. She looked disappointed that they did not see her genius right away. "After tonight, the intrigue surrounding her sudden appearance in London will start, but now I must hide her away and teach her until the opportune time when she can wow the entire ton comes. A bit of mystery never hurt a young lady's popularity."

"Then I hope you'll consider my ball as the first event where you can show her off to society."

Lady Ramsbury looked marquess up and down, then shrugged. "I will consider it. Good evening, Ridlington."

Although he still seemed reluctant to go, the marquess offered them both a swift bow, then left the room. August watched him, frowning, before glancing at her aunt. "You know, you do not have to become celibate for my sake. I'm not sure what Brooks said to you, but—"

"It will be good for Ridlington to spend some time away from me," her aunt said, cutting her off. "Did you know he's twenty years my junior? It's not natural."

"Aunt—"

But Lady Ramsbury did not let August finish. "Shall I show you to your room?" she asked brightly. August reluctantly nodded, following her upstairs.

Her bedroom at her aunt's was much larger than Lucy's and even the one she stayed in at Linfield Hall. There was a sitting area in front of the fire, opposite the bed. A young maid with light brown hair peeking out from underneath her cap stood at attention by the dressing table in one of the room's corner

"Lady August, this is Agatha Wallace," Lady Ramsbury said, gesturing toward the maid, who curtseyed, eyes facing downward. "She will be your lady's maid. I admit Wallace has no experience serving a lady directly, but she is the best chambermaid I have. *And* she knows how to style hair according to my housekeeper."

August smiled at Agatha, who nervously smiled back. "We

can learn together, then. Me how to be a lady, and Agatha how to be a lady's maid."

"We call the servants by their last name at Park Street," her aunt sternly said. August shot her a sheepish look. She supposed that was her first etiquette lesson.

"Well, good night, August," the dowager duchess continued. "Breakfast is at ten in the morning room. We will head to Bond Street right after that."

"Bond Street?" August asked, confused. Her aunt nodded.

"Yes, we must go about finding you new clothes right away." She glanced at August's trunk, which had been delivered from Dover Street and now sat at the foot of the bed. "I'm sure you can't possibly have all that you need in that tiny trunk of yours."

Her aunt said good night one last time, then swept out of the room, leaving August and Agatha alone together. "Shall I take down your hair first, my lady?" Agatha asked, gesturing toward the upholstered chair in front of the vanity.

"Very well," August said, sighing, moving across the room to sit. She looked at Agatha through the small mirror on top of the vanity. The girl reminded her of Jane, petite and pretty with deep-set eyes, a slightly upturned nose, and full lips. August smiled at Agatha through the mirror.

"If I decide to call you Agatha, will you promise not to tell Lady Ramsbury? Wallace feels so impersonal, and if you are going to be bathing and dressing me every day, I'm afraid I must call you by your Christian name."

Agatha moved behind her and began removing the pins in her hair. "You may call me whatever you like, my lady."

As August watched Agatha remove the pins from her hair, she recalled doing the same task herself every night only a few nights ago—how things had changed! Her mind eventually drifted to Brooks, and she wondered what the solicitor was doing at that very moment. He must have been sleeping, probably not dreaming about their scorching kiss earlier in the library that night. He probably didn't think it was scorching at all. She frowned.

Still, Brooks was all she saw later that night after she snuffed the candles, climbed into bed, and closed her eyes. She dreamt of him, the red settee in the library, and all the wicked things he could have done to her there.

BROOKS AWOKE the morning after Lady Ramsbury's dinner party in such a state that he hardly recognized himself. He wasn't the type of man to drink himself into a drunken stupor, but he had the night before. That morning he was paying the price, not just with a headache but also with a deep sense of regret.

He had practically run away from the library—run away from *August*—like the worst sort of coward. After stumbling into his study and closing the door behind him the night prior, he poured himself another drink and lay down on the settee by the window. That's where he found himself the following morning.

He must have fallen asleep without realizing it, for when he regained consciousness, light spilled in from the window, and his glass was only half empty, still in his hand, resting on his chest. Brooks regarded the remaining amber-colored liquid with a look of disgust, getting up and placing it back on the sideboard. He was lucky he hadn't spilled it while he slept.

With an aching head, Brooks remembered why he hardly touched the stuff. He stumbled from the sideboard to his desk, where he sat down, dizzy. He ran his hands through his hair, exhaling deeply.

He couldn't believe he had *kissed* August. He recalled his hands on her waist, his lips against hers. He couldn't forget the feel or taste of her—or the passionate look in her eyes when he finally pulled away from her. That was the moment when he finally regained something of a conscience, realizing he was taking advantage of her and her untamed passion.

Or maybe he was only scared of the hunger he saw in her eyes. August would have let him have his way with her if he had just taken her to the nearby settee and started undressing her. She needed no promise, no sacred vows from him to let him have her. For some reason, that bothered him. August deserved more than her father's solicitor eagerly pawing her when he could offer no hope of love or marriage.

He was fortunate that Lady Ramsbury appeared when she did, leaving him the perfect opportunity to escape without any sort of explanation. At the time, he had none. He still didn't. He could have blamed the alcohol, but what a sorry excuse that was. Quite frankly, he had let what would prove to be a fleeting attraction get the better of him, and in the end, that didn't change his views on love and marriage.

Yet as Brooks lay on the settee with his forearms crossed over his eyes to block out the rising sun, he knew he must apologize. He had done something he shouldn't have and had perhaps gotten her hopes up in the process. If she even hoped for someone like him, cold and aloof. Either way, he could not do such things and not expect any consequences.

The first of which was his mother, loudly rapping on the door of his study a mere five minutes after he woke. "Samuel!" she called from the reception room. "Are you in there?"

Brooks winced but did not answer at first.

"Samuel!"

This time her voice was much more shrill. Brooks sighed. "Just a moment, Mother," he reluctantly called out to her.

Brooks slowly stood up, his entire body aching from a night of excess. He walked to his door and opened it, revealing his mother in her morning gown, a bandeau fashioned around her head. She made a face as if she smelled something foul, her eyes raking over him, but she didn't say a word. "What is it?" he asked.

"What is it?" his mother repeated, shooting him an incredulous look. She put her hands on her hips, a sign that Brooks was in for a proper scolding. "Well, I convinced Lady Ramsbury to let *you* be August's partner in charades, but when she went to find you, you decided to *leave* instead! Because you were *tired!* How could you? Do you know who ended up being her partner? Lord Ridlington, as in the *Marquess* of Ridlington! A man whose name is worth at least three times as much as yours."

Brooks sat there listening, his head aching even more with each word. If he had known August would play charades with her aunt's rumored lover, perhaps he would have stayed. He rubbed his neck, annoyed. "Thank you, Mother, but I am already aware of where Lord Ridlington ranks in society, especially compared to me."

Mrs. Brooks threw up her arms in exasperation, spinning and walking toward one of the settees in the reception room. Brooks followed her without speaking, knowing that sometimes it was best to keep his head down and let his mother talk when she was angry with him. Maybe the last comment had been out of line. She sat down, putting her hands on her knees and shaking her head at the floor.

"Don't you want to be happy?" she asked, looking up at him, her hazel eyes rimmed with tears. He tried not to sigh at seeing how predictable his mother had become. She did this whenever he went out with her, which was part of the reason he stopped going out unless it was by himself to his club. "Or would you prefer to be miserable and alone?"

She bit out the last two words: miserable and alone. Brooks told himself he wasn't either of those two things. And who said he wasn't happy? It wasn't like the ghosts of his dead sister and father haunted him every day, and he certainly did not fear intimacy with others because of that. Brooks sighed, bringing his fist to his temple and closing his eyes. He supposed his mother had a point.

"If I have to leave this world before you make a family of your own, I will haunt you for the rest of your life," his mother practically growled when he did not respond to her questions.

"If it makes you feel better, I have already decided to go to Park Street this afternoon and apologize to August for my abrupt departure," he mumbled, lowering his hand from his head.

His mother seemed to perk up at this news. "Is that so?" she asked. Brooks nodded. "Well, that is a start. Perhaps you can invite her and her aunt to dinner one evening. I doubt it will compare to what they serve on Park Street, but our cook can certainly try."

"I did not say I planned to initiate a courtship by inviting her to dinner," Brooks said sharply, rolling his eyes. He took a deep breath, attempting to diffuse his annoyance. "I only wish to apologize and offer her my friendship—even my services as a solicitor—should she need anything as a woman of newfound fortune."

His mother appeared unimpressed, narrowing her eyes at him. "Your friendship? Your services? What good does that do either of you? She needs a *husband*, not a friend. And who better than you, who rescued her from that dump in Portsmouth!"

Brooks gritted his teeth. "First of all, I did not rescue her. She was doing quite fine without me interrupting her life on behalf of her father. Second of all, the Dunns were respectable people who treated her well, and their house in Portsmouth was as nice as this one." His mother scoffed, but Brooks continued anyway. "And third of all, you and I both know I do not plan to marry, so friendship is the best I can offer."

Mrs. Brooks groaned. "Oh, must you maintain this foolish fancy of yours? You will drive me to an early grave!"

"What foolish fancy?"

"Of being single forever! It's not natural."

Brooks glared at his mother. What wasn't natural, he wanted to say, was the way marriages seemed to collapse all around him. His father and mother's, Lord and Lady Bolton's —even the love match between Lucy and Edward, Charles and Rosamund's cousin, ended in tragedy.

Even if he did wish to marry August, why would he risk her future for his fanciful desires? The husbands he knew ended up beating or cheating on their wives, failing them completely. Hell, it was in his blood, perhaps even all men's blood. If it were up to him, August would never marry.

"I will maintain my foolish fancy for as long as I like," Brooks finally grumbled. He decided he had given his mother his attention long enough. "Now, if you'll excuse me, I must get ready for my morning appointments."

Chapter Sixteen

THE DAY after the dinner party, Lady Ramsbury took August shopping, as promised. After all, there couldn't be any visits from dancing masters or etiquette tutors until her niece procured an entirely new wardrobe. Their first stop was the linendraper, where they bought different fabrics with no sense of economy, despite August's protests.

"You are a wealthy heiress, August," Lady Ramsbury told her, the feather in her hat bobbing to and fro as she turned her chin and nose upward, as she so often did when speaking. "You need to start dressing like one. Do not worry—I have been managing my finances and looking fashionable while doing it for many years. I will not lead you astray in cost or appearance." The dowager duchess offered a reassuring smile. "You only need to trust me."

August watched as her aunt selected plenty of colorful silks for evening gowns, as well as yards and yards of the best muslin that she had ever seen. "Do I need so much muslin?" she asked, uncertain.

Lady Ramsbury looked at August as if she had never heard such a ridiculous question. "You will spend most of your day in muslin. Your morning dress. Your walking dress. Your visiting dress. All muslin."

August still did not see the point. "Is it necessary for me to have so many dresses? I feel as though I'll spend my whole day changing."

"We all have crosses to bear," her aunt muttered, ignoring her as she pointed the shopkeeper in the direction of another floral-patterned muslin. Once she finished selecting fabrics in that material, Lady Ramsbury moved on to wools. August inhaled sharply.

"It is nearly summer!" she exclaimed, causing the shopkeeper to pause. He glanced at her aunt, who gave a curt nod for him to continue. August continued to protest anyway. "Why should I need any wools right now?"

Lady Ramsbury looked over her shoulder, raising a judgmental brow at her tattered red cloak. "It is still the middle of spring, and you desperately need new outerwear," her aunt said flatly before turning away. "And a carriage dress."

"A carriage dress?" August echoed, confused. There were too many types of dresses! "What if I am visiting someone but must first get in a carriage? Do I wear a visiting dress or a carriage dress in that scenario?"

Her aunt turned again, shaking her head, exasperated. "No, no, no! A carriage dress is for *long* journeys."

"What constitutes a long journey?" August asked. She supposed her trip with Brooks was a long journey, but she was trying not to think of him that day. He had already taken up too many of her dreams the night before. She focused on her aunt instead, who contemplated her question.

"Anything over an hour," she finally answered. "For example, if you are going to a house party in the country, you ought to wear your carriage dress, but when you arrive, you should immediately change into your visiting dress. Do you understand?"

August nodded. "Will I be attending any house parties?" she asked, thinking of Rosamund's wedding in June.

"One can only hope," her aunt said in between picking out wools. Finally, they moved on to silks. "House parties truly are *key* to any young woman's success on the marriage mart."

"What do you mean?" August asked, stepping closer to her aunt as if the woman was about to tell her a huge secret.

"Think about it," her aunt said seriously, turning around. "A week or two in a remote countryside palace with twenty or so other people, some of them young and single. I have *yet* to see a house party that ends without an engagement."

The dowager duchess spoke with such authority that all August could do was politely nod in agreement. After they finished there, they moved to the haberdasher down the road —"For trimmings," Lady Ramsbury explained—and then finally the dressmaker. It was late afternoon by the time they finished their errands.

August managed to avoid thinking of Brooks for most of the outing, but when they returned to Park Street, Lady Ramsbury's butler greeted them right away. August's heart started to pound as he spoke.

Brooks was waiting for them in the drawing room.

ALTHOUGH HE SPENT all morning dreading it, Brooks did call on August at Park Street that afternoon. Giving his card to the butler, he was informed that Lady Ramsbury and her charge were out shopping and would not return until later. Brooks pulled his pocket watch out and checked the time, which read half past three, then asked if he could wait.

The butler showed him to the drawing room, the same cavernous room where Lady Ramsbury played Schubert for her adoring fans only yesterday. Brooks furrowed his brow. Was that yesterday? It had felt like a lifetime ago.

He glanced at the furniture by the fire where the group must have played charades last night. Brooks wondered what August thought of Lord Ridlington and if she knew he was one of her aunt's lovers.

"Shall I bring you something to drink, sir?" the butler asked, interrupting his thoughts.

His stomach still felt queasy from the night before. "Perhaps some tea," Brooks suggested, taking a seat in one of the armchairs by the fire. He peered up at the clock on the mantel, wondering how much longer they would be.

Sitting there was worse than all his meetings that day. Brooks had thought those dragged on, but at least his clients had their various business dealings and life problems with which to distract him. Now he only had a cup of tea and finger sandwiches, which made him recall being trapped in Mr. Dunn's study when he first met August. Brooks scowled. Must he always be waiting on this girl?

It was an hour before he heard any signs of life in the entry hall. He nearly dropped his cup of tea on the floor, rising quickly before August and her aunt could enter the room. The younger girl did not look at him, and Lady Ramsbury appeared neither impressed nor irritated upon finding him in her drawing room once more.

"Mr. Brooks," she said in a clipped tone. "I did not expect you back at Park Street so soon."

"I hope you don't mind," he said while they all sat. Brooks glanced at August, who still looked anywhere in the room but at him. "I only wanted to ask how your game of charades went."

When their eyes finally met, August forced a smile. "It was terrific fun. Wasn't it, Aunt?" She turned to Lady Ramsbury, who nodded, then looked back at Brooks. "Lord

Ridlington was my partner, and I must say, he does have a real knack for it. Charades, I mean." She looked at Lady Ramsbury again. "Wouldn't you agree, Aunt?"

"I suppose," she said tentatively before slowly rising, turning to Brooks as she did. "I do not mean to be rude, but I have just remembered I must give urgent instructions to the cook regarding dinner this evening. I'll only be a moment. Excuse me."

Brooks watched Lady Ramsbury's back as she practically floated out of the room, chin pointed upward. As predicted, the dowager duchess was a terrible chaperone, allowing Brooks and August time alone together. Yet there he was, grateful for that moment of privacy with her. He was the worst sort of hypocrite.

"Did you tell her what happened?" he asked in a hushed tone. August was still looking at the empty doorway where her aunt left. Her head snapped back in his direction, her curls bouncing as she did. She glared at him.

"No," she said. "I am not one to cry wolf after I encourage a man. I only wonder why you ran away so frightened when I welcomed your advances with open arms. Were my kisses that unappealing to you?"

Brooks fought back a blush. She would not understand if he told her it was her encouragement that scared him. August probably thought he was like any other hot-blooded man she had met—like the one who took her innocence—but he wasn't. He wasn't like that at all.

"I should not have welcomed them," he said, growing increasingly disgusted with himself as he watched August's shoulders droop. He shook his head, trying to find the right words. "I did not mean to confuse or upset you. You are an attractive girl, and I had a moment of weakness."

"Am I? Did you?"

Brooks found himself tongue-tied as she shot him an

accusatory look, clearly unimpressed by his excuses. She must have enjoyed watching him squirm in the seat across from her, the fire in the hearth making him sweat underneath his jacket, which now felt much too thick for the current season.

"You are—and you do not need the likes of me taking advantage of you," he said.

August stared at him, her mouth slightly open. She looked down, shaking her head, the spite fading from her tone. "It's not taking advantage if I encouraged it... if I enjoyed it."

"A real man would ask you to marry him after that," he said, his voice low. She must understand the rules were different here in Mayfair. She looked up at him, forcing a smile.

"Don't be ridiculous," she said with a wave of the hand. "It was only a kiss. I'm sure I'll kiss many more men before the season is over."

Now it was his turn to stare. How could something so momentous to him mean so little to August? He cleared his throat, rising from his chair while she remained seated, looking up at him with sharp blue eyes.

"Nevertheless, I have come to apologize," he said, the words coming out less confident than he would have liked. August only stared at him. He started to pace the room as a result. "You must remember I have no interest in marrying, and I did not mean to make you think I wanted to be any more than friends."

"Friends?" She repeated the word as if she didn't quite understand it. Still, Brooks stopped pacing and nodded his head as affirmation.

"That's right," he said, suddenly remembering something his mother said. He cleared his throat. "Mrs. Brooks was wondering if you and your aunt would come round for dinner sometime soon. She has already grown very fond of you."

I have grown very fond of you. Brooks shook his head,

ignoring those intrusive thoughts inside his head. He wet his mouth with his tongue after it had suddenly gone dry. "Now, I doubt our cook could compare to Park Street's, but—"

"Dinner at Dover Street!"

A shrill voice came from the hall. Lady Ramsbury appeared back in the drawing room soon after. Brooks half wondered if she went belowstairs at all. Perhaps she wasn't a terrible chaperone after all.

"How charming!" she continued, taking her seat beside August again. The younger girl's eyes remained fixated on him. "I do love that mother of yours, Mr. Brooks. August and I would love to come! Set a date, and we will be there."

Brooks looked at August, hoping for some sort of reassurance from her. "Yes, Mr. Brooks, do set a date," she finally said, a coy smile playing on her lips. "A small, intimate dinner amongst *friends* sounds so lovely right now. Don't you think, Aunt?"

Lady Ramsbury nodded. Brooks remained where he stood, his lips pursing as he regarded her. He very much felt like running again. Instead, he forced himself to stay where he was and nod as well.

"Wonderful," he said. He turned to Lady Ramsbury, who looked rather pleased with herself. He couldn't imagine why. Indeed, there must be other dinner tables at which she would rather see her niece seated that season. "I will have my mother send you the date when she has chosen one."

Chapter Seventeen

Dinner at Dover Street was set for a Saturday evening one week later. By that time, some new gowns had arrived from the dressmaker's, and August had begun her lessons. Pianoforte lessons, singing lessons, drawing lessons, anything and everything to help August become more accomplished. Her aunt even insisted on hiring a French tutor, though August protested that she already knew the language.

"There's always room for improvement," Lady Ramsbury said. "Your good looks, your fortune, your accomplishments. All will make up for having no idea who your mother is in the eyes of the ton."

August frowned. She thought back to her first and only conversation with her father, who remained tight-lipped about her mother's identity. "So my father never said anything to you about her?" she asked her aunt.

The dowager duchess shook her head. "Nothing at all."

August went to her weekly French lessons without complaint, the same with her pianoforte, singing, and drawing lessons. A dance master came not once but twice a week, seeing how dancing was what challenged August the most. She had never even attended a dance in the country or Portsmouth, but she had to prepare herself for Lord Riddlington's ball. Although she could hardly remember the difference between a cotillion and a scotch reel at first, August persisted. She sometimes even found herself dancing in the hallways of her aunt's Park Street mansion, humming a song and counting to herself, practicing long after her dancing master had left.

August practiced while she waited for her aunt in the entry hall the night of their dinner with Brooks and his mother. They were due at Dover Street in a half hour. "It is so refreshing to see a young girl taking her lessons seriously," her aunt said from the second-floor landing.

August abruptly stopped, embarrassed to be caught. She turned and looked at her aunt, who was smiling at her. August demurely clasped her white-gloved hands in front of her, flushing.

She wore all new clothes that evening, all the way down to her stockings, chemise, and stays. Her gown that night was light pink and the frilliest thing she had ever worn, what with its ruffles and floral-shaped appliques across the bodice and skirt. The added feather in her hair had her questioning whether or not she had turned into some sort of exotic bird.

"You look splendid, my dear," her aunt said when she reached the bottom of the stairs. She kissed her niece on the cheek, and despite believing she looked ridiculous, August couldn't stop smiling. She felt like a proper lady on her way to dinner with a man she liked—a man she wanted desperately but shouldn't. Brooks was impossible to decipher, which made him dangerous. One minute he was passionately kissing her in her aunt's library; the next he said he only wanted to be friends.

August and her aunt took the dowager duchess's carriage to Dover Street. Jenkins opened the door and took them to the drawing room, where Brooks and his mother rose to greet them. From the way he stared at her throughout the evening, she thought he might feel the same as she did about her bird-like appearance.

Returning to the drawing room after dinner, August and Brooks sat beside each other in front of the fire. Mrs. Brooks and Lady Ramsbury sat opposite of them, loudly conversing while August and Brooks only listened. When she was sure her aunt wasn't paying attention, August turned to Brooks. "You do not like it," she whispered.

He looked back at her, surprised. "I beg your pardon?"

"My dress. My hair. You do not like it. Any of it. You think I look as ridiculous as I feel."

Brooks smiled, looking down and away from her. He seemed to be chuckling to himself, and August crossed her arms, carefully watching him.

"On the contrary, I think you look beautiful," he said, his eyes meeting hers once more. When August realized he was paying her a genuine compliment, she quickly turned away, blushing. "I even like the feather."

August's head snapped in his direction again, her eyes widening. "Now you are teasing me," she said, fighting back a smile. She glanced at Mrs. Brooks and Lady Ramsbury, who also wore a feather in her hair. "I should ask your mother where she buys her headpieces. As you can see, my aunt has a penchant for feathers."

They both laughed, drawing the attention of the two older women. Her aunt smiled.

"Is August telling you about her dancing lessons, Mr. Brooks?" Lady Ramsbury asked. August looked at her, confused. There was a twinkle in her aunt's eye that made

August suspect the woman was up to no good. "She was awkward at first, but she has improved a great deal in only the past week." Her aunt stood, walking toward the pianoforte in the corner of the room. "August loves to practice. August, why don't you practice with Mr. Brooks? I will play you something."

August felt her face turning red. She was nowhere good enough at dancing to partner with Mr. Brooks, already a full-fledged member of society. Still, he rose, offering her his hand. "I am sure she is already more skilled than me, for I am the worst dancer I know, despite my many more years of experience than her."

She did not respond, staring at his extended hand instead. She nervously swallowed as her aunt sat down at the pianoforte, testing a few keys. Reluctantly, August took the solicitor's hand, letting him guide her to the open space behind the instrument. Mrs. Brooks watched from her seat in front of the fire, smiling at them. August's heart pounded as if it might escape from her chest at any moment.

"Are you certain this is a wide enough space for dancing?" August asked, still uncertain, even as Brooks took her into his arms.

"Do not worry—I have you," he said. Lady Ramsbury launched into a waltz on the pianoforte, and Brooks spun August about the room, holding her much too close for comfort. She was clumsy at first, but eventually, they found their rhythm. She eased herself into the movements, becoming much more confident.

"You are right, Lady Ramsbury," Brooks said. He smiled down at August, who was beginning to feel a little breathless. "She is a quick study."

Lady Ramsbury did not answer, playing for a few more minutes. Mrs. Brooks applauded when she was through, and August and Brooks took a bow. She started to giggle as they did, feeling even more ridiculous than she did five minutes ago.

"She will be a hit at Lord Ridlington's ball," Lady Ramsbury said.

Brooks stiffened beside her. He turned toward the dowager duchess. "Lord Ridlington's ball? Will that be her first outing this season?"

Lady Ramsbury nodded. For a brief moment, his expression was unreadable, then he turned to August and smiled. "Continue practicing, and you shall do fine."

"I asked Lord Ridlington to send you and your mother invitations as well," August told him. His mother gasped from behind her. August turned.

"Oh, how kind of you!" Mrs. Brooks said. "I should love to attend the marquess's ball if he invites us. Wouldn't you?"

Mother and son looked at each other for a moment, appearing as if they were having an entire conversation with only their eyes. "I suppose," Brooks finally said with a slight shrug. "Ridlington would make for a fine client."

August's face fell. She watched as Brooks walked back toward the fire, sitting down once more, leaving her to stare after him. How foolish of her to believe he would attend for her sake alone.

The evening was over soon after that, and Lady Ramsbury turned to her niece when they were safely back inside her carriage, on their way back to Park Street. "Did you have a good evening, August? Brooks seems quite taken with you if you're still hoping to count him amongst your list of suitors this season."

August shook her head. "You are mistaken, Aunt. Brooks and I are only friends. He is not interested in matrimony."

Lady Ramsbury made a dismissive sound, not quite believing her niece. But August knew the truth, and they rode on in silence.

. . .

IN THE WEEKS leading up to Lord Ridlington's ball, the dowager duchess barred all men from her drawing room. The dinner party that took place the night of August's arrival was a final soiree of sorts for Lady Ramsbury and her many friends. She even sent Ridlington away on many occasions, though the man seemed more interested in visiting Lady Ramsbury than August.

"You do not have to turn him away for my sake," August said one day while working on her embroidery by the front window of the drawing room. She watched the discouraged young marquess walk down the street away from her aunt's mansion with his head dipped low.

When Lady Ramsbury didn't say anything, August turned toward her. "Besides, I doubt anyone would think he comes here to see me."

The dowager duchess bristled. "Whether he is here to see you or me, I should not like either of our names to appear next to a man's in the society papers. We must protect your reputation at all costs."

August's shoulders drooped. "Yes, Aunt," she said sullenly, returning to her needle and thread.

Truthfully, August would have liked to have some social interaction that wasn't her aunt or one of her tutors. She hadn't seen anyone else since their dinner with Brooks and his mother a week ago. She wished Brooks would call, but the solicitor seemed to have forgotten her.

One afternoon, though, Lady Ramsbury, visibly excited, glided into the drawing room while August practiced her scales on the pianoforte. "We are to have two guests this afternoon," she said, causing August to freeze. She turned to her aunt.

"Guests?"

The dowager duchess nodded. "You remember Lady Sarah Talbot and Mrs. Ferguson from my dinner party, don't you?"

August narrowed her eyes. She had met so many people that she couldn't recall either woman. Her aunt sighed, shooting August an exasperated look. "Lady Sarah is Ridlington's older sister," she explained. "She is married to a banker, Mr. Talbot. Surely you remember meeting them."

Slowly, August nodded, vaguely recalling her aunt introducing her to a couple in their late thirties that evening. Her husband was friendly enough, but Lady Sarah was quiet. They left soon after dinner.

"Mrs. Ferguson is a widow like me," Lady Ramsbury continued. "Her husband died at the Battle of Waterloo along with my husband's brother."

"And why have you invited them both here?" August asked, furrowing her brow. Before her aunt could answer, a servant walked into the room, carrying four books and placing them on the table between the settees.

August stood up from the pianoforte, walking toward the leather bound tomes. She picked one up, looking inside at the first few pages, before turning to her aunt again. "*The Italian?*" she asked, smiling. "I did not realize you were a fan of Miss Radcliffe."

"I thought we could start a book club for ladies," her aunt explained. "You can practice your conversation skills as we discuss the various texts. It was Lady Sarah's idea."

August raised her brow, wondering why Lady Sarah would care about her conversation skills. "And she chose *The Italian* to start?"

The dowager duchess grinned. "No—that was my idea."

Lady Sarah and Mrs. Ferguson arrived at Park Street only a half hour later. Lady Sarah was much friendlier upon meeting August this second time, kissing her on both cheeks as if they were long lost relations. Although she was in her late thirties, Lady Sarah's youthful good looks hadn't faded quite yet.

Mrs. Ferguson was the first to notice the copies of *The Italian* on the table. She turned to Lady Ramsbury with wide eyes. "I thought we were here to help the girl with her conversation, not corrupt the poor thing!"

"You do not have to worry about corrupting me," August countered. "I have already read it—twice."

Her aunt took one of the books from the table, handing it to August. "Then you can be the first to read today," she said. "We will read a chapter at a time and then discuss."

And such was how Lady Ramsbury's book club began. They spent much more time discussing than reading, often going off on tangents entirely unrelated to Miss Radcliffe or her novel. "Lady August, if you learn anything from this book, let it be this: beware the marriage-minded mothers of the ton," Lady Sarah said after a long discussion about the hero's mother.

Mrs. Ferguson solemnly nodded in agreement. "It's true. Captain Ferguson's mother always thought I was beneath her son. I don't think he would have proposed if it weren't for my connections with your aunt."

"Nonsense!" Lady Ramsbury exclaimed. "Captain Ferguson would have proposed with or without his mother's approval. I only hastened the process." She turned to her niece. "I have never told you, but I'm quite the matchmaker. I can always tell which engagements are coming at the end of every season."

August thought of what her aunt said on their way back from Dover Street. *Brooks seems quite taken with you if you're still hoping to count him amongst your list of suitors this season.*

But then Lady Sarah laughed, interrupting August's reverie. "Do not let your aunt trick you, Lady August. The dowager duchess is only right half the time."

Her aunt scoffed. "When have I been wrong?"

"Why, you were wrong about me and Mr. Talbot! I'm quite sure you were as shocked as everyone else when we became engaged." She turned to August. "Mr. Talbot and I have only been married for five years. I was an older bride, and everyone once thought I would die a spinster, *including* your aunt."

Lady Ramsbury gasped. "That's not true!"

"It's true," Mrs. Ferguson said with a firm nod at August, who bit back a smile without much success. As her aunt and Lady Sarah argued, August looked up to see two men in the doorway of the drawing room. Her eyes widened when she recognized Brooks being led toward them by a footman.

"Brooks!" she exclaimed. The dowager duchess and Lady Sarah ceased arguing immediately. All three older women turned and looked at the solicitor standing behind them. He offered a swift bow. "What are you doing here?"

"I thought I would come and see how your lessons were progressing," he said, looking at the three women and the novels in their hands. He furrowed his brow. "What is this? Some sort of bluestocking society?"

"If you are comparing me to the late Mrs. Montagu, then I'll take that as a compliment," Lady Ramsbury curtly said. Brooks smiled, glancing at the novels in the women's hands.

"I'm not sure Mrs. Montagu's society discussed the works of Miss Radcliffe at their literary breakfasts," he replied skeptically.

"But you like Miss Radcliffe!" August exclaimed, recalling their time in the carriage when she read to him. Brooks flushed underneath August's accusatory gaze.

"True," he reluctantly admitted. He turned to Lady Ramsbury. "I have some business matters to discuss with Lady August. I know you have a rule against gentleman callers before Ridlington's ball, but I thought you could make an exception since I am her solicitor."

August looked to her aunt, who shot Brooks a suspicious look. After a few moments, she finally relented. "Very well," she said.

August followed Brooks to the other end of the room, where a row of bay windows overlooked the street. "So now you are my solicitor?" August asked.

"Haven't I always been?"

She shrugged. "I thought you were my friend."

A set of chairs, a table, and a chessboard sat in the corner of the drawing room. He gestured toward it. "Do you play?" he asked.

August shook her head. "No. Lady Ramsbury doesn't either. It was her husband's. I believe that's the only reason she keeps it there."

"Would you like me to teach you?"

Brooks began walking toward the table and chairs. August watched him, her mouth slightly open as she did. "I thought you had important business matters to discuss with me."

He shot her a rueful look. "I'm afraid that was only a weak excuse to spend time with you, but perhaps if I can teach you how to play chess, we can add that to your list of accomplishments. That's the only way your aunt will approve."

August stealthily looked over her shoulder at her aunt and the other women. They were all leaning in close as her aunt whispered something to them. Sighing, August walked toward where Brooks sat in front of the chessboard.

"You wanted to spend time with me?" she asked. Brooks nodded. "But why?"

Brooks smiled at her, and she realized then that he could be pretty charming when he wasn't acting stubborn or rude. "We are friends, aren't we? I wanted to make sure your aunt wasn't driving you mad with all those lessons she talked about at dinner. I should have known better, though." He glanced over August's shoulder at the women in front of the fire. "It would seem she cannot go too long without holding court."

"It was Lady Sarah's idea, actually," August explained. "To help me practice my conversation skills."

Brooks gestured to the chair across from him. "Sit. You can practice your conversation skills with me *and* play chess."

August sat, and Brooks began explaining the rules of the game. They seemed complicated at first, but after a few moves, she was starting to understand

"Why are you here, Brooks?" she asked after taking one of his pawns with her rook. He immediately retaliated by having his bishop take that same rook. She frowned.

"In chess, you must always be thinking a few steps ahead," he warned.

August glared at him. "That doesn't answer my question."

Brooks sighed. "Can a man not visit his friend after not seeing her for a week?"

"I suppose, but you should know my aunt has become suspicious of you," August whispered as she made her next move. "She thinks you're quite taken with me."

Brooks immediately laughed, causing August to pout. Was the idea of Brooks being interested in her truly that amusing? She cleared her throat. "I would be inclined to agree if I did not know your desire to avoid marriage. You did kiss me, after all."

He froze for a moment in the middle of a move, then quickly completed it, taking one of her pawns. But August did not care. She stared at him. "Why did you kiss me, Brooks?"

His eyes finally met hers, and she held his gaze for a long while. She moved forward in her chair, letting her knees brush against his. He jumped away as if she hurt him.

"Is everything all right over there?" Lady Ramsbury called

out to them. August looked over Brooks's shoulder at her aunt and the two other women.

"Everything's fine, Aunt," August called back. "Brooks was only telling me about an investment I could make with my fortune, and then he offered to teach me how to play chess. Don't you think it will make me even more accomplished if I know how?"

"I suppose," her aunt hesitantly agreed. The three women turned back to each other, leaning in and whispering again.

August turned back to Brooks, smiling. He pursed his lips. "I should not have come," he said, moving to stand up. August reached out, grabbing him by the wrist.

"Won't you stay until we finish our game?" she asked. Whether she liked it or not, she had missed Brooks, and she enjoyed his company. She didn't want him to go. "I will not ask again. I promise."

"Very well," he said, sighing as he sat back down.

Brooks stayed for not one or two but three games, leaving long after Lady Sarah and Mrs. Ferguson did. August behaved the entire time, especially with Lady Ramsbury, who sat at the pianoforte nearby and played for them. When Brooks did finally rise to leave, the dowager duchess smiled at him. "You know, Mr. Brooks, you can call on Lady August whenever you want," she said. "You do not have to feign having business matters to discuss."

August thought she saw him blush. "Thank you, Lady Ramsbury," he said, bowing. "I will remember that for next time. Good evening."

When he was gone, Lady Ramsbury rose from her spot at the pianoforte. "It's just as I said. He's quite taken with you."

August watched her aunt glide out of the room, then sat by herself in one of the window seats until it was time to dress for dinner. Chewing her lip, she watched people traverse the street outside as she considered Brooks's feelings. Even if he had become attached to her, he would never admit it. So what was the point of hoping?

She sighed, massaging her chest. The uncertainty of it all had become a physical tightness there, and that couldn't have been healthy. She hoped she met men who *wanted* to marry at Ridlington's ball. Surely her feelings for Brooks would be a thing of the past in no time at all.

Chapter Eighteen

As April turned into May, August fell into what she found to be a most pleasant routine while living with her aunt. She still rose earlier than Lady Ramsbury every morning, unable to break the habit she developed at school and later in Portsmouth. August used the extra hour before Agatha came to her room to write letters.

She still maintained frequent correspondence with her friend Jane, who was in her last year at Hardbury. She also occasionally wrote to Mrs. Thorpe, her old headmistress, and the Dunn family. Mr. Dunn hired a new governess, who, according to Charlotte, could never compare to Miss Summer. August begged her two former pupils to be kind to the poor woman.

All her former companions had become very invested in August's debut at Lord Ridlington's ball, making August increasingly nervous for the event. Her lessons were going well enough, and Lady Ramsbury's book club was an entertaining diversion.

Meanwhile, Brooks's occasional appearances at Park Street only served to confuse her. He always claimed he was simply checking in on her—as all good friends do—but her aunt had other ideas. "I might as well reject Ridlington's invitation," the dowager duchess mused one day over dinner after Brooks had left. "You will be engaged before the night of the event even arrives."

August tried not to get her hopes up. Brooks was quite stubborn, and no amount of flirting on her end could ever break his seemingly impenetrable shield of cool indifference. Yet he still came once or twice a week to play a few rounds of chess, usually in the late afternoon after he finished working.

Thus was August's new life. According to Lady Ramsbury, all was going according to plan—until one day when Agatha was helping August get dressed, and they heard the dowager duchess shrieking from her bedroom. The two women exchanged terrified looks. August immediately rose from her seat at her dressing table, leaving her room and flying down the hall in nothing but her stays, chemise, and stockings. Her cloth curlers were still in her hair.

"What is the matter, Aunt?" August asked after swinging open the door to Lady Ramsbury's bedroom without so much as knocking. August found her aunt pacing across the room, still wearing her nightgown and wrapper. She held a single broadsheet in her hand, manically waving it around in the air.

"What is the *matter*?" the dowager duchess echoed in disbelief. She continued to pace the room, looking at her niece with wide eyes. She shook the broadsheet, the thin paper crackling as she did. "*This* is the matter."

Lady Ramsbury lifted the broadsheet to eye level and began to read. "*Perhaps most notable of this season's debutantes is Lady August Finch, the illegitimate daughter of the late Earl of Bolton, recently taken in by her distinguished yet notorious aunt, the Dowager Duchess of Ramsbury.*"

Her aunt paused a moment, inhaling deeply. August took

the opportunity to speak. "Well, they haven't said anything untrue, have they?"

"I am not finished!" Lady Ramsbury snapped. Her eyes turned back to the paper. "*Lady Ramsbury seems content to keep her niece hidden from society until Lord Ridlington's ball next week, perhaps administering the much-needed polish that would make this country girl worthy of her rumored twelve thousand pound inheritance.*"

Lady Ramsbury let out a loud, angry groan before continuing any further. August winced at the sound. "*After all, this writer has it on good authority that Lady August was once known as Miss Summer, a governess from Portsmouth by way of Hardbury School for Girls, a mediocre establishment for females of questionable origin.*"

August winced again, but the author of the piece still hadn't written anything untrue. But how they came to discover all this information, August had no idea. Her aunt was purposefully vague when introducing August to her friends a month ago at dinner.

"*This writer also has it on good authority that Lady August is the product of an affair between the late Lord Bolton and Lady Sarah Rowe, now known as Lady Sarah Talbot.*"

Lady Ramsbury lowered the broadsheet from her gaze, her eyes meeting her niece's. August became lightheaded, stumbling over to the bed and sitting down as she clutched her stomach. She turned to her aunt. "W-what? Lady Sarah is my mother?"

The dowager duchess nodded, folding the broadsheet and placing it on her bedside table. "You must finish getting dressed. We will call on the Talbots at once. If Mr. Talbot did not know... if he chooses to censure his wife for this..." August watched her aunt, who sighed. "Mr. Talbot is a very powerful banker amongst the Mayfair set. If he does not want the result of his wife's indiscretion out in society, not even I can stop him."

August thought back to how quiet Lady Sarah was at dinner the first night they met. She hardly even remembered the woman when she came to Park Street a week later. Perhaps Lady Sarah always knew August was her daughter, which would explain why she asked Lady Ramsbury to host a book club. August chewed her lip, looking at her aunt.

"Perhaps Mr. Talbot already knew," she said. "Couples surely discuss such things, don't they?"

Lady Ramsbury laughed bitterly. "I would not count on it. You do recall Lady Bolton's reaction to your existence, don't you?" August frowned as her aunt continued. No wonder Brooks despised the idea of marriage. August and the ton certainly had two very different opinions on what it should be. "Come, now. Go and finish getting dressed. We will leave at once."

When August returned to her room, Agatha was still standing by her dressing room table, waiting for her. "Is everything all right, my lady?"

August attempted a smile. "Everything's fine, Agatha. Please, pick out one of my visiting dresses. We are to call on Lady Sarah this morning."

Agatha's eyes widened. "So early?" she asked, clearly concerned. "Will you not at least have breakfast first?"

"Come, Agatha," August ruefully replied. "You know my aunt. When she sets her mind upon something, nothing will deter her—not even breakfast."

Agatha nodded and walked toward the wardrobe while August sat back down at the dressing table. She watched Agatha through the mirror that rested on top of it.

"Do pick out my best one," August told her. If she was going to meet her mother's husband for the first time, she wanted to look her best.

Once she finished dressing, August met her aunt in the entry hall. She paced across the marble floors, her mood much unchanged since August first came to her in her bedroom. Her aunt brightened—but only slightly—when she saw August descend the staircase.

"There you are," she said, clapping her gloved hands together. She wore one of her characteristic ostrich plumes on top of her head. "I have already had the carriage pulled around front. We will leave at once."

August nodded, joining her aunt by the front door. One of the servants pulled it open for them, but an out-of-breath man standing on their doorstep prevented them from leaving. August nearly gasped when she saw him. "Brooks!" she exclaimed. "What are you doing here?"

"I came as soon as my mother brought me the paper," he said, removing his hat and striding straight past them into the entry hall. The two women spun around, watching him, both with very different expressions on their faces. Lady Ramsbury appeared irritated, while August could hardly contain her delight.

"Do you mean—"

"Are you all right?" Brooks asked, his blue eyes focused on August. "I know you wanted to know the identity of your mother... but to find out like this..." He trailed off, shaking his head. He pursed his lips, looking from August to Lady Ramsbury, who had taken a fan from her reticule and begun wafting it in front of her face quite vigorously. "I should have known. I should have remembered!"

August furrowed her brow, confused. "What do you mean?"

He sighed. "When I was younger, I once overheard Lord and Lady Bolton arguing about a woman. A woman named Sarah Rowe." He shook his head. "I did not recall it until now." He glanced at Lady Ramsbury. "It's no wonder she wanted to start a book club. She probably wished to get to know you without having to reveal herself."

Lady Ramsbury cleared her throat. "And that's what makes me nervous. If she did not want to reveal her true relation to August, surely her husband does not know about the girl's existence. And if he does not take kindly to it, who knows what trouble he will cause. Men are such jealous creatures."

August watched Brooks bristle at her aunt's last statement. Then, he seemed to notice the women dressed in much too fine of frocks for a morning walk through Hyde Park. "Are you going somewhere?" he asked, narrowing his eyes, his voice uncertain.

"We are calling on the Talbots," August explained, nervously glancing at her aunt, who had lifted her chin at least three additional inches in the air as she regarded Brooks. The solicitor looked confused.

"At this hour?" he asked.

Lady Ramsbury nodded. "I must ensure Lady Sarah is all right. Regardless of her secret, she is a dear friend, and I will not allow her husband to mistreat her over this news. And if she is all right, I must discern Talbot's intentions toward August. Ridlington's ball is only a week away, and I will not have any more surprises."

August watched Brooks nod in agreement. "Very well," he said, glancing at August. His gaze made her heartbeat quicken. "I will come with you."

Her aunt huffed beside her. "That will not be necessary. I have this well in hand, sir. I am the girl's guardian, after all—not you."

"And I am the girl's solicitor," Brooks argued. "What if Talbot wants money in exchange for his support, or even just to ignore his wife's indiscretion? You know how bankers are. I will not let him rob the poor girl blind!"

Lady Ramsbury scoffed. "You can come with us if you admit if it's for purely selfish reasons alone."

Brooks contorted his face. "Selfish reasons?"

"Yes," the dowager duchess replied, nodding once. August looked back and forth between her aunt and the solicitor as if she were watching a particularly intense game of battledore and shuttlecock, a popular game amongst the girls at Hardbury during the summer.

"And what selfish reasons are those?" Brooks asked, practically fuming from the ears as he took a step closer to Lady Ramsbury. She groaned.

"Just admit you care for the girl!"

Brooks gritted his teeth. "I never said I didn't."

The dowager duchess groaned again. "You know what I mean. Just admit it! Why else would you have run here first thing in the morning after reading the latest scandal sheet?"

"I did not run," Brooks said, putting his hands on his hips.

"Do not lie, Brooks. Why else would you be panting as you do? I can see the sweat on your brow—not to mention your jacket."

"I beg your pardon! It's hot outside today."

The dueling pair seemed to have reached an impasse, growing quiet as they glared at each other. The only noise was Lady Ramsbury's fan moving quickly in front of her face. August sighed. Brooks would never admit to such tender feelings as caring for someone like Lady Ramsbury meant. Her aunt did not know Brooks like August did. He would never concede to any sort of accusation that might demand a proper proposal.

"If Brooks would like to come, he can, with or without admitting anything," August finally said. Her two companions turned to her as if they had forgotten she was standing there. August sighed. "Try to remember it's *my* future at risk, won't you? I will take all the support I can get."

She spun on her heel, leaving the entry hall through the still-open front door. She did not bother turning to look if they were following her. Instead, August let one of the footmen help her into the carriage. Her aunt and Brooks soon joined her inside. When the carriage finally lurched forward, August realized Brooks was sitting in the opposite direction of where they were going. She frowned, knowing that would make him ill.

"Would you like to switch seats?" she asked him quietly, but in such close quarters, her aunt overheard anyway. The older woman suspiciously looked from August to Brooks, who smiled slightly.

"It's a short ride," he said. "I will be fine."

August smiled back at him and nodded, then turned to her aunt. The older woman watched her with narrow eyes. "What?" August asked.

Her aunt only shook her head before turning to look out the window. August did the same, trying to ignore the tension inside the carriage. Lady Ramsbury may have been annoyed at Brooks, but August was too busy reveling in his kindheartedness. He came to her when she needed him most, just as a scandal that might damage her future irreversibly was brewing.

Perhaps there was hope for them after all.

When they arrived at the Talbots' home in Grosvenor Square, the butler tried to turn them away at the door.

"Lady Sarah does not take social calls until three o'clock, ma'am," the mustached man told the dowager duchess, who would not accept such a rule. Instead, she procured a small calling card from her reticule, handing it to him. He glanced at it, then looked back up at her with horrified eyes.

"Tell your mistress that the Dowager Duchess of Ramsbury would like to see her on a most urgent matter," Lady Ramsbury said sweetly. August watched the butler's Adam's apple bob in his throat as he nervously swallowed. "Surely she won't make me wait until the afternoon."

"Of course, Your Grace," he said with a slight bow, opening the door wider so they could wait in the entry hall. A portrait of Lady Sarah and her husband hung on one of the walls. August studied it, noticing similarities in their features that she hadn't recognized before, their fair hair and square jaws being two of them.

The butler did not keep them waiting long, returning to the entry hall to lead them into the drawing room, where Lady Sarah—August's mother—sat on a settee in front of the window, still wearing her morning gown. A pug stood on the cushion beside her, barking at them as they entered the room, causing Sarah to scold him. "Jasper! That is no way to treat our guests."

The dog whined, then eventually curled up beside her. Sarah gestured to the empty settees that flanked her. "Please, sit. It would appear you have read the latest scandal sheet as well if you have decided to call this early."

Lady Ramsbury gave a firm nod. "We have."

Nervous, August tried not to fidget, though it was hard not to. The woman sitting before her was her mother, a person she believed was dead for the longest time. Now, August couldn't decide if knowing Lady Sarah for the past month made it worse or better. Their familiarity with each other had become somewhat tarnished now that August knew she kept such a secret from her.

Sarah glanced at Brooks. "I'm surprised to see you here," she said.

"I am Lady August's solicitor," Brooks replied matter-of-factly. Whether he had a right to be there or not, Brooks was a calming force for August. She wanted him there, whether it made sense or not. But Sarah still looked confused.

"Do we have a legal matter on our hands, Mr. Brooks?" she asked.

"We might."

August glared at him. "Brooks," she warned.

Sarah looked at August. The girl blinked back at her, seeing all the similarities between their features now. "I apologize that you had to find out this way," Sarah said ruefully. "I meant to tell you eventually, but there was never an opportune time."

"So it's true, then?" August asked. "You are my mother?"

Sarah nodded, and Lady Ramsbury sighed. "Does Mr. Talbot know?" the dowager duchess asked. Sarah turned to her, tilting her head to the side.

"Yes, my husband knows." She looked back at August, who watched her mother with wide, hopeful eyes. "He's always known. I could never marry a man without feeling like I could explain what happened all those years ago with Lord Bolton." She laughed slightly. "Perhaps that's why it took me so long to marry."

"So he does not mind?" Lady Ramsbury carefully asked. Sarah quickly shook her head, and relief washed over August.

"No, he does not mind, though I imagine someone thought he would with that article published this morning," she said. "Nevertheless, you do not have to worry about Mr. Talbot. You will have my husband's full support in society—if that even means anything to you."

"Believe me, it does," the dowager duchess interjected before August could answer. "A rich and powerful man such as Mr. Talbot? It certainly helps a great deal."

"In fact," Sarah continued, still looking at August, "my husband has been trying to help me find you these past five years without much luck. Imagine my surprise when you showed up at one of Lady Ramsbury's famous dinner parties one day."

August's chest swelled. "You have been searching for me for the past five years?"

Sarah sadly nodded. "Much longer than that, I'm afraid—ever since my father died. You see, he was the one who made me give you up. After he died, I became desperate to find you—if you were even still alive. Arthur—Mr. Talbot, I mean—was the one who found the orphanage where we suspected my father left you. They had a record of a babe who was found there the morning after you were born." She smiled slightly. "They named her August Summer."

August frowned. "But that was five years ago! I was still at Hardbury School for Girls five years ago. Did they not tell you where Lord Bolton eventually sent me?"

"No," Sarah said, shaking her head. "The orphanage could only tell us that August Summer had been released from their care in 1801." She sighed sadly. "They wouldn't even tell me who took you, no matter how much money we offered them. I assumed your father might have grown a conscience and found you himself at that time, sending you to school somewhere. I am glad I was right about that, though I wish he would have told me. Mr. Talbot wrote to him many times on my behalf, but the earl never responded."

"Why not?" August asked, growing angry with her father. She regretted being so kind to him when she met him, even if he was ill. "What happened between you and the earl?"

Sarah hesitated, glancing at Lady Ramsbury, but the dowager duchess offered no assistance. She looked to Brooks next, who only shrugged. "You might as well tell her the whole sordid affair," he said. "She will not rest until she hears it all."

Sarah sighed, nodding. August carefully watched her mother while she spoke. "I was eighteen when I met Lord

Bolton. He was as old as I am now, not to mention married, but I was quite taken with him, and he with me. I was young and foolish, and we began an affair."

August recalled her foolish desires when it came to Henry. She wondered what would have happened if she stayed in Wilton. Would she have fallen victim to a fate similar to her mother's?

"I'm not sure what I was expecting," Sarah continued. "Bolton would never divorce his wife and risk a scandal for me, and my father would not accept his well-bred daughter becoming an older man's mistress—even if that man was an earl. Eventually, none of that mattered. I fell pregnant, and the earl abandoned me. I was angry, of course, when my father took you away from me—but at least he did not abandon me after I was ruined."

"And Mr. Talbot?" August asked. Her mother smiled, appearing so serene that August imagined the past didn't matter to either of them. Only people in love must have been able to smile that way.

"My angel," she said dreamily. "He was the one who encouraged me to get to know you even when I was frightened. I had so many doubts, which is why I did not reveal myself right away."

August frowned. "Doubts?"

"What if you did not like me?" She glanced at Lady Ramsbury. "What use am I when you have a powerful dowager duchess at your side?"

Lady Ramsbury scoffed. "A powerful dowager duchess is nothing compared to a banker who holds half of Mayfair's money!"

"Ah," Sarah said, turning away and nodding. "But that is my husband, not me."

August frowned. "Mother—"

"August will be better off with the support of your

husband *and* you, Lady Sarah," her aunt said, interrupting her. "There is no doubt that aristocratic blood flows through her veins now. I trust you and Mr. Talbot are attending your younger brother's ball next week?"

But Sarah wasn't listening. She was too busy staring at August. "You called me Mother," she said.

August nodded. "Is that all right? I could call you Lady Sarah—or even Mrs. Talbot—if that's what you prefer."

Sarah smiled, shaking her head. "Mother is perfect."

Chapter Nineteen

BROOKS CAREFULLY WATCHED as August interacted with Lady Sarah, now knowing that the banker's wife and member of Lady Ramsbury's book club was her mother. Although Mr. Talbot wouldn't be causing August any problems, there was still the question of who told the scandal sheet writer about August's past and her relation to Lady Sarah. Someone meant to cause trouble for August, and Brooks wanted to know who.

He said as much to the women gathered in Lady Sarah's drawing room. August had moved to sit beside her mother, and Jasper now sat in August's lap, happily accepting her pets on top of his head.

"Who else would have known that August was your daughter?" Brooks asked. He glanced at Lady Sarah, thinking of Lord Ridlington. "Your brother, perhaps?"

Surprisingly—or perhaps not—Lady Ramsbury was the first to come to his defense. "He would never do such a thing!" the dowager duchess exclaimed.

Brooks arched a single brow at her. "You have used August as an excuse to keep him away from Park Street while openly entertaining me for the past month. Perhaps he wants her gone so he can go back to monopolizing your attention."

Lady Ramsbury glared at the solicitor. "I can rescind my open invitation to you anytime, sir."

Brooks glared back as Sarah cleared her throat. "I do not think my brother has done it either, but I have wondered who might have, and I think I might know who it could be." Brooks turned to her, listening intently. "It has to be Lady Bolton. She knew of our affair, and from what August has told me of her, the woman was angry that her husband wanted his daughter to take her place in society. The countess probably thought this article would prevent her from doing that."

Brooks grew still. He didn't want to think of Lady Bolton doing such a thing. She had been so kind to him as a child. How could she be so cruel to a poor, defenseless woman now? He did not want to consider it.

Brooks rose abruptly, looking at Sarah and August. "I apologize, ladies, but I should go. I have been away from my office for too long. I'm glad everything's settled." He swiftly bowed. "Give Mr. Talbot my regards."

He turned, quickly leaving the room. He was halfway down the hall when a female voice called out his name. He stopped, wincing before turning to face her

"August," he said. She looked pretty today, of course, her cheeks and lips a perfect shade of pink. Brooks couldn't understand why he was still torturing himself by becoming involved in her life, but here he was. He just couldn't stay away. "What is it?"

She smiled at him, and he softened slightly. She seemed to have that effect on him, made worse when she reached out to touch his hand—very lightly, just enough to make him begin to melt. "I wanted to say thank you," she said. "It was very kind of you to come to my aunt's this morning and then here to my mother's. I do appreciate your friendship."

Brooks took back his hand. *Friendship.* He nearly laughed out loud. Instead, some sort of pathetic sputtering sound came from his lips. She watched him, concerned. "Are you all right?" she asked.

Regaining his composure, he nodded. "Yes. But I really must be going now. Good day, August."

He felt her eyes on his back as she watched him leave the house. They seemed to have burned a mark there, one that he felt his entire journey home. When he finally reached Dover Street, Jenkins had opened the door before Brooks had even reached the front steps. "You are eager, Jenkins," he observed as he handed him his hat and coat.

"Mr. Edward Swinton is here to see you, sir," Jenkins replied before quickly dashing away. Brooks froze, watching him go.

"Oh," he muttered, glaring at the butler's back as he disappeared down the hall. *Coward*, Brooks thought to himself. He had not seen his brother-in-law—as well as the cousin of Charles and Rosamund on their mother's side— since Lucy died last year. Brooks recalled telling the man— quite firmly—that he never wanted to see him again after his sister's funeral. So why was Swinton here?

He angrily strode into the reception room, ready to throw the pompous ass out onto the street. Swinton sat there waiting for him. He sat facing the opposite direction of the entry hall, but Brooks immediately recognized him due to his hair color, the same shade of red as his aunt's.

"Swinton," Brooks said, trying not to grit his teeth as he came into his brother-in-law's view. "What are you doing here?"

Despite Brooks's cool greeting, Swinton grinned at him, rising and extending his arms at his sides as if inviting an embrace. "Brooks!" he exclaimed.

But the solicitor only stared at him, unmoved. Swinton's

friendliness would not fool him. He trusted the man with his sister's happiness, and Brooks could not forget how that turned out. "What are you doing here?" he asked again.

Swinton dropped his arms, bringing his hands behind his back, though his grin did not fade. "Does family need an excuse to visit family? I was in town and wanted to see how you are doing."

"You are not my family," Brooks snapped, turning on his heel and heading toward his study. Hearing Swinton following him, he almost slammed the door in his face, but he supposed it was better to work this out now before Swinton involved Mrs. Brooks, who would surely take Swinton's side, sentimental as she was.

"Come now, Brooks," Swinton said. The solicitor sat down at his desk, feeling his jaw tense. His brother-in-law continued. "Surely a year is long enough to let tempers cool after what happened."

Brooks looked up at him, horrified. "My little sister is dead. Do you honestly think I am over it? Are you?"

Swinton furrowed his brow, pulling out one of the chairs in front of Brooks's desk and sitting down. "Of course not. I loved your sister. But I was hoping that after a year, you might have finally realized I am not at fault for her death—and neither are you." Brooks stared at him. He knew he was acting stubborn, but he couldn't help it. He missed his sister too damn much, and he had to blame someone. Swinton sighed. "I suppose that was too much to hope for."

"Indeed," Brooks said, reaching for his pen and his pot of ink. His brother-in-law glared at him, but Swinton should have been used to his complete lack of feeling by now. "If you'll excuse me, I have work to do."

But Swinton would not leave. He remained seated in the chair across from Brooks's desk, carefully watching the solicitor. "Where were you this morning, anyway?" Swinton finally asked. "I was waiting for over an hour. It's not like you to be away from your office for so long—especially not before luncheon."

Brooks sighed, dropping his pen. He made a steeple with his hands, bringing it toward his chest. "I was helping a friend."

Swinton raised his brow. "A friend?" he repeated in disbelief.

Brooks glared at him. "Is it so hard to believe I might have one?"

"A little," his brother-in-law replied, smiling slightly. Brooks's glare deepened, and Swinton shot him a sheepish look. "You have never been the most social creature, Brooks."

Brooks huffed but did not bother trying to argue. He would much rather change the subject. If Swinton discovered Brooks had become so preoccupied with some country girl eight years his junior, his brother-in-law would never let him hear the end of it.

"What are you doing in London?" Brooks asked, hoping to distract Swinton with questions about himself. "Where are you staying?"

"I'm staying with my aunt in Berkeley Square," Swinton replied. Brooks stiffened at the mention of Lady Bolton. "She needed a calming force for Charles, and I thought it was high time I came out of hiding in Surrey. The memories there weren't doing me any good."

"So Charles and Rosamund have come to town as well?" Brooks asked. He wondered if Rosamund would call on her sister. He was sure August would have liked to see her.

"If I'm honest, Rosamund is the reason I'm here."

Brooks raised his brow. "Is she all right? Has something happened with Rutley? You know how I despise that man."

"Yes, I do," Swinton replied, snickering. "You hold grudges for far too long, my friend."

"We are not—"

"We are not friends," Swinton finished for him, causing Brooks to purse his lips. "Yes, I know. But rest assured, Rosamund is just fine. It's her sister that I came to inquire about."

Brooks felt the hair on the back of his neck stand up. He rubbed it with his hand, attempting to drive away any tenseness that came whenever someone mentioned August. It didn't work. He dropped his hand, sighing. "So they told you about August," he said.

Swinton nodded. "Rosamund was hoping I would get to know her. She thought my approval might convince my aunt to give the poor girl a chance. What do you know about her?"

Brooks stared at his brother-in-law for a moment, then shrugged, attempting to be as emotionless as possible. "She is Lord Bolton's illegitimate daughter. Should I know more?"

He did not like the smug look forming on Swinton's face. "I have it on good authority that you call on her at her aunt's house on Park Street quite frequently."

"Who told you that?" Brooks asked, his face falling.

"Lord Ridlington."

Brooks grimaced. "That weasel," he muttered to himself. Meanwhile, his brother-in-law laughed.

"Why have you become so close to the chit?" he asked. "It's very unlike you, Brooks. You have had women, of course, but I have never seen you so... enamored."

He said the last word with such an arrogant grin that Brooks nearly walloped him. "I am not enamored," he said, his denial sounding flimsy even to him. "And she is not some *woman* as you so carelessly put it. I am her solicitor, and I am only looking out for her. She's come into a great deal of money, and plenty of foolish men will want it. Plenty of people would like to see her fail as well—your aunt included."

Brooks thought of the article that Lady Bolton must be behind.

"I agree," Swinton said innocently. He brought his hand to his chest. "I only wish to improve my aunt's opinion of her. Can you introduce me to her?"

Brooks did not hesitate. "No."

Swinton pursed his lips. "Surely you want the girl to have a good relationship with her family. I am practically her cousin as well."

"Hardly," Brooks replied, clenching his jaw.

Swinton sighed. "Well, I suppose I could call on her at Park Street without you. I have always been a favorite of Lady Ramsbury. Surely she would entertain me for a few minutes this afternoon."

"You cannot do that," Brooks said, grimacing. "Lady Ramsbury isn't accepting any male guests until after Lord Ridlington's ball. You can meet her there like all the other Mayfair dandies."

"Mayfair dandies?" Swinton asked, laughing slightly. But Brooks ignored him, causing Swinton to sigh again. "I'm sure she will make an exception for me like she has for you." He rose from his chair, and Brooks nervously watched him, rolling his pen between his forefinger and thumb.

"Fine," Brooks finally said. The force with which he said the word nearly made Swinton jump. "I call on her some days at five. You can join me today if you are free."

Swinton raised his brow. "Such an intimate time to call on someone. Will you be attending Lord Ridlington's ball as well?"

"August would like me to go, but I haven't decided yet," Brooks said without thinking. He winced when he saw the look of glee on Swinton's face.

"My." Swinton placed his hand on his hip as he carefully regarded Brooks. The solicitor shifted uncomfortably in his chair. "I wonder what Lucy would say if she could see you. We always wondered if you would ever find yourself besotted with someone."

"I think you ought to go now," Brooks replied icily. He did not look at Swinton when he did. Talking about Lucy was difficult with anyone but especially her former husband.

"I will be back at half past four," Swinton said. "Give your mother my love. Perhaps I will come by again sometime this week to call on her."

"I like it better when you remain in Surrey," Brooks grumbled, causing Swinton to laugh as he left the room.

"Until this afternoon, Brooks."

Chapter Twenty

THE EVENING after discovering Lady Sarah Talbot was her mother, August sat in one of the bay windows of her aunt's drawing room, blissfully happy. She hummed to herself, working on a piece of embroidery, remembering how she left Linfield Hall so unsure of herself. But somehow, she had made a family for herself in London, all without the help of Charles or Lady Bolton.

She triumphantly grinned. She did not need them. She never needed them, and if they were the ones who told that scandal sheet writer about her past... Well, they had failed. She would have her debut whether they liked it or not.

But as August worked, the figures of two gentlemen walking down the street caught her eye. She squinted through the window, recognizing Brooks but not his unfamiliar red-haired companion. August turned to her aunt, who sat playing at the pianoforte like she did most afternoons when Lady Sarah and Mrs. Ferguson did not come for their club.

"Mr. Brooks is here, and he's brought someone with him," August said.

Lady Ramsbury immediately stopped playing, looking

over her shoulder at her niece and appearing confused. "He's brought someone with him?"

August nodded before turning back to look out the window. Brooks and his mysterious companion drew closer, and August heard her aunt get up from the pianoforte. "He has red hair," August said before gasping suddenly. "Is that...?"

She recalled the miniature on Lucy's bedside table. The red-haired gentleman. She wondered if that was him!

"Red hair?" Lady Ramsbury asked, suddenly standing behind August, peering out the window over her shoulder. "That looks like Mr. Edward Swinton, Brooks's brother-in-law. He's also Lady Bolton's nephew."

August's head snapped in her aunt's direction. "Lady Bolton's nephew? Why would Brooks bring him here?"

"I have no idea. Now come away from the window. We cannot appear as if we were waiting for them to arrive."

August nodded, taking her embroidery and moving to sit in front of the unlit fireplace, where she pretended she wasn't expecting any guests along with her aunt. Eventually, the butler appeared. "A Mr. Samuel Brooks and a Mr. Edward Swinton here to see you, Your Grace," he said.

"Send them in," Lady Ramsbury said with a curt nod. August watched as the butler disappeared through the doorway, then waited for Brooks and Mr. Swinton to appear. When they did, August knew Mr. Swinton was the man she saw in the miniature right away. He had the same red hair, strong nose, and narrow blue eyes, which seemed to study her as carefully as hers did him. August demurely turned away, knowing she could not stare at him for too long. Brooks probably already noticed and would scold her later for the impropriety of it.

"Brooks!" Lady Ramsbury exclaimed. "I see you are still making good use of that open invitation of yours, even after this morning." August watched as Brooks grimaced. Mr.

Swinton shot his companion a sly look. He probably had no idea that Brooks was at Park Street and later the Talbots' house with them that morning. "You even brought a friend with you!" Lady Ramsbury looked at Mr. Swinton with a smile. "How are you, darling? I have not seen you in town for at least two years now."

"I hope you do not mind me coming, Your Grace," Mr. Swinton said. "I am staying with my aunt and cousins. Rosamund has told me so much about Lady August, and Brooks was kind enough to offer to introduce me when I called on him earlier today."

August glanced at Brooks, who appeared pained. Looking between the two of them, she wondered what happened to make him look that way. August knew right away that Brooks did not want to bring Mr. Swinton there—so why did he?

"Mr. Swinton is Lady Bolton's nephew," Brooks explained. August nodded as if Lady Ramsbury hadn't already told her. "He's also my brother-in-law." He practically muttered the words. August turned to Mr. Swinton, frowning.

"Mrs. Brooks was kind enough to tell me about Lucy when I stayed at Dover Street. I am so sorry for your loss, sir. I did not realize she was married at the time."

Mr. Swinton laughed slightly. "Brooks likes to pretend I do not exist. He always bestowed plenty of brotherly affection upon his little sister when she was alive, but none upon his brother now that she's gone."

August's lips twitched as she watched the two men sit down. "Brooks can be very stingy with his affection. I would not take it personally."

Swinton glanced at Brooks, who wore the same sullen look he frequently did. "Did I hear Lady August say she stayed at Dover Street?" Swinton asked, sounding surprised. He turned back to August, a quizzical expression on his face.

"It was only for one night," Brooks finally said. August nodded in agreement.

"Yes," Lady Ramsbury interjected, her laugh like a birdlike trill. "Brooks wasn't quite sure if I could manage my niece's debut." The dowager duchess made a sweeping motion with her hand. "But look at her. Isn't she lovely?"

August's eyes met Mr. Swinton's, and she found herself blushing underneath his intense gaze. She quickly looked away, but there was Mr. Brooks, staring at her as well. She narrowed her eyes at him. Was he jealous? She turned back to Mr. Swinton, forcing herself to smile at him. Let Brooks see her smile at other men, she thought. He ought to get used to it with Lord Ridlington's ball quickly approaching.

"She is lovely," Mr. Swinton finally said. "Very lovely."

"Did you say you are staying with your cousins in London?" August asked, still forcing herself to smile. "I did not realize they were in town."

"We only just arrived a few days ago," Mr. Swinton explained. He began to frown as he continued. "Rosamund told me she wishes to see you, but my aunt and cousin have forbidden it. I was hoping by getting to know you, I might change their opinions. I have always had a way with my aunt and cousin Charles."

August raised her brow. "Is that so?" she asked. Mr. Swinton nodded. "Well, I'm afraid you are wasting your time. I could care less if I have the approval of Charles or Lady Bolton. I have done very well for myself in town, thanks to my aunt and my mother and her husband."

The pleasant look on Mr. Swinton's face faltered. August glanced at Brooks out of the corner of her eye to find him covering his mouth with his hand. August bit her lip, imagining his smile underneath it.

"Your mother and her husband?" Swinton asked. "Rosamund said they had no idea who your mother was."

"I gather you do not read the scandal sheets then, Mr. Swinton," August said. "My mother's identity was announced to the whole world this morning in a broadsheet. She is Lady Sarah Talbot, wife of the banker, Arthur Talbot. Do you know Mr. Talbot?"

"I know the Talbots," Swinton said, nodding. Truthfully, his performance was superb. He acted as if he was learning this information from August for the first time, but August knew the truth. She was sure Lady Bolton was the one who informed the scandal sheet writer about her background. Them arriving in town only a few days ago confirmed it. The timing of it was too much of a coincidence.

"They are quite fond of me," August said. Well, Lady Sarah was. She only met her husband once, but August was sure they would adore each other once they got to know each other.

Brooks rose from the settee, turning toward Mr. Swinton. "Come, Swinton. We have taken too much of Lady Ramsbury and her niece's time."

Swinton reluctantly stood. "I hope you will save me a dance at Lord Ridlington's ball next week, Lady August."

"Will you be there?" August asked.

"I will."

August sighed. "I suppose I could, but only if you bring my sister with you. I should like to see her, and it's not fair for Lady Bolton to keep her all to herself."

Swinton nodded again, moving to leave while Brooks lingered for a moment. He looked down at August, smiling slightly. "Good evening," Brooks said, dipping his head before exiting the room with Mr. Swinton.

After the men left, Lady Ramsbury turned to her niece. "When did you become so vicious, my dear? Not that I didn't enjoy that spectacular show."

August cast a sidelong glance at her aunt. "I know a pawn

when I see one, and Mr. Swinton is nothing more than a pawn. If Lady Bolton and I are two queens in a game of chess, I will not let her capture me, no matter how hard she tries."

"And who is Brooks? Your valiant knight?"

August flushed. "I don't know. I hadn't considered it." She abruptly rose. "I'm going upstairs to change. I will see you at dinner."

"SHE CERTAINLY SAW STRAIGHT THROUGH YOU."

Brooks joined Swinton on the front steps of Lady Ramsbury's mansion, unable to keep himself from smiling. August never ceased to surprise him, this time most delightfully so. He rather enjoyed watching her put Swinton in his place.

"I don't know what you mean," his brother-in-law muttered, glaring at him. "I had no idea Lady Sarah Talbot was her mother. I do not read the scandal sheets."

Brooks carefully watched Swinton. "We all suspect Lady Bolton was the one who started the rumor."

"If she did, she did not tell me." Swinton sighed. "Surely you believe me, Brooks. I only wanted to help Rosamund."

Brooks was unable to tell if Swinton was telling the truth or not. "Then convince your aunt to allow Rosamund to attend Ridlington's party. I know August would like to see her."

Swinton nodded. "Do not worry, Brooks," he said, clapping the solicitor on his upper arm with his hand. "If that's what the lady wants, I will see to it." Swinton looked over his shoulder at Lady Ramsbury's front door, then turned back to Brooks. "She is beautiful, isn't she? I'm not sure what I was expecting, but it wasn't that. Those lips!"

Brooks's eyes widened, and he promptly spun on his heel, walking down the steps. His brother-in-law quickly followed him, calling his name and laughing, but Brooks would not stop.

"Good night, Swinton," he said, hoping the man wouldn't follow him any further. But Swinton was walking beside him soon enough, their long strides matching one another's.

"You must forgive me," Swinton said. He bit back a smile, his facial expressions not matching his words. "I only wanted to see how you would react. I have never seen you in love."

Brooks stopped abruptly, and Swinton nearly tripped over his own two feet. "I am not in love," Brooks said, his irritation growing by the minute. He wished Swinton would have stayed in Surrey. "What a silly notion."

"Come now, Brooks," Swinton said, tilting his head to the side as he thoughtfully regarded the solicitor. "Surely it's not so bad. I gather she's rather fond of you as well. Perhaps you should ask her to marry her before one of Lord Ridlington's far wealthier, much more aristocratic friends do."

But Brooks shook his head. He knew he could not, even when the idea of August eventually marrying someone else stung. "I have no interest in matrimony. You know that."

Swinton sighed, bringing his forefinger and thumb to the bridge of his nose and pinching it. "How could I forget," he muttered, closing his eyes and shaking his head. When he opened them again, he dropped his hand from his face. "Fine —do whatever you want. But will you join me for dinner at my club? Long before I married your sister, we used to be friends. You can confide in me if you would like."

Brooks narrowed his eyes. "If I confided in anyone, it wouldn't be you."

"One drink," Swinton said, lifting his forefinger in the air. "Have one drink with me. I have not been in London in two years, and I would like my time here to be at least somewhat enjoyable. You know how dreadful Charles and Rutley can be.

Unlike them, you become much better company the more you drink. Much more *fun*, if you will."

Swinton started to snicker, and Brooks rolled his eyes. "You are not doing a very good job convincing me, Swinton."

"Please." Swinton brought his hands together in mock prayer. "Think of how happy it would make Lucy. She loved both of us so dearly. She would not have wanted—"

"Enough," Brooks said, cutting him off. As much as he hated to admit it, Swinton was right. Lucy would have wanted them to be friends. She wouldn't have wanted him to blame her husband for her death. But he did not want to talk about it—not then or ever. "I will join you for one drink."

ONE DRINK TURNED INTO TWO, and then two drinks turned into three, and then Brooks was thoroughly drunk. He had not been so drunk since Lady Ramsbury's dinner party, but he didn't want to think about that night. He would remember the way August felt in the library, his hands and lips on her skin, and Brooks was desperately trying to forget all that.

But it was there in Swinton's club that he overheard *him*, a stranger with her name on his lips as if he knew her. Brooks squinted, turning toward a nearby table, trying to make out the men sitting there. There were three of them, and the one in the middle was the man in question. He seemed young, with chestnut-colored hair and a splattering of freckles across the bridge of his nose.

Brooks pointed toward him, looking back at Swinton. He was sure his brother-in-law was equally foxed. They had been laughing like nothing terrible ever happened to Lucy only a few moments ago, but now this mysterious freckled man had broken his reverie.

"Do you know who that is?" Brooks asked, still pointing.

Swinton took a swig of his brandy, then narrowed his eyes, staring at the man in question.

"No idea."

"Listen," Brooks said, using his head to gesture toward the three men sitting at the table nearby. Swinton leaned forward.

"I never dreamed of proposing," the freckled one said. "My father would never allow it, but I told her I loved her. Before she took a position as a governess in Portsmouth, she told me she returned those feelings—with her body, at least."

"You mean…?" one of his companions asked. The freckled one nodded, and they all snickered. Brooks resisted the urge to go over there by taking up his glass. The alcohol burned the back of his throat.

The freckled one shrugged. "Sorry, lads, but Lady August and her twelve thousand pounds are engaged to me. We plan on announcing it at Lord Ridlington's ball. At least we will if she knows what's good for her. Not even the daughter of the late Lord Bolton and Lady Sarah Talbot can survive such a mark on her reputation."

Brooks could no longer stop himself. He rose immediately, closing the distance between him and the other table in only a few strides. Yanking the bastard up by the cravat, Brooks violently shook him. The unnamed gentleman yelped. Although Brooks did not know his name, he knew who he was right away. He was the one who took August's innocence and somehow managed to let her walk away from him.

"What is your name?" Brooks growled.

"H-Henry," the man sputtered. "H-Henry F-Fitzgerald."

"Mr. Fitzgerald, I do not want to hear Lady August Finch's name on your lips again. If I do, I will do more than threaten you. And if you try to blackmail that poor girl into marrying you at Ridlington's ball, I will see to it that you're arrested. Do you understand?"

Henry somehow managed to nod despite the vicelike grip that Brooks had around his cravat. "Y-yes, s-sir."

Brooks let go of him, unceremoniously dropping him back on his chair. He landed with a loud thump. Brooks looked around, realizing then that the entire club was watching them. When he caught Swinton's eye, though, his friend looked like he wanted to laugh. His hand covered his mouth, only somewhat hiding his glee.

"W-who are you?"

Brooks turned back to Henry. "I am Lady August's solicitor."

Chapter Twenty-One

August awoke that night to what she thought was the sound of light tapping on her balcony door. She tried to ignore it, rolling over in bed. It must have been an animal, or perhaps she only imagined it, but then the knocking became more insistent. Groggily, August rose from her bed, blinking until the door to the balcony came into focus. Her eyes widened when she saw the shadow of an unknown man.

She looked around the room, desperately searching for something that she could use to protect herself. Her eyes landed on the metal candelabra on her bedside table. She quickly removed the half-melted candles, then hoisted the branched candlestick above her head as if it was a weapon.

August quietly pulled back her bedclothes, swinging her legs over the edge of the mattress and stepping onto the soft carpet of her bedroom. She tiptoed across the floor, closer to the balcony door, where the shadow continued tapping.

But as she drew closer, the figure grew clearer. Her arm holding the candelabra dropped to her side, and she stared outside in disbelief. "Brooks?" she asked.

August closed the remaining distance between her bed

and the balcony door, unlatching the lock and opening it. "Brooks," she said again, her voice a shrill whisper. He stumbled inside, and she knew right away he was drunk. August placed the candelabra on a nearby table. "What are you doing here?"

"I needed to speak to you," he said, not bothering to lower his voice. August hushed him, stepping forward to cover his mouth. She felt his lips curl against her palm before she quickly pulled her hand back. He was looking down at her, smiling.

"It could not wait until tomorrow?" she asked. She walked back toward the balcony, shutting and latching the door outside once more. When she turned around again, Brooks was still smiling. When it became clear he would not answer her first question, she tried another. "How did you know this was my room?"

"You once told me your bedroom had a balcony overlooking your aunt's garden," Brooks explained, stepping toward her. She stood motionless in front of him, feeling the heat of his body next to hers. He smelled of brandy, the same way he did that night in the library. She narrowed her eyes at him.

"Have you been drinking?" she asked. Brooks nodded. "Where?"

"Swinton's club."

August narrowed her eyes further. "You have been consorting with the enemy."

Brooks scoffed, waving his hand. "Swinton is harmless. He will make sure Rosamund comes to Ridlington's ball." Suddenly, his eyes became serious, and he grabbed August by her elbows. She gasped out of surprise.

"Brooks!"

"But I'm not here to talk about Swinton," he anxiously told her. "I have met the real enemy, August." She arched his brow at his furtive tone, all the while letting him lead her toward the bed, walking backward until they were sitting down together, their legs touching. August looked toward her bedroom door, then turned back to Brooks, chewing her lip.

"You should go, Brooks," she said. "If Lady Ramsbury finds us, you will be in terrible trouble."

"Henry Fitzgerald," Brooks said suddenly. August's eyes widened.

"What?" she asked. "What did you say?"

He nodded vigorously. "It's true, August. I have met your former lover, Henry Fitzgerald."

She nearly shuddered. "Please do not call him that. It makes me feel ill." But then August stared at him, her mouth opening and closing like some sort of fish. "But where did you meet Henry?"

Brooks sighed impatiently. "At Swinton's club. I overheard him telling some other patrons about you. About..."

He shot her a sheepish glance, and August resisted the urge to roll her eyes. "Yes, I understand." *Men,* she angrily thought to herself. "But what did you do? Did you do something to Henry?"

He nodded again. "I threatened him. I told him he couldn't blackmail you into marrying him, and if he tried, I would have him arrested."

August's eyes widened. "He's going to blackmail me into marrying him? Oh, Brooks, that's terrible news! What am I going to tell Lady Ramsbury?"

But Brooks pressed a single finger to her lips. She stared at him. "Do not worry, my love," he told her. She furrowed her brow, confused. What had he just called her? "I will not let him do anything to you."

Brooks removed his finger and pulled August to his chest, crushing his lips against hers. Although she was confused, August kissed him back, unable to resist the almost magnetic pull between them. He cupped the side of her face with his large hand, then smoothed her curly hair with his palm.

He began to speak in between peppering kisses across her collarbone. Everything was moving so fast, but she still happily threw her head back, his hand supporting her neck. "I cannot bear the fact that you gave yourself to that boy, yet he probably never showed you true pleasure."

"Mmm," was all August could say, closing her eyes, letting his kisses bring her somewhere else. She felt him lift the hem of her nightgown, snaking his hand underneath it. He trailed deft fingertips up her inner thigh. She whimpered.

"Let me show you," he breathed against her skin. "Let me touch you."

"Please," August begged, still somewhere else. She had wanted this for so long, and even if he was drunk and not thinking straight, how could she tell him to stop? His fingers quickly found her wet center, skillfully exploring her until he found the spot that ached the most.

His touch there was what awakened her. She finally opened her eyes to the reality of the situation she found herself in. August didn't want this. She didn't want to deal with this man's regret in the morning. August could not be a regret, especially not his. She reached for his arm.

"Stop," she said. Brooks froze immediately, lifting his head from her neck. They stared at one another, both sets of eyes hooded with desire. August thought she might cry if she went through with what she wanted to say.

"Stop?" he asked. Slowly, August nodded. He backed away from her as if he had been stung by the simple word. He stood up from her bed and immediately began to pace, running his fingers through his hair.

"Brooks," she said reassuringly, recognizing the panic in his eyes right away. He stopped pacing, looking at her.

"I thought... you said..."

She shook her head, rising from the bed and taking his hands into her own. August brought his knuckles to her lips, kissing them. She looked up at him through her eyelashes, and he stared down at her as if he was completely mystified.

"I do not want you like this," she finally explained.

"But you said…"

She shook her head. "I wanted you that night in the library. I do not deny it. I want you even now. But I know you now, Brooks. I truly know you. I will not be a regret tomorrow morning—not when I love you so—or at least when I *think* I love you so."

Brooks pulled his hands away from her, taking a step back. "What?"

"Have I sufficiently terrified you, Brooks?" she asked. "I am falling in love with you, Brooks, and that's nobody's fault but your own. You cannot have me unless you marry me. Any other way will surely break my heart because I want you for many more reasons other than carnal ones."

He blinked, and she realized right away what she had done. So that was what it took to sober him: merely the truth.

August wasn't sure when she began loving him. Perhaps it was when he danced with her in his drawing room. Or maybe it was later than that, over one of their games of chess. It even could have been when he showed up at her door that morning, so deeply concerned for her that he ran there.

"You know I do not wish to marry," he said.

She nodded. "I do."

He reached for her again, holding her by the waist. "But you do want me."

"I do," she replied, nodding again.

"Then why do you demand something I cannot give you?" He shook his head as he pushed a loose strand away from her face. "You will see. I will have you, and our need for each other will subside. Soon you will realize you don't want to marry me but someone else. Someone much more deserving of you."

Now she was the one to shake her head. "But I must demand it, for I know my feelings will not subside. I will not settle for anything less than all of you. I'm sorry, Brooks."

He turned away from her then. The moonlight spilling into the room from the balcony's glass door outlined his broad shoulders. He looked down. "Fine. It was foolish of me to come in the first place. Forgive me, August."

He walked toward the balcony door, but August called out for him. He froze but did not turn to look at her. "Will you still come to Lord Ridlington's ball next week?" she asked.

He sighed. "Of course."

He unlatched the balcony door, disappearing into the night. Closing it behind him, she wondered how he managed to get up there. But such questions were soon forgotten when she returned to bed. She reached underneath her nightgown for the spot that ached, thinking only of her lust for him.

Chapter Twenty-Two

AUGUST DID NOT TELL anyone about Brooks's midnight visit, though her aunt, Lady Sarah, and Mrs. Ferguson incessantly commented that Brooks was nowhere to be found in the last days leading up to Lord Ridlington's ball. August kept mum, refusing to comment on the subject altogether, except to say that Brooks was a busy man and was probably dealing with clients other than her.

"Do you think he will still come to Ridlington's ball?" her mother asked the day before the grand event, her brow creased with worry.

"He said he would," August replied. "I have no reason not to believe him."

And that was after she rejected his advances, though she was sure her rejection hurt her more than it hurt him. But she could settle for nothing less than what she truly wanted, and if that meant she must meet someone new at Ridlington's ball, then so be it.

The night of the ball, August expected to be nervous. Instead, she found herself quite excited, despite what Brooks told her about Henry. August hadn't told her aunt yet and wouldn't dare unless it became necessary.

Truthfully, she feared her aunt's disappointment. Even a forward-thinking, modern woman such as Lady Ramsbury had her limits. And if anyone could understand August's foolishness almost three years ago, it would have been her mother, Lady Sarah, but even then, August could not bring herself to tell anyone.

But she would not worry about such things that night —*could* not. As the carriage approached Ridlington House, August's heart pounded with anticipation. She repeatedly smoothed her lavender skirts and touched her jeweled headband, thankful for its lack of feathers.

"Do not fidget so much," her aunt scolded from across the carriage.

August nodded, trying to sit still, but soon enough, she was wringing her hands in front of her. She looked at her aunt with pleading eyes. "Are we almost at the front door?" August asked, leaning her head against the carriage's glass window, trying to see in front of them. The carriage lurched forward, moving another place in line. August nearly fell face forward into her aunt's lap.

Lady Ramsbury sighed. "We will be there soon," she said, watching August straighten herself and slide back into her seat. "You must calm yourself."

August looked out the carriage window again, this time at the gentlemen and ladies walking down the sidewalk, all dressed impeccably for the evening. "How can I?" she asked, turning back to her aunt. "Isn't this the moment for which you have been preparing me? I couldn't contain my excitement even if I tried."

"Just try to remember your etiquette lessons, dear," Lady Ramsbury said while shooting August a censuring look. "The acceptance of society is a tremulous thing. We cannot afford any mistakes tonight."

August nodded, trying not to worry about what Brooks said about Henry or if Brooks would even show up at all that night. The carriage eventually arrived at the front door, and a footman approached to open the door and help them out. August looked up, her mouth slightly open as she admired the white stone mansion illuminated by torches mounted on its outer walls. The large front doors were wide open, and she could hear the commotion of the party inside.

Her aunt took her by the arm and guided her forward. They elbowed their way through the throngs of people gathered in the entry hall and on the stairwell, which led to a second-floor landing and another set of wide-open doors. They waited in line with other guests outside the ballroom, each party holding their invitation and then handing it to one of the footmen, who would guide them inside and call out their names to the rest of the guests.

August tried not to look too much in awe of her glittering surroundings, but she practically shook with excitement. Her aunt tightened her grip around her arm.

"Calm yourself," Lady Ramsbury scolded again.

When they finally reached the front of the line, Lady Ramsbury handed their invitation to another footman, then followed him into the ballroom. The sheer size and brightness of the room struck August at once. Multiple chandeliers hung from the ceiling, illuminating the gleaming wooden floorboards beneath.

"The Dowager Duchess of Ramsbury and her niece, Lady August Finch!" the footman announced.

It was nothing like August imagined. The music did not suddenly stop, and people continued to dance without paying much mind to the newcomers. But those in the middle of conversations did turn and look at them. August thought her heart might have skipped a beat walking into the room, and she glanced at her aunt out of the corner of her eye, finding the woman meeting the room's collective gaze with a confident stare.

August attempted to smile, but the sea of people seemed endless. She wondered what they all might be thinking—if they thought she, the illegitimate daughter of an earl and a marquess's daughter, deserved to be there at all. Judging by the way some turned and whispered to their companions with such shrewd looks on their faces, she knew some probably didn't.

But before August could panic too much, three familiar figures appeared amongst the crowd, walking toward them. Lord Ridlington, her mother Sarah, and Sarah's husband, Mr. Talbot, had come to greet August and her aunt. August gave her best curtsey to Ridlington, much less awkward than it was a month ago when she first came to town.

"Thank you for inviting me tonight, my lord," August said. Ridlington smiled at her, but she noticed right away his gaze kept drifting toward her aunt. August tried not to giggle at the obviousness of his affection when Lady Ramsbury did such an excellent job ignoring it. "It's an honor to be here."

"It's an honor to have you here," Ridlington replied. He cast a sidelong glance in the direction of his older sister, Sarah. "You are my niece as much as Lady Ramsbury's, aren't you? I do hope you'll save me a dance." His eyes flitted toward the dowager duchess. "You as well, Your Grace."

"Ah, but you forget I am nothing but an aged chaperone now," Lady Ramsbury said, causing Ridlington to frown. "I will be far too busy supervising to partake in any dancing."

"We can take turns watching August if you would like to dance, Your Grace," Sarah said, swiftly coming to the aid of her younger brother. "Either way, I'm not sure my brother will take no for an answer." August's mother then gestured to the tall man with thick side-whiskers standing beside her. "You remember my husband, Mr. Talbot, don't you, August?"

August demurely nodded. "Of course," she said, smiling. "It is lovely to see you again, Mr. Talbot. I do hope we can become better acquainted."

Before Mr. Talbot could answer, August felt a small gloved hand with slim fingers on her shoulder. She turned, finding two familiar faces: Rosamund and her fiancé, the Duke of Rutley. August's eyes widened upon seeing them.

"Oh, Rosamund!" August immediately embraced her older sister. "You came!"

Rosamund smiled. "You can thank my fiancé and my dear cousin Edward for that. They somehow managed to convince my mother to let me come if they escorted me." She glanced over her sister's shoulder at Lady Ramsbury. "How do you do, aunt? It's been far too long."

"Indeed," the dowager duchess replied. She stepped forward, pressing a kiss to her older niece's cheek, then nodded at the duke. "Your Grace."

August and her aunt regarded Rutley with equally suspicious gazes. So her sister and the duke were still engaged. August glanced back at Rosamund. "Is Charles here?"

"Thankfully, no," Rosamund replied, frowning. "I wouldn't be able to keep him away from the card room if he were." August thought she saw her sister's eyes flicker toward Lady Sarah. "Why don't you come with me to the refreshment table? I will show you the lay of the land."

August glanced back at the Talbots. Her mother gave an encouraging nod, so August faced her sister again, smiling. "All right."

"I also find walking around the room is the best way to capture a man's attention." Rosamund winked. "Wouldn't you agree, Aunt?"

"Indeed," Lady Ramsbury said.

With that, Rosamund whisked her sister away, guiding her to the refreshment table at the other end of the ballroom. There was not much opportunity to talk at first as they fought their way through the crowd. Multiple young men shot leering gazes at them, and August started to wonder where Brooks was and if he would come at all. When they reached their destination, and she still hadn't spotted him, August sighed before looking at her sister. "Did you say that your cousin Edward is here?" she asked.

Rosamund mischievously grinned, looking around the ballroom. "Yes, he is here, though I'm not sure where at the moment," she said. "Why? Are you interested in my cousin? I heard you met briefly with the help of our friend Brooks."

August flushed. She was sure Mr. Swinton was a spy for his dreadful aunt, but that didn't mean she couldn't dance with him, especially if Brooks didn't show. "No," she quickly replied, causing her sister's grin to broaden even more. "Why are you smiling at me like that?"

"If you were interested, I have it on good authority that he might be as well," Rosamund discreetly whispered. August tried not to look too horrified.

"What? Didn't his wife only die a year ago?"

Rosamund frowned. "Yes, but he cannot mourn forever, can he? Poor Lucy. She was my friend as well, you know. I miss her dearly."

August took a step closer to her sister, looking around to make sure no one was listening. "How did Lucy die, Rosamund? Brooks does not like to talk about her, but his mother said something about a long illness."

"Come now," she said quietly, patting August on the arm, all the while forcing a smile and laughing slightly. "It's not right to talk about such things at parties. Have a drink with me!"

August reluctantly nodded, even though, in her experience, drinking made people foolish. Case in point, Brooks, who—by the way—still hadn't arrived. But Rosamund handed August a cup of punch anyway. Her sister took one as well, immediately bringing it to her lips. August looked at the red liquid inside the silver cup and hesitantly took a sip, following her sister's lead. She smacked her lips together, finding herself pleasantly surprised. The beverage was like a fruitier version of the table wine Lady Ramsbury served at dinner every night. She took another sip.

"It's good, isn't it?" Rosamund said with a smile, watching her. August nodded. "Try to drink it slowly, or our aunt will accuse us of being too silly."

August looked for her aunt over the crowd of people. She found her at the other end of the room, still standing with Ridlington, the Talbots, and the duke.

"Although I'm pleasantly surprised to see you here," August murmured to her sister, "I hope you made no deals with the devil to come."

Rosamund followed her sister's gaze, a look of recognition passing over her face when she saw the duke. She sighed. "I suppose I should tell you not to refer to my future husband as the devil."

August raised her brow. "Then you have not tried to cry off again? Is this for our brother's sake? When will you marry?"

"Next month as originally planned," she grumbled before drinking more punch. "I told my brother I would not do it unless he invited you to the wedding as well as the house party before. You and Lady Ramsbury should expect your invitations shortly."

August reached for her sister's hand, taking it and squeezing it. "I'm so sorry, Rosamund. To marry someone you do not love for the sake of Charles! I cannot imagine a more cruel fate. I wish—"

"There you are!" her sister exclaimed, interrupting her when someone caught her eye over August's shoulder. She watched her sister's face brighten.

Brooks, August immediately thought, but when she turned, she saw Mr. Swinton instead. She tried not to let her disappointment show on her face, but the sinking feeling in her stomach was still there, invisible to everyone but her.

She hated feeling so wretched over Brooks, especially when she knew he did not like balls or want to marry. He probably thought the better of coming and wouldn't show. After all, he made it quite clear the other night that he did not want her enough to marry her, only bed her.

"You look beautiful this evening, Lady August," Swinton said with a slight bow of the head. August forced a smile. She supposed if Brooks was not an option, she had to start her list of potential suitors somewhere—if only she trusted Swinton.

"Thank you, sir," she replied as she curtseyed. She glanced at her sister, then back at him. "You have held up your end of the bargain by escorting my sister here, so I suppose I owe you a dance."

Swinton looked pleased, and August took another drink. She now knew why Brooks sometimes drank to excess. Alcohol gave her a certain amount of courage that she did not always have.

"So you remembered," Swinton said. "If your sister is not opposed to releasing you from her company, perhaps you will do me the honor of the next one, then." He extended his hand toward her, and August stared at it, uncertain. Rosamund smiled beside her.

"I am not opposed," her sister said. "I suppose I should find Rutley."

"But Rosamund—"

But her sister already left, and when August turned back to face Swinton, he was still offering her hand. She reluctantly took it, letting him escort her to the center of the ballroom. The freshly polished wooden floors shimmered beneath their feet.

As she stood across from him at the center of the dance floor, she tried to remember all the steps to the scotch reel, visualizing them in her mind as the orchestra readied their instruments. When the music began, she let her body guide her, and her mood quickly improved with each jaunty step.

"You are better at this than I thought you would be," Swinton remarked after a few moments.

August shot him a bemused look. "I'm not sure if you're trying to be kind or rude, Mr. Swinton. Kind because you offered to dance with me despite those preconceived notions that I would be a poor dance partner—or rude because you had those preconceived notions at all."

Swinton chuckled. "I did not think you would be a poor partner. I only did not realize you would be more skilled than me."

"Well, I have been practicing very hard."

They continued in silence. At one point, August thought she saw Brooks in the corner of the room, but he disappeared as soon as she could take a second look. Swinton must have seen the disappointment on her face. "Is something the matter, Lady August?"

She forced a smile. "Not at all. I only thought I saw Brooks in the corner, but then he disappeared. I must have imagined it. I should not have believed him when he said he would come." She sighed. "You must know how he hates balls since you are his brother-in-law."

"Yes, Brooks is quite the curmudgeon," he replied with a wry grin. "I believe he grows worse every year I know him. He seems to have developed an attachment to you, however."

"Me?" August asked incredulously, her face becoming warm. He smiled, looking down at her.

"Yes, you, and I can't say I blame my brother-in-law."

August did not respond, unable to find any genuineness in Swinton's compliments. If Brooks *was* attached to her, what sort of friend was Swinton, shamelessly flirting with her while they danced? More importantly, why wasn't Brooks *here* if he liked her as Swinton claimed he did?

But she must move past that. She would not spend the whole night pining over stupid Brooks. "Is this room not rather warm?" she asked Swinton when the dance finished. "Is there somewhere we can go and get some air?"

Swinton nodded, offering her his arm. She took it, walking beside him through the crowd to a pair of glass doors, which opened onto a balcony overlooking Ridlington's gardens. August noticed other couples standing in the shadows behind him as they came to the balcony's railing. Torches illuminated the gravel pathways, shrubbery, and flower bushes below. At the center, water in a circular stone fountain trickled softly.

They looked on in silence. August supposed it would have been romantic if she felt anything for him. She frowned, thinking about Brooks.

"I have a proposition for you," Swinton said, his voice cutting through the hushed atmosphere. August turned, surprised. She had almost forgotten he was there.

"Oh?" she asked. The moon was in just the right spot in the cloudy sky so that the light shone directly upon his face. His cheeks dimpled when he smiled at her. To another woman, he might have been attractive. Lucy, for one, must have loved him.

"I have convinced Lady Bolton and Charles to let you and Lady Ramsbury dine with us one night next week," he explained. "I have not even told Rosamund yet. I wanted to tell you first."

"My!" August said caustically, turning back to the garden below. "You have changed their minds rather quickly."

He chuckled. "I told you I have a way with my aunt, and I can be very persuasive when I want to be." He paused a moment. "Besides, I think they might pity me. I have not been so excited about a new acquaintance in a long time." August eyed him suspiciously. "Do you think you and your aunt would like to come?"

August sighed. "I will think about it," she said, realizing she would need much more courage if she would be facing his bizarre advances for the rest of the evening. "Do you think you could get me more punch from the refreshment table?"

"Of course," he replied with a gracious bow of the head. "I will be back soon."

He turned and left the balcony, and August stood alone with the other two couples in the shadows. She smiled ruefully at them, though they didn't notice her. She sighed again, looking out into the garden until a familiar figure in the doorway caught her eye. August spun around, facing it.

"Henry?" she asked, dread spreading in her gut. He looked the same as ever, tall and broad-shouldered, with a splattering of freckles across the bridge of his nose. When he stepped closer to her, he practically stumbled, and she realized right away he was drunk. She thought back to what Brooks told her about him. Her pulse quickened.

"What are you doing here, Henry?"

"August," he said, his lopsided grin spreading from ear to ear. He reached out for her, but she stepped away. He lost his chance with her a long time ago.

"Why have you been telling everyone at your club about us?" she asked, her voice low. "You can try your best to ruin my reputation, but you cannot blackmail me into marrying you just because I'm rich now and you suddenly want me as your wife."

Henry straightened, regarding her with a frown. "Who told you that? Your solicitor?" He laughed slightly, and August stepped further away. Still, he followed her. "Did it shock him to learn the truth about you?

August glared at him. "What truth is that?"

A condescending grin formed on Henry's lips. "That you are nothing more than a wanton country girl, hardly a true lady at all."

August flinched, his words stinging her. "That may be true, but I doubt Brooks gives a damn!"

Henry clucked his tongue. "No wife of mine will curse like that. Perhaps I should punish you for it."

He lunged for her, somehow managing to grab hold of her wrists. She struggled against his grip, but he held her so tightly that she couldn't break free. She winced. "Henry, let go! You're hurting me." But he did not let go. Instead, he laughed and only drew closer.

"You and I had something special, August," he said against her neck, his breath tickling her skin. He smelled of brandy and snuff. She tried to pull away, but he cornered her at the edge of the balcony. August glanced at the other couples in the shadows, but as soon as they noticed her precarious situation, they promptly scattered, practically running back into the ballroom. She cursed them inwardly, peeking over Henry's shoulder at the door. She hoped Swinton would be back soon.

"I have not stopped thinking of you since the day you left," Henry murmured, nuzzling his head against her neck. She groaned with anger.

"Please, Henry," she said, trying to shove him away from her, but he was as solid as a brick wall, completely unmoving no matter how much force she used. "You and I both know that couldn't be further from the truth. You only wish to marry me because I have money now!"

But he continued to nuzzle her neck, planting wet, sloppy kisses on her skin. Realizing she still had free use of her legs, she swiftly raised her knee with all her might, aiming for his groin. The kisses ceased, and he let out a loud moan, stumbling backward.

She feared his retaliation and considered running while she had the chance, but a large hand covered one of Henry's shoulders soon after she hit him. Someone jerked him even further away from her, throwing him to the ground in the process. August closed her eyes, only hearing the struggle that was playing out in front of her.

When she was brave enough to open her eyes, she expected to see Swinton standing there, their beverages discarded at his side after he sprung into action. Instead, a fair-haired gentleman stood over Henry's limp body. August gasped. "Brooks!" she exclaimed.

But he did not acknowledge her—not yet. Instead, he crouched beside Henry, the vicar's face bloodied and bruised, lifting him roughly by the cravat until they were face-to-face. August thought she heard Henry whimper. She would have as well if Brooks looked at her like that.

"I should preface this by saying I do not like having the same conversation twice," he told Henry. "Trust me when I say you do not want to meet me a third time. If I ever see you touch her again, I will kill you. Do you understand?" When Henry did not answer right away, Brooks violently shook him. "Do you understand?"

"Y-yes, sir," Henry stammered.

"Good," Brooks said, dropping Henry on the cold stone of the balcony floor. He quickly got to his feet and rushed toward the ballroom, scampering away like the rat he was. Swinton appeared then, holding two cups of punch in his hands, nearly dropping them as Henry shoved past him. He looked at Brooks.

"Was that...?"

Brooks nodded, then turned to August, who stood beside him, somewhat in a daze. She hadn't expected him to arrive in such a fashion that night.

"Are you all right?" Brooks asked, reaching for her elbow, gently holding her steady. She stared at him, nodding. She wanted to say something, like how thankful she was for him, but nothing came out, feeling as though she couldn't form even half a sentence at the moment.

Brooks moved to speak again, but Ridlington suddenly appeared on the balcony, a nervous expression on his face. "The three of you must come with me at once."

Chapter Twenty-Three

BROOKS NEARLY DIDN'T COME that night. After the embarrassing incident where he drunkenly scaled August's balcony and barged into her bedroom in the middle of the night, Brooks wasn't sure he could face her again. Her rejection still stung, but how could he blame her? She knew what she wanted... and now it appeared she might get it.

Brooks and August sat in two matching armchairs across from Lord Ridlington's large desk. They were far away from the ballroom in his study, where Lady Ramsbury, Lady Sarah, and Mrs. Brooks relentlessly interrogated them from behind the marquess's desk. Ridlington and Mr. Talbot stood together in one of the room's corners. For a private matter, the room certainly felt crowded.

Rosamund nervously hovered behind them, and where Rosamund went, the duke was never far behind. Swinton was there as well, and as much as his presence irritated Brooks, his brother-in-law certainly needed to be there. This incident was as much his fault as anyone else's. If he hadn't left August alone on the balcony, they wouldn't have been in this mess.

Thus it was a good thing Mrs. Brooks poked and prodded

her son until he finally dressed that evening and rented a hack to take them to Ridlington House. If Brooks hadn't happened upon the balcony at just the right time, who is to say what could have happened to August. Brooks shuddered at the thought.

August explained who Henry was to their interrogators right away, after which Ridlington told them that the bastard bolted from the ballroom sometime after Brooks leveled him with his fists. That was just as the gossip started to travel throughout the ballroom and the rest of Ridlington House.

The other couples on the balcony that night heard August's name and saw what happened, and they told the story to anyone who would listen, doing the newcomer no favors with their lack of discretion. Although no one could name the man who attacked August, this was not a scandal her reputation could simply recover from when the night was over. They must take some sort of action to protect her, or at least that was what her aunt, the dowager duchess, said.

"I'm sorry, Aunt," August said, her voice frantic. "I should have told you as soon as Brooks discovered his intentions this evening."

Lady Ramsbury cast a nasty glare in Brooks's direction. "You knew about this?" she asked, her shrill voice causing him to wince. Brooks reluctantly nodded.

"Samuel Brooks!" his mother exclaimed with a gasp. "Why didn't you tell anyone?"

Ridlington stepped forward then. "Yes, why didn't you? I could have uninvited the stupid bastard."

Brooks's face grew warm. He didn't know what to say. Over the past few days, he hadn't stopped thinking about what happened in August's bedroom. As a result, he nearly forgot about Henry Fitzgerald's plan. Perhaps Brooks also expected the man not to do anything after he threatened him at the club. But as it turned out, that wasn't the case, and now

August would pay for it. Brooks sighed, trying to think of some excuse for his stupidity.

"I didn't want to embarrass August any further," he finally said, glancing back at Ridlington. He turned to face the three women staring down at him with narrowed eyes. "I thought I could handle the situation myself."

Lady Ramsbury made a sound of exasperation. "Clearly not!" She turned to August then, her face softening. "Why didn't you tell me, my dear? I could have helped you."

Brooks looked at August, seeing the tears start to form in the corner of her eyes. His chest tightened. He did not want to see her cry, especially not over that bastard Fitzgerald. He nearly reached for her hand, but after briefly glancing up, he noticed Lady Sarah watching him like a hawk, so he resisted.

"I-I'm sorry, Aunt," August said again, this time practically sputtering the words. "I was em-embarrassed, and I-I d-did not want you to t-think any less of m-me!"

"Oh, August," her mother said, sighing as she came around the side of the desk. Lady Sarah kneeled next to her daughter, reaching for her shoulders. She gently held them, then shot a surreptitious glance in Lady Ramsbury's direction. "Surely you did not believe *we* would think any less of you."

"Regardless of what anyone in this room thinks of Lady August, her debut has unfortunately been ruined," Rutley said, his booming voice startling Brooks, "as will she if she does not leave this house engaged."

August's eyes widened, and she frantically looked from her mother to her aunt. They did not say anything, only sadly smiled. August grew panicked as she thought of being tied to Henry for the rest of her life.

"B-but I cannot marry Henry!" she said. She turned to Brooks, whose chest tightened once more upon seeing her tears. Whatever strange emotion he was feeling made him uncomfortable, and he didn't like that. "He is awful!"

"There may be ways out of that," Rutley said. Both August and Brooks turned to look at him. Even Rosamund stopped pacing long enough to turn and stare at her fiancé.

"What do you mean?" Rosamund asked, furrowing her brow.

Rutley glanced over his shoulder at the marquess in the corner of the room. "Ridlington said it himself earlier." He turned back to August and Brooks. "No one knows who attacked August, but everyone saw Brooks and Swinton leave the balcony with her. People will think it's one of them who had their way with her, not Fitzgerald."

Brooks quickly faced forward, unable to look at Rutley any longer. There was the solution he feared the most. His shoulders tensed as Rutley continued. "If Brooks or Swinton agrees to marry her—mark my words—the ton will forget about this in a week."

Brooks looked up, meeting his mother's eyes immediately. How quickly they changed from concern to hope. Meanwhile, Brooks felt as though he might be sick. He didn't dare look at August, though he felt her eyes burning a hole in the side of his face.

"I will marry her."

Brooks tightened his jaw, his head snapping around to look at Swinton. But his brother-in-law ignored his menacing gaze, focusing his attention on August. When Brooks glanced at her, she was staring at Swinton, her mouth slightly open, probably in shock at his ridiculous proposal. Brooks turned back toward Swinton, glaring at him.

"If she will have me, of course."

"She will *not* have you," Brooks said before he could think the better of it. Everyone turned and looked at him. His shoulders grew tense underneath their collective gaze. "I will not allow it. Not after what happened to my sister when she was your wife."

A feminine voice answered him. "Then you will have to marry me."

Brooks froze. When he looked to his right, August was staring at him, her bright blue eyes capturing his. She did not smile when she said it. She must have known forcing him into marriage would not earn his love, and wasn't that what she said she wanted from him?

I will not settle for anything less than all of you. But why would August want such a thing? Surely he would only disappoint and fail her.

"I cannot marry you," he finally said, turning away.

"Brooks!" his mother and Rosamund exclaimed at once. Let them be disappointed in him, but even Swinton was better for her than him.

But August squared her shoulders, resolutely facing forward, barely sparing the other man a second glance. "And I cannot marry Mr. Swinton, so I suppose I will have to live in ruination, forced to think about my one terrible night out in society for the rest of my life."

Brooks glared at her. "Do not be so dramatic, August." Her head snapped in his direction, and her nostrils flared at his insult. "You will marry Swinton, and you will—"

"Brooks. Swinton. A word outside, please."

The duke was the one who interrupted him. Brooks and Swinton simultaneously looked at him, confused. "Out in the hall," Rutley said, gesturing toward the door.

Reluctantly, Brooks stood up and followed him, Swinton not far behind. When they left the room, Brooks could faintly hear chatter, laughter, and music coming from the ball-room at the front of the house. He narrowed his eyes at the duke, annoyed.

"Is it wise to speak out in the open like this?" Brooks asked.

Rutley pursed his lips. "This will only take a moment. Someone needs to talk some sense into you, and I didn't want to embarrass you in front of the ladies."

Brooks flinched at the duke's insult but didn't say anything. The man always did like to hear himself talk. He was sure there was nothing Rutley could say to change his mind, but Brooks decided to let him speak his piece.

"I was once afraid of matrimony," Rutley said. Brooks blinked, willing himself not to burst out laughing.

"Here we go," he muttered, looking down at the gold carpet beneath their feet and shaking his head.

"My fear made me do foolish things, and by the time I realized how awful I had been to the person I loved, my fiancée no longer wanted to marry me. Do you want the same thing to happen to you?"

Brooks did not answer, and Rutley groaned at the solicitor's lack of response. "Let me approach this a different way, then. Do you want August marrying *him*?" He jerked his thumb in Swinton's direction. When Brooks still did not answer, the duke gritted his teeth and turned toward Swinton. "Tell him about Lady Bolton and Charles."

That got Brooks's attention. He looked at Swinton, his brow furrowed. Swinton sheepishly looked back at him. "Tell me *what* about Lady Bolton and Charles?"

His brother-in-law sighed. "There's a reason the countess invited me to town with them—the same reason I called on you at Dover Street to ask you questions about August. Lady Bolton asked me to court the girl so that I may marry her and give her twelve thousand pounds back to Charles."

Brooks stared at him, outraged. "And you agreed?" he asked in disbelief. Such treachery was fouler than he expected from any of them, especially Lady Bolton. Lord Bolton's decision to leave his illegitimate daughter twelve thousand pounds had undoubtedly changed the countess.

Slowly, Swinton nodded. "Try not to be mad, Brooks," he pleaded. "I was trying to help my cousin pay off his debts. Men have agreed to worse things than arranged marriages."

"But did August ever agree? What right do you have to marry her for her money just to hand it back to her lousy excuse of a brother? Even if you tricked her into marrying you, she would not have forgiven you once she found out the truth. She would have been miserable for the rest of her life."

Rutley interjected before Swinton could respond. "And does that change your mind as to who should be marrying August after tonight?"

Brooks stiffened, then slowly turned his head in Rutley's direction. So that was why the duke called them out there. He knew he could change Brooks's mind with this information. But there was something that confused him. Brooks squinted at Rutley and Swinton.

"But why are either of you telling me all this?" he asked. He looked at Swinton. "Won't Lady Bolton and Charles be displeased with you if I end up marrying August?" He then turned to the duke. "And wouldn't it be better for you if Swinton married August rather than me so Charles can pay off his debts?"

Swinton and Rutley exchanged guilty looks. Swinton turned to Brooks, sighing.

"Once I saw how besotted you were with August, I could not stand the idea of coming between the two of you," Swinton explained, the beginnings of a smile playing at his lips. "Lucy would not stand for it. I pretended to go along with Lady Bolton's plan, all the while thinking of ways to force your hand. Unfortunately, Henry Fitzgerald got to it first."

Brooks stood there in silence. It was beginning to look

more and more like he would be the one to marry August. He breathed deeply, then glanced at Rutley. "And you? What is your motivation?"

The duke smiled ruefully. "I am only trying to prevent you from making the same mistakes I did." He paused a moment, thoughtfully tilting his head to the side. "And if it appears I'm the one who convinced you to marry August, Rosamund might start thinking of me in a kindlier manner than she does at the moment."

A sudden realization dawned on Brooks as Rutley spoke. "You love her, don't you?" he asked. Rutley nodded, but Brooks still shook his head in disbelief. "You have changed."

"Sometimes one must change to find lasting happiness." The duke cleared his throat." Now, are you ready to go back in there and make the right decision?"

As he considered Rutley's words, Brooks hesitated. He did not like change. As for this idea of lasting happiness? It sounded impossible. He glanced at Swinton, who regarded him with a hopeful gaze. How could this man endorse marriage after what happened?

Perhaps Brooks would never understand, yet he still nodded his head as he started to think of August, who looked at him so hopefully and told him she wanted all of him regardless of what she already knew about him. He looked at Rutley and Swinton.

"I will do it."

AUGUST SAT in Lord Ridlington's study, feeling frightened and small. What began as a promising evening spun out of control quickly, and she regretted not telling anyone other than Brooks about Henry. Although her solicitor came to her aid many times in the past, August feared this would be where he drew the line. He would not marry her.

August impatiently waited as the man in question spoke to the Duke of Rutley and Mr. Swinton in the hall. Her sister paced the room, frequently looking toward the shut door that separated them. "What could they be talking about?" she wondered aloud, not once or twice but three times.

"He will marry you, August," Mrs. Brooks told her with a firm nod of the head, though they both knew her son was unpredictable. "He will come to his senses and marry you."

But August had her doubts. There was something that Brooks feared, and it was more than just matrimony. Perhaps it was intimacy altogether. Either way, for some reason, he did not think he was good enough for her, and August didn't like that. How could she make him see he was plenty good enough for her and then some?

Eventually, the door opened, and Brooks and the others filed into the room. August turned forward, unable to meet his gaze. She was terrified of what he had to say. She said she could not marry Swinton and meant it, but what was there to do if she became ruined in the eyes of society? Would her aunt still want her?

She would have to take her twelve thousand pounds and leave town. She would rent a cottage in the country where no one knew her name or anything about her so-called wanton ways. She would live in peace and forget all about Brooks. Perhaps Jane could come live with her and keep her company.

"Well?" Lady Ramsbury asked, her eyes flickering between each of the three gentlemen who had just been out in the hall. Eventually, they landed squarely on Brooks. "Will you marry her?"

August still couldn't bear to look at him. She closed her eyes, waiting for his response.

"Yes," he said. August's eyes shot open, and she exhaled for the first time in what felt like forever. Slowly, she turned to look at him, and his unsmiling eyes met her hopeful ones.

"Yes," he repeated. "I will marry her."

August abruptly faced the other way, blinking. Her eyes found her aunt, who wore a triumphant smile. But a creeping sense of doubt snuck up on August, settling in her stomach. This was not what she intended or even what she wanted—not like this, anyway.

When she told Brooks she wanted to marry him only a few days ago, she hoped he would come of his own free will. Now she felt like she was forcing him into something, all because of something stupid she had done with Henry Fitzgerald a few years ago. She felt tears welling in her eyes once more as she thought of his disgusting mouth upon her neck.

"Are you all right, dear?"

Her mother was beside her again, her eyes full of concern. August supposed she should have appeared overjoyed at the news. Brooks just agreed to save her reputation, and she didn't have to marry Mr. Swinton—or Henry—as a result.

"I suppose I'm only a little overtired," she said, forcing a smile. "There's been so much commotion this evening."

Her mother smiled back, looking as if she understood. She turned to the dowager duchess, who was in the middle of a conversation with Mrs. Brooks.

"You must call on me at Park Street tomorrow afternoon," Lady Ramsbury said. Both women seemed to be buzzing with excitement over this sudden turn of events. "We can discuss all the details then."

"Your Grace," Lady Sarah interrupted. "August is tired. Although the night is young, I believe she's experienced enough excitement for one evening. Mr. Talbot and I would be happy to escort her home if you would like to stay here at the party."

The dowager duchess and Mrs. Brooks turned, their faces

falling when they saw August's wretched state. Lady Ramsbury gave a single nod. "I will take her home. Come, August."

August did not dare look at Brooks as they left Ridlington's study, unable to look at him after what happened, and they made a swift exit through the front of the house. August was very aware of the other guests watching them as they walked through the entry hall. Her aunt must have noticed it as well. "Do not worry, dear," she said. "I'll arrange for an engagement announcement to be put in all the papers."

August didn't respond, and when they finally reached their carriage on the street outside, they rode home in silence. Upon arriving at Park Street, August tried not to collapse at the bottom of the staircase. To her surprise, her aunt told her to go to the drawing room rather than sending her to bed. She then asked one of the footmen to bring them two glasses of milk and a plate of biscuits.

"Do be generous with the number of biscuits," she added as he walked away. August tentatively followed her into the dimly lit drawing room. They sat in silence until the footman returned with a tray. When he left, the dowager duchess took a glass and one of the biscuits, dipping it into the thick white liquid and taking a bite.

"Have some," her aunt said, gesturing toward the biscuits. When August didn't budge, Lady Ramsbury sighed. "It will make you feel better."

August looked at her aunt, frowning. "I'm not sure biscuits and milk will make me feel better after what happened this evening, Aunt."

The dowager duchess sighed again. "Would you like to talk about it instead?" When August didn't reply, she added, "I could tell you the things I have been plotting to ruin Henry Fitzgerald's life instead if you would like."

August's eyes widened. "W-what?"

Lady Ramsbury looked as if she was disappointed. "You

didn't think I would let him get away with what he did to you this evening, did you? I know his father well. I will make sure Mr. Fitzgerald returns to that little village of Wilton of yours humiliated and dishonored—and that he stays there as well. No lady in London will have him once I'm finished dragging his name through the mud."

August blinked, helplessly reaching for a biscuit and taking a bite. "You can do that?" she asked in between chewing.

Her aunt squared her shoulders. "A wealthy dowager duchess like me can do anything, dear."

"Oh, Aunt! But aren't you disappointed in me? I did something no dignified lady would do. It's no wonder he attacked me!"

Lady Ramsbury narrowed her eyes. "I will not have you saying such things—not while you're still under my roof. Men have been categorizing us since the beginning of time. We are either pure and innocent or sullied and virtueless. Well, I refuse to be either, and I prefer men who do not care—as should you."

August immediately thought of Brooks. She wondered if he cared. She frowned, remembering the night he came to her, ready to take her without committing himself to her. How did he categorize her? He must have been in anguish knowing he would have to marry her now, knowing what she had done with Henry.

"I feel as though I have trapped Brooks," August said, her blue eyes filled with fear as she looked at her aunt. "He never wanted to marry, and now he is stuck with me. *And* I feel as though I have wasted your time. All those dresses and lessons for me to be ruined and then engaged in one night!"

Lady Ramsbury sighed. "I have known Samuel Brooks since he was a little boy. You must be patient with him. He has his reasons for believing matrimony isn't for him, but he does care about you. Once he sees every relationship doesn't have to be like his parents, he will open up to you. I'm sure of it. As for the dresses and lessons..." Her aunt shrugged. "The goal of any girl's season is an engagement and marriage, isn't it? We have only gone about yours in record time."

August bit back a smile at Lady Ramsbury's joke, but her mind automatically returned to the subject of Brooks. "But don't you think I have trapped him?"

Her aunt laughed. "Of course not. He's lucky I didn't force him to marry you earlier after I caught you kissing in the library."

August nearly gasped, her cheeks turning pink with embarrassment. "You saw that? Oh, Aunt, why didn't you say anything? I'm so embarrassed!"

"I thought it would be best if the two of you came to some sort of arrangement on your own time." The dowager duchess smiled. "After a servant told me he saw him scaling your balcony in the middle of the night, I knew it was only a matter of time." She took another bite of her biscuit. "I had not, of course, accounted for the incident with Mr. Fitzgerald, but in the words of Shakespeare, all's well that ends well."

August's blush only deepened upon hearing her aunt's words, but she ignored them, knowing there was something that wasn't quite making sense. "What do you mean every relationship doesn't have to be like his parents?" she asked. "Did something happen between Mr. and Mrs. Brooks?"

Lady Ramsbury hesitated. "I'm afraid that's a subject for your future husband to discuss with you," she finally said. "What I will tell you is the late Mr. Brooks wasn't a good man. There is plenty of pain in that family's history—the untimely death of his young sister Lucy included—but I'm a firm believer that your marriage will be a turning point for all involved, so do not fret, August. Even if Brooks feels trapped now, he won't feel that way for long."

Chapter Twenty-Four

NEWS OF BROOKS and August's engagement traveled quickly. Despite not seeing or hearing from them since he went to Linfield a month ago, Lady Bolton and Charles were the first to call on Brooks at Dover Street to congratulate him—or so they said. Mrs. Brooks had already left to visit Lady Ramsbury at Park Street, so Brooks saw them in his study.

"I suppose Swinton and Rosamund told you the news," he said as his two visitors took their seats across from him at his desk. Charles had dark circles under his eyes, but his mother appeared impeccable as always, her red hair piled high on top of her head.

"They did," Lady Bolton said, smiling brightly. She looked at him as if he was still the same little boy she found hiding in her husband's study all those years ago. But things had changed since then, and Brooks no longer trusted her, not after what Swinton told him last night and how she treated August in the past.

"We had no idea you felt so strongly about the girl, nor she about you," Charles said. Brooks pursed his lips, not appreciating the smug look on his former friend's face. "If we had known, we might have taken our proposal to you instead of cousin Edward."

Brooks didn't like where this was heading. If they thought he would happily hand over August's inheritance to them, they were sadly mistaken.

"Is that so?" he asked. He chose to pretend he had no idea what proposal they meant—as if Swinton and Rutley hadn't revealed everything to him last night. It was hard to believe the duke had somehow grown a greater conscience than the countess or her son, but here they were, already angling to take his future wife's money, their engagement less than twenty-four hours old.

Lady Bolton nodded. "As you know, the health of our estate is not what it used to be," she said.

"I wonder whose fault that is?" Brooks asked, his tone sardonic as he cast a sidelong glance at Charles. The young earl shifted uncomfortably in his chair.

"Yes, well," he said awkwardly, "what my mother means to say is that I will still owe Rutley eight thousand pounds after he marries Rosamund. If you agree to return August's inheritance to me after you marry her, I'll have plenty to pay back the duke."

And then some, you conniving rat, Brooks thought. He resisted the urge to say the words aloud, watching as Charles forced a grin and nervously passed his hat between his hands. "So what do you say? Won't you help an old friend?"

A stone-faced Brooks stared at Charles. "I'm not sure your father's intention was for August's future husband to hand her inheritance back to you as soon as they married." His eyes flickered from his former friend to Lady Bolton. Both their faces slowly fell. "I'm sorry, but I cannot give you the money. It belongs to my wife, and I intend it to be hers even after we marry."

Lady Bolton started to laugh. "You cannot be serious. You

and I both know it does not *belong* to your wife. My husband was not in the right frame of mind when he decided to leave it to her." She glanced at her son. "Charles was his pride and joy, not some bastard child who I hear is as wanton as her mother. He did not mention or even think of her until that terrible illness slowly stole away his facilities for three months."

Now Brooks felt forced to say something. His jaw tensed. "You will not talk about my future wife that way, especially when I know you were the one who spread the rumor about the identity of her mother. I imagine that didn't go how you planned either, did it?"

Lady Bolton stared at him in shock. Brooks stared back at her, unmoved. They must know he wouldn't change his mind. For better or worse, August would be his wife, which meant she was his responsibility now more than ever. He couldn't stand the idea of betraying her by giving her money to Charles either.

"You are wasting your time," Brooks said. "I will not do it."

Lady Bolton grew pale. "But Samuel—"

"Your son said it yourself, Lady Bolton. I feel strongly for the girl. I will not do something that puts her at a financial disadvantage."

Charles looked ready to burst, his face turning red. "You seem to forget who helped start *your* family business."

Brooks scoffed. "I didn't forget. It was your father, who—"

"No," Charles said sharply, interrupting Brooks. "It wasn't my father. It was the Earl of Bolton. It was the title, not the man. And now that the title is mine, I can easily tear down your business as quickly as my father created it. What will you do without your wealthy clients, Brooks? What sort of income will you have?"

Brooks wavered—at first—but then he addressed Charles with a direct and fearsome gaze. "I will find other ones. I have grown sick of Mayfair, anyway. And if I still cannot find clients, perhaps my wealthy wife will let me depend on her. You ought to try finding one of your own, Charles."

Brooks then abruptly rose from his chair, walking toward his study door and pulling it open. He gestured toward the empty reception room. "Now, I think it's time for you both to leave. I have work to do."

Lady Bolton and Charles stood up, walking toward the door. Charles lingered a moment, looking at his old friend with angry eyes. "You will regret this, Brooks."

"There is plenty to regret but not this," he said, slamming the door behind them. He turned, wandering toward the sideboard in his study, pouring himself a glass of brandy. He nursed it for the rest of the afternoon while he worked—or at least *tried* to work. He found himself frequently sighing, leaning back in his chair, and running his hands through his hair.

Brooks was restless, and the brandy was not having the desired calming effect on his nerves. He wondered what August was doing. In the past, he would have left Dover Street by now to call on her. They would play chess and tell each other about their days. He wondered if they would ever achieve that sense of normality again or if he would be forever tense, fearing what might happen next.

In the middle of his anxious reverie, he heard a commotion in the entry hall. Assuming it was his mother, he stood up and went to greet her. She was smiling and humming to herself as she handed Jenkins her hat and pelisse. "How was she?" Brooks asked from the doorway of the reception room, still holding his glass of brandy.

His mother jumped, bringing her hand to her chest when she saw him. "Samuel!" she exclaimed. "You startled me."

Then, she raised her brow. "Do you mean she as in Lady Ramsbury or she as in your betrothed?"

Mrs. Brooks giggled happily at the last word, causing Brooks to roll his eyes. "Either," he replied, very much unamused. His mother's face fell when she realized his mood hadn't improved since morning.

"Both are very well," she said, glaring at her son. "Have you given any more thought to a date?"

No. Brooks took a sip of brandy. He supposed there was no use delaying it, and if Charles truly intended on driving his clients away from him, marrying his wealthy fiancée sooner rather than later made sense.

"As soon as possible," Brooks said. His mother's face brightened at his sudden turn of mood. "Do you think the dowager duchess could procure a special license for us?"

His mother's face brightened even further. "I can certainly ask," she said, walking toward her son and grabbing his free hand. He resisted jerking away as his mother stood on her tiptoes and pressed a kiss to his cheek. "I'm so proud of you, Samuel Brooks."

Proud of what—marrying someone? He wanted to ask. How ridiculous. Nevertheless, he forced a smile and nodded instead, bringing the glass of brandy to his lips once more as he watched his mother ascend the stairs, smiling and humming the entire way.

Brooks and August were married within a week. Lady Ramsbury happily paid for a special license, unwilling to take any chances given the solicitor's fickle heart. The wedding was a small affair at St. George's, with the same people in attendance that were in Ridlington's study. August said she would have liked to invite the Dunns and her acquaintances from Hardbury, but there was no time.

After the ceremony, the dowager duchess hosted the wedding breakfast at her mansion on Park Street. Charles and Lady Bolton didn't attend either event, though Lady Ramsbury did invite them. No one but Brooks, Swinton, and Rutley knew what they were planning before August married the solicitor. Still feeling guilty over agreeing to deceive August, Swinton offered Brooks use of his house in Surrey for their honeymoon. He would remain in town until they returned so they could have some much-needed privacy.

Brooks almost said no, but then he realized it would be nice to have some time alone with August before she started living with him and his mother. He may have been approaching his marriage with some reluctance, but he was still a man. He would rather his mother not overhear him exercising his husbandly rights, and he planned to do so frequently—especially at first.

Still, thoughts of their wedding night made him nervous. He had not laid with a woman in a long time, and he did not want to disappoint her. He never wanted to disappoint her, but he was sure he would at some point or another. Now that they were alone in Swinton's carriage on their way to Surrey, such thoughts dominated his mind. They reminded him they hadn't been alone together since that night in her bedroom when he behaved abominably.

Although they sat next to each other so Brooks wouldn't grow ill facing the wrong direction in the carriage, he still felt queasy. There was a heaviness between them, but neither addressed it, at least not until August finally turned and looked at him when they were about halfway to Surrey.

"I am sorry if you feel like you were forced into this," she said. "That was never my intention. Although it might be hard for you to believe, I always wanted you to come on your own accord."

"I did come on my own accord," Brooks said, not thinking

twice. She slowly smiled at him, then faced forward. He admired her side profile, taking in her strong jawline, plump lips, and rosy cheeks. Soon, she would be his, and he wondered if she was thinking the same thing.

August looked at him again, her blue eyes thoughtful as they raked over his face. "I know you did not want a wife, but I promise I will try and be a good one. Whatever you need of me—do not hesitate to ask."

His lips twitched, fighting back a smile. He glanced at August's hands, which rested in her lap, clasped together. He reached for one, taking it for himself, gently squeezing it. She inhaled sharply. "It was never whether or not you would be a good wife that worried me," he said.

She crinkled her brow. "Then what was it—what *is* it—that worries you?"

He turned away, sighing—but he still held onto her hand. "Many things worry me, but most of all, I worry I will not be a good husband."

"Why?"

His head snapped in her direction once more, his gaze serious. "My father was not a good husband."

August looked as though she might laugh. "And what do your father's skills as a husband—or lack thereof—have to do with you?" His face fell, and he turned away, letting go of her hand. August wouldn't understand—how could she?

"Forget I said anything," he muttered, looking out the window. The sun hung low in the sky, and the carriage moved slowly. The roads were still muddy from rain earlier that week. They wouldn't reach Swinton's house in Surrey until suppertime.

Suddenly, he felt August's gloved palm on his cheek. She gently guided his gaze in her direction, finding her upturned face very close to his. His eyes landed on her lips. He realized then if he wanted to kiss her, he could. She was his wife now.

Nothing was stopping him, and that knowledge sent a jolt straight to his groin. He nervously swallowed.

"You will make a fine husband, Samuel Brooks," she said. "I'm sure of it."

"Is that so?" he asked, lifting his hands to twirl some of the loose curls that framed her face between his fingers. Slowly, August nodded, chewing her bottom lip.

He could not stand it any longer, and she must have known what she was doing to him, chewing on her bottom lip like that. Brooks quickly bent his head until his lips crashed into hers, and she responded almost immediately, wrapping her arms around his neck. Meanwhile, his hands hungrily explored the curves of her lower back, her breasts, and her neck. He broke away from her for a moment, and they both loudly panted. Brooks leaned forward.

"I like it when you call me Samuel," he whispered against her neck. He peppered a trail of kisses from her earlobe to the swell of her bosom. When he looked up, she was smiling with her head thrown back and her eyes closed.

"Samuel," she said breathlessly. "Samuel."

He moaned, reaching for her, needing to taste those luscious lips of hers once more. He grabbed her by the waist, pulling her toward him until she was sitting on his lap, her skirts bunched up around her waist. He felt her bare thigh graze against the hardness forming in his breeches, and she gasped.

"Is this what you wanted, August?" he asked against her chest, lifting his palms to her breasts, gently rubbing his thumbs over her nipples until they became two erect points. "Is this what you wanted that night in your bedroom?"

"Yes," she replied, unabashedly moving in a slow back-and-forth motion on his lap until he was stiff with need.

"If you keep doing that, I'll take you right here in this

carriage," he warned. August opened her eyes, looking down at him. She grinned.

"What if that's what I want?"

Little minx, he thought, grunting. If she wanted him to take her right then and there, he could, and he would. He didn't give a damn if the postboy out front heard them. She was his wife. No sense of propriety stopped him now.

Brooks reached in between them, deftly undoing the buttons of his breeches until his hard length sprung free. August gasped again as his most intimate part brushed her inner thigh, this time with no fabric to separate their bare skin.

"Are you sure about this?" he asked, holding her close. There was some sense of hesitation, a tiny voice telling him he should wait to bed his new wife until they were actually in a bed, but August didn't seem to give a damn about such things. He marveled at his dumb luck in finding her.

"I'm sure," she said, leaning forward and kissing him, taking his face between her hands. He moaned against her mouth and grabbed hold of her hips, lifting and positioning her over him.

Slowly, he lowered her until he was inside her. She grabbed onto his shoulders, and he gritted his teeth as her fingernails dug into his upper back through the fabric of his jacket. Although his hands remained tightly fastened around her hips, she rode him on her own accord. All the while, August's eyes remained locked on his.

He had never experienced something so wonderful, so intimate. He arched his neck against the curve of the carriage seat, closing his eyes, thinking of nothing but how it felt to be inside her. He did not want it to end, but his climax came quickly—*too* quickly. He groaned as he released his load deep inside of her, shuddering beneath him. She grew still, pressing kisses to his forehead, brow, and cheekbones.

When August retook her seat beside him, she nestled into his side. He sighed happily at the feel of her against him, leaning over to kiss the top of her head. "I know I'm not a virgin, but I hope that was... adequate," she said into his chest with a hint of uncertainty.

He took her chin between his finger and thumb, gently forcing her to look at him. "That was more than adequate. That was wonderful."

She smiled at him, burying her face into his chest once more. When she eventually fell asleep, Brooks carefully watched her, counting her breaths and the different shades of blonde in her hair until he forced himself to face forward. He swore to himself that he wouldn't lose his head over her, though anyone with half a brain could make a solid argument that he already had. He swallowed hard at the prospect.

August was still sleeping when they finally arrived at Hart House. Brooks gently woke her, helping her out of the carriage and bringing her inside. The dimly lit entry hall hadn't changed since he last been there, with its gray stone floors and walls of dark wood.

For a moment, Brooks wondered if he made the right decision bringing August there. He remembered his sister Lucy descending the wooden staircase on her wedding day three years ago. He glanced at August. She and his sister had been the same age.

"Mr. Brooks."

The housekeeper, Mrs. Godwin, appeared out of the shadows. She smiled at him, her skin crinkling around her brown eyes. "It is a pleasure, sir. I was beginning to think we would never see you at Hart House again."

Brooks felt August's curious gaze. He did his best to ignore it. "I was thrilled when Mr. Swinton wrote to say you and your new wife would be staying with us a few days," Mrs. Godwin continued. She looked at August.

"Allow me to introduce my wife, Lady August Brooks," he said, the words feeling foreign on his tongue. She had not even been Lady August Finch for all that long. "August, this is Mrs. Godwin. She has been the housekeeper here since I was a little boy."

The older woman nodded. "It's true. Your husband and Mrs. Swinton—God rest her soul—used to visit Hart House all the time as children."

August followed Mrs. Godwin's gaze toward the portrait of Swinton and Lucy hanging in the entry hall. Brooks looked at it as well, frowning. August walked toward the painting until she was only a few feet from it. When she glanced back at him, she smiled.

"I have never seen Mr. Brooks's sister," August told the housekeeper. "She is beautiful—just like his mother."

Brooks tilted his head to the side, studying Lucy's portrait and noticing the similarities between her and his mother as well. They shared the same dark hair, strong brow, and defined chin. But Brooks had no desire to dwell on the dead —not that night, anyway. He turned to Mrs. Godwin. "Have you prepared supper?" he asked.

The housekeeper nodded, taking them further down the hall and into the dining room. At first, they ate in silence, all the while Brooks desperately thought of something to say. He knew he should tell her something about Lucy. Hart House was her home for two years, after all. But nothing came to him. August must have realized it was bothering him, for she put down her knife and fork in the middle of her meal, looking at him intently.

"I wonder why you chose this place for our honeymoon," she said. "Aren't the constant reminders of your sister difficult for you?"

Brooks put his knife and fork down as well. He took his

napkin, dabbing his mouth with it. "Swinton insisted after what happened."

August raised her brow. "Oh?"

He sighed, knowing he would just have to tell her. "There is something I haven't told you," he slowly said. She frowned, carefully watching him as he spoke. "There was a reason Swinton wanted to call on you at Park Street and dance with you at Ridlington's ball."

Brooks explained everything then, from Swinton's confession at Ridlington House to Charles and Lady Bolton's visit the day after the ball. August's frown only deepened the more he spoke. "Do not worry," he said, reaching across the table for her hand. "I will not give them your inheritance. That money should be yours to do with however you sit fit."

August drew her hand back, shaking her head. "But your clients," she said. "Surely you need your income more than I need my inheritance. From the beginning, I have said I didn't want to cause anyone trouble. I should give the money back."

Brooks pursed his lips. "I will repeat what I told you the first time, then. We must rid you of this self-sacrificing behavior of yours. I will not have you throw away your future for Charles."

"But it's not for Charles. It's for you, and my future *is* you. I will not allow him to turn all your clients against you."

"I will find new clients."

"Nevertheless, it's my money, and it should be *my* decision. I want to give the money back to my brother."

Brooks stared at August, feeling his temper rising. She may have been a little minx, but she was also stubborn as hell. Couldn't she see he was doing this for her? He took a deep breath.

"Well, the money became mine the moment you married me," he said, picking up his knife and fork again. He carved into a piece of roast beef. "And I'm here to protect your best interests. I will not let you waste your inheritance on Charles, who will only fall into debt again the moment he pays off Rutley."

But August would not listen. "That may be so, but at least your practice—"

"Enough, August." Their eyes met, and she was glaring at him. He glared back at her, her nostrils flaring as he did. She rose abruptly, the wood legs of her chair scraping against the floor as she did. "Where are you going?"

"I am going to bed," she angrily said. "I will not eat with someone so... so... hypocritical!"

He furrowed his brow. "Hypocritical?"

"Yes!" she exclaimed. "Hypocritical! You cannot tell me the money is mine to use however I please and then not let me do what I want to do with it. It's not fair!"

"August—"

But she turned to the two footmen who attended their dinner. They stared back at her with wide eyes. "Could one of you show me the way to my bedroom?" she asked.

"No, it's fine," Brooks said, rising from his chair and throwing napkin on his still half full plate. "I will show her the way."

He walked around the table, offering her his arm. She reluctantly took it, following him out of the dining room and back into the entry hall. They climbed the stairs to the second floor, and he took her to the bedroom he always used when he stayed at Hart House. She seemed surprised when he closed the door behind him. He arched his brow at her.

"Did you think I would be sleeping in a different room?" he asked. "On my honeymoon?"

She blushed. "N-no. Of course not."

He slowly walked toward her, and she backed away until she ran into the bed, her knees buckling as she did. She landed on the mattress with a thump.

"Since we are on our honeymoon, I think we should agree not to talk about your money or your family until we return to town," Brooks said. "After the past two months, I have grown tired of both subjects. Perhaps we could begin focusing on other topics, such as our mutual desire for one another."

He reached for her, but she backed away. Narrowing her eyes at him, she crossed her arms across her chest. "Fine, but that does not mean I forgive your hypocrisy."

He couldn't help but smile at her obstinate nature. So he got on his knees, slowly making his way toward her across the floor. Her eyes grew panicked. "W-what are you doing?" she asked.

"One could say I'm groveling," he said, still smiling. "Won't you forgive me, August?"

Her blush deepened, and she quickly turned away. "I will not!"

Still, he made his way toward her. "I have been thinking about the carriage."

"H-have you?"

He nodded. "I was very selfish. I thought I would return the favor."

She furrowed her brow. "What do you mean?"

"You'll see," he said, his torso now between her knees at the edge of the bed. He reached for her shoes, removing them slowly. Then, he roughly grabbed her by the waist, pulling her forward until her bottom was on the edge of the bed. She yelped.

"Brooks!"

"Lean back," he told her. She hesitated, nervously searching his face for some sort of explanation. He sighed. "Trust me."

Slowly, she leaned back. Brooks grabbed hold of her skirts, lifting them around her hips to reveal a pair of shapely stocking-clad legs. He took one ankle and lifted it, kissing the inside of her calf and thigh. His lips came close to her center, then he abruptly pulled away, switching to the other leg.

"Brooks," she whispered, lifting herself onto her forearms, looking down at him.

He knew he must have been torturing her. He was torturing himself by taking his time, but he wanted to make this memorable for her. He carefully hooked her legs over his shoulders, leaning forward and kissing around the delicate folds of her sex. She squirmed beneath his touch.

Slowly, he licked the length of her, tasting her wet heat. She gasped as he used his tongue to explore her, the tip of it dipping in and out of her delicate folds. When he finally touched her most sensitive spot, she moaned. He took her between his lips, gently sucking.

"W-what are you doing to me?" she breathlessly asked, throwing her head back. He continued to devour her, slipping two fingers inside her and sliding them in and out in a steady rhythm. She moaned again, her hips jerking upward toward his mouth. He could tell she was close.

"Brooks... What is..."

He felt her intimate muscles contract around his fingers. She whimpered, covering her mouth with her hand as she looked down at him. Their eyes met for a moment before she threw her head back once more, removing her hand from her mouth and crying out with full force.

When her climax subsided, he hastily stood up, unbuttoning his breeches and pulling his hard length free once more. He grabbed her by the hips and thrust himself inside of her, closing his eyes as he did, overcome with lust. Her mews of pleasure eventually drove him over the edge, and when he finished, Brooks fell onto the bed beside her, out of breath. He turned on the side of his head to look at her. She was staring up at the ceiling, eyes wide with wonder, her chest rapidly rising and falling.

"Do you forgive me yet?" he asked.

August turned and looked at him, grinning mischievously. "A few more of those, and perhaps I will."

He raised his brow. "Is that so?" He yanked her toward him, and she giggled as he nuzzled her neck. "If that's the case, then we must get you out of this dress."

Chapter Twenty-Five

ALTHOUGH THEIR PHYSICAL intimacy grew the day and night of their wedding, August still had the feeling that Brooks was hiding parts of himself from her. After making love for the first time in bed, August noticed multiple long, thin scars across her husband's back.

"What happened?" she asked, her eyes full of concern as she lightly traced the wrinkled and discolored skin with her fingertips. Brooks moved away from her so quickly that she thought she might have hurt him. He reached for his shirt, deserted haphazardly on the floor at some point, and quickly pulled it over his head.

"Nothing for you to worry yourself over, darling," he said, turning back around to face August. He bent over her naked form, pressing a kiss to the center of her crinkled brow. When he pulled away, she looked up at him, displeased with his answer.

"But Samuel—"

"Do not ask me again, August," he said, his voice low and full of warning. They stared at each other for a moment, and then he climbed into bed with her. She crossed her arms, pursing her lips as she did.

After he snuffed the candle on the bedside table, she turned on her side, folding her hands between her head and the pillow and closing her eyes. If he did not want to open up to her, she would not open up to him. But then she felt his firm body slide behind her. He wrapped his arms around her waist, pulling her close. He began to kiss her neck, and she knew she could not resist him, even if he had only married her out of duty.

August still recalled the night he visited her bedroom on Park Street. She told him she loved him that night. He had yet to say those three words in return, not even after he came inside her that evening. But August already knew that love and lust were two separate things, and she wasn't sure she could settle for her husband's desire alone.

Now he was nuzzling his face against her neck, his hot breath and soft lips filling her with want once more as he reached for her breasts. He gently squeezed them, and she felt his manhood grow hard against her back as he ground his body against hers.

August shivered as he brought one of his hands from her breast to her thigh. He carefully wrapped his hand around her knee, lifting her leg to allow him better access to her wet heat. He positioned himself at her entrance, and she moaned as he slowly thrust inside her, filling her to the brim.

"Brooks," she whispered. "This feels…" She could not find the right word. None could do the sensation of having her husband make love to her justice. But it wasn't making love, was it?

"Amazing?" Brooks tried to answer for her. She made a slight whimpering noise as he continued to slide in and out of her, maintaining a steady and pleasurable rhythm. With one hand still holding her by the knee, his other drifted from her breast and down her stomach until it found the bundle of nerves just above where their bodies joined. He lightly stroked her there while simultaneously kissing her neck and whispering sweet words that filled her up until she thought she might burst.

As the pleasure built in August's lower stomach, she held onto the feeling as long as she could, not wanting the steady climb to her peak to end. When it finally did, she cried out, her legs shaking as she became like jelly in Brooks's hands, which began to deftly roam across her torso and breasts, gently kneading and squeezing in all the right places. His climax came not long after hers.

She remained quiet as he slipped out of her, leaving nothing but warm dampness behind. If she wasn't so content, she might have felt empty. He kissed her shoulders. "I think I could fuck you all night long," he murmured against her skin.

August felt herself grow cold. "Is that all you want of me?"

Brooks must have felt her growing sadness. He forced her to face him. "Surely you don't believe that."

She looked away, not sure what to believe. Brooks pulled her closer, holding her tight against his frame until she felt him fall asleep beside her. Perhaps he could learn to love her, she thought. She would be a good wife, and he would learn to love her eventually. She smiled to herself, hopeful for the future, and finally fell asleep.

BROOKS AWOKE EARLY the following morning, his wife still tucked against him underneath the crook of his arm. He listened to her gentle breathing, admiring the slight tilt of a smile playing at her lips. He considered waking her using his lips alone but then decided against it at the last minute.

He had used her enough in the past twenty-four hours, unleashing months of pent-up desire. Even he could admit he was attracted to August from the moment they met, but that didn't change the fact he had never wanted a wife.

But now he had one, sleeping soundly beside him, the soft curves of her naked figure so enticing that he had to force himself away from her, lest he wanted to spend all morning in bed. He exhaled deeply, running his fingers through his hair, already mussed from sleep and sex.

Quietly, he crept out of bed, carefully lifting the bedclothes so as not to disturb his sleeping wife beside him. She shifted slightly when his feet hit the creaking floorboards beside the bed. He carefully stood, tiptoeing across the room and gathering his clothes.

Some air, he thought, would do him good. He quickly dressed, took one last look at August's sleeping form, then left, gently shutting the door of their bedroom behind him. He walked down the hall, heading for the backstairs.

Brooks knew his way around Hart House intimately from frequently visiting as a child and later as an adult to see his sister after she married Swinton. He took the stairs to the ground floor, opening the back service door and slipping into a small courtyard.

Hart House, a two-story brick house surrounded by trees and green shrubbery, was small compared to Linfield Hall. The quaintness made Brooks all the more fond of it, and he found himself reminiscing about his sister Lucy and how she ran around the small garden in the back as a child and then later hosted tea parties for her neighbors when she was older.

There wasn't a day that passed that Brooks didn't think of his sister. Despite the cruelty of their father, he never broke his daughter like he had his son. It wasn't until she lived at Hart House for a year that she started to change. The effusive girl he once knew became withdrawn, even when he visited from town. Whenever Brooks pressed Swinton for an explanation, the insufferable man only laughed it off as nothing.

Brooks knew now he should have pressed harder. He hadn't discovered the number of miscarriages she faced during her two years of marriage until later, once she already died. That was what drove Lucy's melancholy, and Swinton said the local physician prescribed her laudanum for her nerves. One evening she took too much and...

That was where the reminiscing became painful, where Brooks refused to think anymore. He walked through the garden at Hart House, leaving through the iron gate at the back of the gray stone wall that ran the perimeter. Behind the house was a small meadow, which, if he crossed, would take him to the road that led to the nearest church.

The sun was just barely above the horizon as he approached the churchyard, and birds had just started singing from the treetops. The church itself was quiet, and Brooks walked across the line of graves in the yard until he found his sister's. He picked up some dried flowers resting on top of her headstone, reducing some petals to dust between his fingertips.

"You must be wondering why I'm here," he said after a moment. Brooks was not a religious or spiritual man, and he knew his sister could not hear him, but he felt like talking to her anyway. "Especially after I told your wretched husband I would never speak to him again after we buried you."

Brooks paused. He had been furious at Swinton. Why hadn't Swinton told him about Lucy's plight? Brooks had always been able to cheer her. He protected her from their father for twenty years, and he could have saved her from this if he only knew about it.

"I would not say I have forgiven him, but he did come round Dover Street looking to reconcile," Brooks continued. "I suppose we are speaking now, though his actions remain gravely disappointing for someone I once believed to be one of my best friends. He's just like Charles in that regard.

Surprisingly, I find myself liking Rutley more than both of them as of late."

He shook his head, realizing he hadn't come here to tell her about his childhood friends that used to gather in the old forester's lodge at Linfield. "Truthfully, Lucy, I'm here on my honeymoon. Swinton lent me the house while he's in town with his aunt and cousins. Hard to believe, I know, me being married, but I swear it's true."

Brooks thought of August back in their room. He smiled slightly, wondering if she was still sleeping. Perhaps he would have the chance to wake her with only his lips after all.

"I think you would like her," Brooks said, taking another dried flower petal between his fingers. He watched the dust fall to the grass beneath his feet. "She is Lord Bolton's illegitimate daughter. You must be shocked, of course, but you must have known if I ever did marry, it would not be to some fine society girl. She's from the country in Hampshire. Her name is August."

He paused again. If the vicar came out the church's front door, he would think Brooks was unwell—and perhaps he was. "I am just rambling now," he said, smiling down at his sister's grave. "The truth is I'm not sure how to be married, Lucy, no matter how thrilled you might be to hear this news. I did not propose because I wanted to but because I had to."

And Brooks was sure August understood as much. He couldn't even figure out if he loved her not. "I already feel like a failure of a husband," Brooks muttered. "And can you blame me? I have only had failures as examples—Father, Lord Bolton, Swinton."

He pursed his lips, tears welling in his eyes. He quickly blinked them away, then reached out to put one hand on the top of Lucy's headstone. He closed his eyes, standing there silently for a few moments before pulling away and heading back toward the house.

. . .

WHEN AUGUST WOKE the next day, she found herself alone. She reached behind her for Brooks but only found emptiness. Sighing, she got out of bed, putting on her nightgown and wrapper and then pulling back the curtains covering the windows.

The windows of their room overlooked the garden and a meadow after that. In the distance, August could see a road that probably led to the nearest village. Looking around the room and frowning, she wondered where Brooks was.

August walked toward the bedroom door, opening it and peering outside. Seeing no one, she stepped out of the room, leaving the door open behind her and wandering down the hall, looking inside the other bedrooms out of curiosity. Upon finding the largest one, she suspected it might have belonged to Swinton. August stood in the doorway, wondering if Brooks's sister once slept there as well.

Pulling her wrapper tighter around her shoulders, August searched for signs of Lucy. She knew so little of Brooks's younger sister but wished that wasn't the case. His mother said a long illness took her, but August had no idea what it could have been. Lucy looked like the picture of health in the portrait downstairs.

Her curiosity getting the better of her, August stepped inside Swinton's room. She walked toward the bedside table, opening a small drawer and looking for any hints of who Lucy might have been when she was alive. When August found nothing, she scanned the room again, her line of vision landing on a small writing desk underneath one of the windows.

She walked toward it, opening the drawers and searching through them until she found a collection of old letters in one of them. Beneath the letters was a small leather bound book.

August ignored the letters and took the book, opening it and skimming through the pages, which contained neatly handwritten text. Each entry was dated, and August realized right away what it was: Lucy's diary.

A sudden noise startled her. She quickly closed the book and put it back in the drawer on top of the letters. After shutting the drawer, she turned around and left the room, going out into the hall. She nearly jumped when she saw Brooks standing in front of their room. When he turned and noticed her standing there, he smiled

"There you are," he said, walking toward her. When he realized what room she had just come out of, he narrowed his eyes. "What were you doing in there?"

August immediately shook her head. "Nothing," she replied. "I only got turned around and thought that was our room. I went downstairs to ask Mrs. Godwin when breakfast would be ready."

"What time did she give you?"

August blinked. Brooks stared at her, looking perplexed and having no idea she was lying. "An hour," August finally said. "She said it would be ready in an hour."

Brooks nodded, then reached for her hand, gently pulling her back down the hall toward their bedroom. "Good," he said. "We can accomplish much in an hour."

August arched her brow. "Accomplish?"

He did not answer, only guided her to the bedroom, shutting the door behind him. When he turned to face her, she giggled at the mischievous look on his face. Even if her husband did not love her, he certainly wanted her. "Where have you been, anyway?" she asked as he slinked toward her. "You weren't here when I woke up."

"I went for a walk," he replied, kissing her neck. He slipped her wrapper off her shoulders, letting it fall to the ground.

"You went for a walk?" August echoed incredulously. "How far did you go?"

Brooks chuckled, sliding a hand from her waist up to her breast. "Does it matter? I am here now. I would like to focus on being here."

August thought about protesting, but her husband's skillful ministrations with his hands and tongue quickly distracted her. She forgot all about his absence that morning after they finally tumbled onto the bed together, both of them completely naked.

But August did not forget Lucy's diary next door. After they finished, she watched her husband dress, biting her lip as she studied the scars across his back. When he turned and looked at her, she smiled brightly at him, pretending that nothing in the world could bother her at that moment, not even her husband's secrets. He smiled back, walking toward her to press a gentle kiss to her lips.

AUGUST AND BROOKS returned to London a week later. While they were gone, Mrs. Brooks had her son's belongings moved out of his old bedroom and into his father's former room, which had remained untouched since his death. August immediately noticed her husband's displeasure over this decision, seemingly made without him while he was gone.

"I'm not sure why you are so upset with her," August said later when they were alone. Mrs. Brooks's old bedroom had become August's, and she and Brooks laid in her new bed together the night after they returned to town. Brooks came through the adjoining door between their two rooms soon after they retired for the evening. August thought he would have grown tired of her by then, but she happily accepted that he had not.

"I do not like my father's room," Brooks replied simply.

"Why?"

Brooks shot her a warning look. "Must you always ask why? All I know is that I cannot sleep there."

August frowned at him. "Does that mean you are sleeping here this evening? And the evening after that?"

"You look as if you think that's a bad thing," he said, chuckling. "I knew you would grow tired of me eventually, but I thought you might last longer than one week."

She laughed. "That's not what I meant at all!" She paused a moment, her expression becoming sheepish. "I just don't understand why you feel as though you can't sleep there. It's just a room, after all." August gasped suddenly, a playful smile forming on her lips. "Are you afraid it might be haunted? Is that it? I did not take you to be a believer of such things, but—"

Brooks silenced with her a kiss. "You talk too much," he grumbled against her lips before pulling away and sighing. She carefully watched him as his eyes drifted back toward the door that connected her room to his.

"You have never told me why you dislike your father," August said. Brooks turned back to her, his expression unreadable. "You *do* dislike him, don't you?"

They stared at each other for a long moment until Brooks finally shrugged. "I do not think of my father enough to like or dislike him." He leaned forward, pressing another kiss to August's lips. When he pulled away, their faces remained very close. He played with a strand of hair that framed her face. "Won't you like it if I stay here with you every night, sweet August?"

Slowly, August nodded, knowing she wanted him close; she couldn't help it. They fell asleep soon after that.

The following morning, Brooks was gone, probably already downstairs in his study working. Not ready to ring the bell for one of the maids quite yet, August reached over to the bedside table. She took out the stolen leather bound book from Hart House that she hidden in the drawer. August had been reading Lucy's diary in secret, feeling as though she finally had some measure of insight into Brooks's life from Lucy's words.

The diary was how she discovered the late Mr. Brooks was not the kind man she once thought he was. He was also a wretched abuser who drank too much, inclined to violence against his wife and son. Although Brooks would not tell her himself, August now knew where he had gotten those marks across his back.

As for Lucy's mysterious illness and death, that was less clear. She was approaching the last of the entries, and by that time, Lucy had fallen pregnant three times but had yet to have the baby she so desired. The later entries had become much shorter and slightly melancholic in tone, and August worried what she might discover at the end of the diary.

Suddenly, the door to August's bedroom opened, and Brooks appeared in the doorway. He smiled at first, but his face seemed to fall when he noticed the leather bound book in August's hands. She shut it tightly, trying to slow her racing heartbeat.

"What are you reading?" he asked, leaving the door open as he stepped toward the bed, all the while narrowing his eyes at her.

"N-nothing." August winced at the way she stuttered her response. She knew it had been wrong to take Lucy's diary from Hart House or even read it all, but there she was, feeling like a child who got caught stealing sweetmeats.

"I recognize that book," Brooks said, walking around to stand at his wife's bedside. He snatched Lucy's diary from her. "I gave it to my sister as a wedding gift."

Brooks flipped through the pages, then looked down at August. She could tell right away there was a growing fury inside of him. "Have you been reading my sister's diary?" August turned away, unable to look at him any longer. The tightness in her chest was becoming so unbearable that she thought she might cry, but her husband was relentless. "Answer me."

She looked back at her husband, frightened by his demanded tone. "I-I'm sorry. I only thought I might learn something about you by reading it."

Brooks appeared flabbergasted by her confession, and perhaps rightfully so. August swallowed, crossing her arms across her chest. "And did you?" he asked.

She crinkled her brow. "Did I what?"

"Learn something," he practically spat, his impatience growing.

August's face became warm, and she looked away. When she finally turned back, there were tears in her eyes. "I learned that your father used to beat you and your mother," she said. "I suppose that's where you got those scars, the ones you won't tell me about even though I'm your wife and see you naked every night."

Brooks's nostrils flared. "You had no right to read this— no right at all!" He brought his hands to his hips, still holding Lucy's diary. She expected him to yell at her more, but he only sighed, his shoulders drooping as he did. "Now I remember now why I never wanted to marry." He shook his head, and August waited, thinking he might have heard her heart pounding in the quiet bedroom. "You never truly know the person until it's too late."

He began to walk away, and August scrambled out of bed, following him. "Brooks!" He stopped in front of the door but did not turn to face her. "You seem to be forgetting that I do not know you at all either. I am sorry for what I did, but can you be sorry for always shutting me out and hiding things from me? I only wanted to understand you better." When

Brooks did not answer, August's face fell. "But I suppose that's impossible now. You will shut me out for good after what I have done."

He suddenly turned around then, and she took one step back, frightened by the anger on his face. "You're right," he said. August flinched, but Brooks continued anyway. "I will shut you out for good, just as I should have a long time ago. Perhaps I wouldn't have ended up with this sham of a marriage as a result!"

August glared at him. "Do not blame me for our marriage! You did not have to marry me. No one forced you, least of all me. I would have gladly been ruined and kept my money to myself instead of having some stupid husband. But now it all belongs to you—and you won't even let me do what I want with it!"

"It does belong to me, and rightfully so! I'm going to need that money if things continue as they do. Did you know I have lost ten clients because of your brother Charles?"

She frowned at him, shaking her head. "How could I have known that? You never tell me anything that's bothering you. You prefer to keep your pain to yourself, not caring at all how it might affect me or your mother or your friends."

He did not reply, and they fell silent, staring at each other. His eyes eventually fell on the unmade bed. He turned toward August. "Perhaps it's better if this marriage remains one in name only."

August furrowed her brow. "What do you mean?"

"I will not bother you tonight or any other night in the future." He glanced at the door that led to his father's bedroom, then back at August. "Do you understand?"

She did not answer at first, too surprised that their argument would end this way. When they disagreed about her inheritance a week ago, he had not merely cast her aside. Not like he was trying to do now. August stepped forward, one hand outstretched. "But Brooks—"

Brooks quickly maneuvered himself so he was out of her reach. She dropped her hand, letting it fall to her side. "I have work to do," he said eventually. "You should get dressed. My mother will expect you down for breakfast soon."

With that, he spun on his heel and left the room, closing the door behind him. August turned and walked toward the bed. She stood at its edge a moment, considering falling on top of it and loudly weeping. Instead, August walked toward the bellpull, pursing her lips. If Brooks did not want her, she would return to her aunt's house.

"I'll show you a sham of a marriage," she muttered to herself.

Chapter Twenty-Six

AUGUST ASKED AGATHA, who came with August from her aunt's to Dover Street, to tell Mrs. Brooks that she would take her breakfast in bed that morning. Then she had her show her the service entrance so she could slip out of the house undetected.

The day was fine, so August walked to Park Street, eager to see her aunt. Lady Ramsbury's butler seemed surprised to find August standing on the other end of the door when he opened it.

"I know it's early, but I must see my aunt," she said, stepping around him and into the entry hall. The butler nodded and had her wait there while he alerted her aunt to her unexpected arrival. August paced the entry hall, impatient.

When the butler appeared again, he motioned for her to follow him. He guided her toward the morning room, where August assumed her aunt was eating breakfast. She hoped the dowager duchess wasn't too cross with her for calling so early.

But August forgot all that when she discovered her aunt was not alone. Lord Ridlington sat at the morning room table with her. The marquess looked over his paper at her, grinning as she turned an awful shade of red. "Lady August! Or should I call you Mrs. Brooks now? What a pleasant surprise either way."

August glanced at her aunt, who did not quite meet her gaze. August turned back to Ridlington, feeling embarrassed. "I apologize, my lord. I have called much too early. I will return in the afternoon."

"Nonsense!" Ridlington exclaimed. He gestured to the seat across from him. "Sit down. How was your honeymoon?"

Her aunt still wouldn't acknowledge her, so August reluctantly sat down. "It was lovely, thank you."

"Would you like any breakfast?"

August shook her head. "I'm afraid I do not have much of an appetite this morning."

This seemed to capture her aunt's attention. The dowager duchess finally turned and looked at her, then turned back to the marquess. The two of them exchanged a look that August couldn't quite read. Ridlington turned back to August. "Ah," he said with a nod, folding his paper and placing it beside him. "What has our friend Brooks done now?"

August bristled. "What makes you think my husband has done anything?" she asked, turning toward her aunt, who wore a skeptical gaze. They stared at each other for a long moment before August finally burst into tears. The dowager duchess sighed, looking at Ridlington.

"Perhaps you ought to leave," she said. "Auntly duty calls, I'm afraid."

Ridlington reluctantly nodded. August watched through tears as he stood and bent over her aunt, pressing a single kiss to her cheek. August muttered apologies to the marquess as he turned to her next, handing her a handkerchief. When she tried to give it back to him, he shook his head, placing a hand on her shoulder and squeezing it.

"You keep it for now," he said. "I will have it back the next time I see you."

August nodded, watching him leave the room. She turned back to Lady Ramsbury, who carefully watched her niece with a concerned gaze. "What is the matter, dear?" she asked. "What has happened?"

August told her everything then—the scars across her husband's back and her discovery of Lucy's diary. She saw the disappointment in her aunt's eyes when August told her about taking and reading the latter. "You should have let him confess the issues with his father and sister himself," she firmly said. "You have forced his hand once more, and now he is upset."

"Once more?" August asked incredulously. Her aunt did not have to answer for August to realize the woman was referring to her marriage. August shook her head. "But that isn't fair! I didn't *force* him to marry me."

The dowager duchess shrugged. "Nevertheless, that's most likely how he's feeling at the moment. But you shouldn't fret, my dear. He will come around. He always does, doesn't he?"

August thought back to all the times she thought they would part, but Brooks remained anyway. It started from the moment he brought her to Linfield Hall to see her father, and he decided to stay to ensure she was comfortable with her new family. She never did understand it.

"Why, though?" August asked. "Why does he always insist on having me near, yet still at least an arm's length away?"

Lady Ramsbury tilted her head thoughtfully, considering the question. "It must be frightening to love someone when you grew up surrounded by such a tenuous relationship."

Love someone? August furrowed her brow. "That's where you're mistaken, Aunt," she replied, shaking her head. "Brooks does not love me."

"Give him time, August," the dowager duchess said with a nod. "Let him come to you. He always does."

Before August could respond, the butler appeared in the doorway once more. He cleared his throat. Her aunt toward him, furrowing her brow. "What is it?" she asked.

"Your other niece—Lady Rosamund—is here to see you, Your Grace," he said before glancing at August, whose face was blotchy from crying. "I'm afraid she seems upset as well."

Lady Ramsbury looked at her butler, confused. "Another distraught niece? There must be a full moon tonight." August looked at her aunt sheepishly, all the while wondering why Rosamund was there. "Show her to the drawing room. We will meet her there."

The butler nodded, then left the room. August and her aunt swiftly rose from their seats after he left. "Do you think it's Rutley?" August asked.

"I do not know, but I expect we are about to find out."

When they reached the drawing room, Rosamund was sitting on one of the settees. She wrung her gloved hands over her lap, looking surprised when she saw August with their aunt that morning. "Rosamund!" August exclaimed, moving toward her sister, who rose to greet her. They embraced. "Are you all right? What happened?"

Her sister looked from August to Lady Ramsbury, her gaze full of suspicion. "I could be asking you the same thing," she said. "What are you doing here?"

August dismissively waved her hand, not wanting to bring up her issues with her husband if Rosamund was there. What if Charles or Rutley had done something to her? "Never mind me. I was only having breakfast with our dear aunt. Is everything all right?"

Rosamund glanced back and forth between her aunt and her sister, shaking her head as she did so. Her lips trembled as she spoke. "I cannot do it. I cannot marry him."

"Are you certain?" Lady Ramsbury asked, guiding her older niece back to the settee and helping her sit. August took one of the chairs across from them. Meanwhile, her sister nodded.

"I will not throw my life away for Charles," she said, shaking her head. "Not after all he did. The incessant gambling is terrible enough, but after I heard his intentions for you and Swinton? As well as Mama outing Lady Sarah as your mother? I cannot do it."

"Have you told Charles this?" the dowager duchess asked.

"Yes," Rosamund replied with a nod. "He is furious. I suspect he will be following me here with my mother and the duke at any moment." She looked back and forth from her aunt and sister with pleading eyes. "You mustn't let them convince me to change my mind. I will be miserable if I marry Rutley."

August furrowed her brow. "But why, Rosamund? You once told the duke yes. You never explained to me why you changed your mind."

Her sister sighed. "I have loved Robert since I was a little girl, and I was thrilled when he proposed. But he kept pushing back the wedding date. It didn't take me long to discover why. He never did want to give up his wild ways until only recently when I threatened to cry off." August frowned. So the duke had been unfaithful. "He says he has changed, but I do not trust him. I *cannot* trust him."

"I understand," August replied softly. She looked toward her aunt, who had stood up again. She was pacing the room, carefully watching them.

"Are you certain about this, Rosamund?" Lady Ramsbury asked. "You will lose your dowry, your mother, your brother."

Rosamund nodded. "I understand, but I will have you—won't I?" Her gaze then traveled to August. "And you as well."

"Of course!" August exclaimed, moving to sit by her sister.

August reached for her hand, squeezing it, and the two younger girls then looked toward their aunt, who momentarily stopped pacing. The woman sighed.

"You can stay at Park Street however long you need," she told Rosamund. "Ridlington will be upset again, but my niece is more important than him." Rosamund looked at August, confused, but her half sister only shrugged in response. Rosamund would discover their aunt's secrets soon enough. Meanwhile, Lady Ramsbury reached for the handbell on one of the tables in the drawing room, ringing it. "I will have the servants go and gather your things."

SITTING AT HIS DESK, Brooks angrily stared at Lucy's diary. It was all he could do after his argument with August, though he would have liked to throw himself into his work instead.

Unfortunately, there was hardly anything to be done. After losing so many of his clients, Brooks did not have any appointments that day, even though he would have loved the distraction of someone else's problems.

It wasn't until the afternoon when he heard a light rapping at his door. Just as his mother entered his study, he quickly moved Lucy's diary from the top of his desk to one of its drawers.

"What is it?" Brooks asked, recognizing the concerned look on his mother's face right away. The older woman sat down in one of the armchairs across from his desk, sighing as she did.

"Your wife did not come down to breakfast," she said. "She took it in her room. Do you have any idea why?"

Brooks dipped his head and began rubbing his temples with his thumb and middle finger. He had told August that his mother was expecting her. She probably stayed in her room on purpose. His mother would now ask him questions until he finally had to admit he was wrong. He looked back up at her.

"No, I do not," he said, dropping his hand on his lap. His mother only narrowed her eyes at him.

"She has not been downstairs all day. Have you done something already, Samuel? You both appeared so happy when you returned yesterday."

Brooks rolled his eyes. "Why must you assume it's me who has done something wrong?" He thought of his wife stealing his poor sister's diary. "Perhaps *she* is the one who has done something wrong."

His mother laughed—she laughed! Brooks couldn't believe her audacity. "I doubt that very much," she said when she was through. Her son glared at her, then opened his drawer, reaching into it and pulling out his sister's diary. He dropped on the desk between them. His mother looked at it, confused. "What is that?"

"Lucy's diary. August found it at Hart House. She took it and has been reading it in secret for the past week, all because I would not tell her where I got the scars on my back." He shook his head, his temper rising. "This is one of the reasons I never wanted to get married! There are certain things I do not wish to share with anyone. *Anyone!*"

His mother grew pale. They had never spoken directly about his father's abuse, but Brooks could not stop himself this time. It was a conversation they never dared to have before, even though they desperately needed to, and he was tired of skirting around the subject. "I have always regretted being unable to shield you from your father's abuse," his mother said, her lips trembling. "I wanted to leave him, but I had nowhere to go. The best I could do was send you to Linfield Hall or Hart House whenever the Finches or Swintons would agree to it."

Brooks sighed. He knew it was never his mother's fault,

but that did not make him any less angry. "You did the best that you could do," he said. Their eyes suddenly met.

"Did I?" She paused a moment, looking down and shaking her head. "You always told me you do not believe in marriage, and I suppose I have never blamed you. You have not had many good examples to follow—that I understand. But I like to think your life was not devoid of love altogether." His mother looked up again, her discerning gaze landing squarely on him. "I surely did not fail so horribly as a mother that I left you incapable of loving a sweet girl like August."

He gestured toward the diary in protest. "But she—"

"But she dared to try and know you better than you are presently allowing her, even though she's your wife."

Brooks pursed his lips. "You do not understand."

"What don't I understand? That girl loves you, regardless of your scars or your uncanny ability to push people away. Do not let my dead husband's abuse stop you from being happy, Samuel. Have you even told her how Lucy passed?"

"We agreed not to tell anyone how Lucy passed."

And aside from Swinton and them, no one knew the truth. There was nothing but the long mysterious illness, actually an instance of acute melancholia that may have ended in suicide by laudanum. But they could never know what Lucy was thinking that evening before she went to bed. Perhaps she wanted to die—or maybe it was only a terrible accident.

"She is your wife," his mother said, interrupting his thoughts. "You cannot keep such secrets from her and expect a happy marriage." Brooks sighed. He knew his mother was right, but that didn't make him fear intimacy any less. "You must try, Samuel. For August's sake, you must try."

"I will go check on her then," he said, nodding. His mother's triumphant smile did not escape his notice as he left the room to head upstairs, but Brooks did not feel entirely out of the woods yet. When he reached August's door, he lightly knocked.

"August? May I come in?" He waited, but there was no answer. He knocked again. "August?" Still, there was nothing. Brooks tried to open the door, but his wife had locked it. He struck the door with his knuckles for a third time, much more loudly than before. "August! Let me in this instant."

"She's not there, sir."

Brooks almost jumped. He turned to find August's lady maid, Agatha, standing in the hallway. He narrowed his eyes at her. "What do you mean she's not there?"

"She left for her aunt's house on Park Street early this morning," Agatha explained. Brooks bristled. So she had tried to leave him already. Had she indeed given up that easily? "She asked me to take her through the back door and not say anything."

Brooks attempted to hide his embarrassment by nodding. He placed his hands behind his back and forced a smile. "Very well. Did she say when she would return?"

The maid shook her head. "No, sir."

Brooks nodded once, then went back downstairs, where he gathered his jacket and hat and immediately left for Park Street.

AUGUST DECIDED to stay at Park Street until someone inevitably came looking for Rosamund. She didn't know if it would be Charles, Lady Bolton, or the duke, but she expected someone would come eventually, especially after her aunt sent servants to Finch Place to gather Rosamund's things.

Sitting in the drawing room, the three women heard a commotion in the entry hall. They expected Charles or the duke to come barging into the room after that, but an angry-looking Brooks appeared instead, Lady Ramsbury's butler trailing closely behind him.

"Brooks!" August exclaimed, standing immediately. She saw her aunt and sister exchanged panicked looks out of the corner of her eye. "What are you doing here?"

His eyes widened. "What am *I* doing here?" he asked, wildly gesturing toward himself. "I could ask you the same thing! You left Dover Street without saying a word."

August refused to play the role of the villain this time. She would not feel guilty for leaving after what Brooks said to her. "Must I tell you all my comings and goings? I believe you were the one who said our marriage would be one in name only. Why should you care if I leave without a word?"

Her husband's nostrils flared, and he glanced at Lady Ramsbury and Rosamund. He was probably embarrassed that she would say such a thing in front of them, but she remained calm, sitting back down in her chair. Her aunt and sister sat very quietly across from her. "If you think I will let you run away from me, you are sorely mistaken. You must come with me back to Dover Street at once."

August raised her brow. "Who said anything about running away? Can you not see that we are in the middle of a crisis?"

It finally seemed to dawn at him that Rosamund shouldn't have been there either. His annoyance seemed to subside, and he looked at her, bowing slightly. "Lady Rosamund. What brings you to Park Street? Is something the matter?"

August answered before her sister said anything. "She is leaving the duke. My aunt has sent for her things. We are waiting for someone to arrive and cause a scene." She raked her eyes over Brooks. "Imagine my surprise to see you and not Rutley or Charles."

Her husband glared at her, then turned the dowager

duchess. "I apologize for the trouble my wife has caused you. I will be taking her back to Dover Street now."

"No!" August exclaimed. Brooks turned to her, his brow arched. "I will stay until I know my sister is safe here."

Brooks pursed his lips, then tossed his hat on one of the empty chairs. "Very well," he said. "I will wait with you."

They said nothing, sitting in silence. Every so often, August and Brooks's eyes would meet, but she would quickly turn away. She did not want to think of him or why he chose to follow her to Park Street. She was too concerned about her sister, especially when they heard a carriage stop in front of Lady Ramsbury's Park Street mansion a few moments later. August stood up, walking toward one of the front windows. She saw the duke step out first, followed by Lady Bolton and Charles.

"They are here," August told her aunt and sister. She turned back toward the window, discreetly watching their visitors until her eyes briefly met Lady Bolton's. She quickly backed away, returning to the room's center to sit with her aunt, sister, and Brooks.

Lady Bolton entered the room first, with Rutley and Charles following close behind her. The butler barely had time to announce the group before the countess addressed Rosamund directly. "Rosamund," she said, "you will abandon this silly game of yours and come with us this instant." She looked from her daughter to the duke, then back again. "The two of you will get married at the end of this month, just as you agreed to and wanted three years ago."

"No," Rosamund replied, her gaze and tone dripping with defiance. August and Brooks exchanged nervous looks. "It's too late."

"You little—"

Lady Bolton lifted her hand, turning her chin over her shoulder at her son, effectively silencing him. Charles looked like a little boy, sullen after being chastised. She turned back to the group sitting in the drawing room, her eyes eventually falling on Brooks and August.

"I should have known you two had something to do with this," she said, shooting them a vicious glare. Brooks scoffed.

"I had nothing to do with this," he muttered. He glanced at August. "I am only here because my wife wanted to support her sister."

Lady Bolton and August's eyes met. The younger girl stared back defiantly, refusing to be afraid of her father's widow. Eventually, Lady Bolton turned toward her daughter once more. "If you do this, you will lose your dowry. Your brother and I will disown you. You will not *find* a better husband than Lord Rutley."

But Rosamund shook her head. Her voice cracked as she spoke. "To think I no longer recognize my mother. You of all people should know why I can't marry him!" She shook her head again, narrowing her eyes at her mother. "At least you pretended to know before you discovered Linfield was at risk due to your own son's idiocy. I cannot marry someone who I know is incapable of honoring his vows!"

Rosamund looked at Rutley now, who stared back at her, jaw set. He appeared more disheveled than usual, and August suspected the man regretted whatever decisions had led to this moment of Rosamund finally leaving him. Her sister turned back to Lady Bolton. "Tell me, Mama, would you have agreed to marry Papa if you knew he would have taken mistresses?"

Lady Bolton paused. "Yes," she finally said. "Because it was my duty to bring honor to my family—to become a countess. Now you must bring honor to yours by becoming a duchess. Do your duty, Rosamund."

Rosamund made a sweeping gesture toward August, startling her aunt beside her. "What about your duty to honor my dead father's wishes? He told us to love August, to treat her as one of our own. It may have been a foolish wish from a dying man who felt guilty for his sins, but I have done as he asked. Can you honestly say you have done the same?"

"Do not bring her into this," Lady Bolton warned, though she did not look at August. Her eyes remained fixated on her daughter instead. "She is part of the reason we are in this mess. If my husband hadn't left her—"

Rosamund groaned, interrupting her. "This is not mine or August's fault. This is Rutley's fault for betraying me, and Charles's fault for gambling away twenty thousand pounds! Perhaps you ought to arrange his marriage for him instead of me or August." Her mother bristled, and Rosamund laughed slightly. "You did not think I was unaware of what you wanted Edward to do, did you? Our cousin told me everything." She shook her head. "I hardly even recognize you anymore."

Lady Bolton remained stone-faced as she addressed her daughter. "I would have been doing her a favor, allowing my nephew to marry her given her past."

August nearly said something to defend herself, but Rosamund loudly groaned before she could. "What happened to you? You used to be kind, but now you are a hypocrite, all over a son who is just like the man who betrayed you. I do not understand!"

"And what will I do when Rutley turns us out of the house?"

"What will any of us do when Charles falls into debt again?"

Lady Bolton moved to speak once more, but Rutley's booming voice pierced the room like the cannon, interrupting her. "Enough! No one will be turning anyone out of their houses." Lady Bolton turned to face him. Rosamund looked at him as well, her mouth hanging open slightly. Meanwhile, Charles still cowered behind the duke.

"Rosamund no longer wants to marry me, and nothing any of us can say will convince her otherwise."

August watched Rosamund's face, a mixture of confusion and surprise coloring her features as the duke spoke. "Lady Bolton, I will ensure your protection regardless of your son's financial situation. You do not need to bully your daughter into marrying someone she no longer wants." He turned to Charles next. "As for you, we will discuss your debt and how you might pay for it tomorrow morning. I release your sister from our engagement—no scandal necessary."

Everyone stared at the duke, completely speechless. Out of everyone, Rosamund appeared the most shocked. Her former fiancé turned to her last, approaching her at the center of the room. "I am sorry for the pain I have caused you, Rosamund. Consider this my first step in atoning for my sins. I hope one day, you might forgive me."

He took her hand and closed his eyes, bringing her knuckles to his lips and pressing a kiss there. When the duke let go, he nodded at Lady Ramsbury, then swept out of the room without another word. Lady Bolton and Charles remained in the drawing room, silent.

With a sigh, Lady Ramsbury rose from the settee. "I think it best if Rosamund stays with me for a while, Lady Bolton." The dowager duchess placed a protective hand on her niece's shoulder. "She will return to you when she's ready."

"Rosamund—"

"My aunt is right, Mother," she said, not allowing Lady Bolton to finish. "I wish to stay in London with my aunt and my sister nearby. I will write to you when I am ready to return to Linfield."

Lady Bolton turned toward her son, who remained surprisingly quiet throughout the entire exchange. "Come, Charles," she said. They swept out of the drawing room.

August suddenly remembered something, rising to follow

them into the entry hall. She found Charles and Rutley at the center muttering obscenities at each other. Lady Bolton stood off to the side, dabbing her eyes with a handkerchief.

"Charles," August called out, walking toward them. All three of them looked at her, each of them appearing equally confused to find her standing there. "How much of my inheritance must I give you so you will stop telling my husband's clients to take their business elsewhere? I do not think he will let me write a check for twelve thousand pounds, but perhaps we can strike a bargain."

Charles sputtered, seeming surprised by the offer. "W-what?"

August frowned at him. "You know, if you at least tried to be a good brother, I might have given you all of it before Brooks married me, but now, what's mine is his. You and I both know there's only so much I can do. He's quite stubborn."

Another voice joined the conversation. "I *am* quite stubborn—as are you."

August raised her brow, and she turned and saw Brooks standing behind her, not realizing he had followed her out in the entry hall. Surprisingly, he appeared to be smiling. He looked directly at Charles. "Unfortunately, I cannot allow my wife to give you anything, even if you do agree to her terms. My business will be fine with or without the Earl of Bolton."

Charles glared at him. Meanwhile, Rutley cleared his throat, looking at August as he did. "Nevertheless, I will make sure Charles keeps Mr. Brooks's name out of his mouth for as long as he owes me money."

August smiled up at him, suddenly feeling as sorry for him as she did for Rosamund. "Thank you, Your Grace."

The duke nodded at her, then both men replaced their hats and left through the front door, Lady Bolton following not far behind them.

Chapter Twenty-Seven

BROOKS AND AUGUST walked home in silence until they reached the front door of their home on Dover Street. It was then that Brooks reached for her hand, pulling her close before they walked up the front steps.

"Why did you leave without telling me?" he asked. He brought one hand to the side of August's face, tracing her jawline with his thumb. Her heartbeat quickened, especially when she realized he looked as if he might kiss her. She pulled away and looked down, not wanting to give in to her lust until they finally spoke.

"I thought you wouldn't care, but I was always planning on coming back." She looked back up, capturing his steady gaze with her curious one. "You knew that, didn't you?" He stiffened, and August frowned. Now she was the one reaching for his face, cupping his cheek with her palm. "I will always come back for you, Brooks, just like you will always come back for me." She shook her head. "I am sorry for reading Lucy's diary. It was wrong of me. I only hope you trust me one day to tell me the story yourself."

She forced a smile, then dropped her hand and turned,

walking back up the stairs. August tried to believe her aunt when she said Brooks would come around. Perhaps he might share his true self with her one day. But before she could get to the top of the stairs, he reached for her once more. She stopped, his fingers firmly wrapped around her wrist. "Wait," he said.

August turned to face him, surprised. She stepped down, standing on the step above him so that they were at equal heights. Releasing her wrist, his hands skimmed over the fabric of her dress until he found her waist. He held onto her and briefly turned his face away.

August knew he was trying to tell her something, so she gently put her hands on his shoulders, then slid them up to his neck, using her fingertips to force him to look at her. She frowned when she saw his blue eyes rimmed with tears.

"My father used to beat me with a birch rod, especially when he was drunk," he finally said. August's heart dropped into her stomach, and her mouth went dry. She had no idea what to say. "My mother used to love him, you know. What if I become like him?"

"Oh, Brooks," August said, pulling him close by wrapping her arms around his neck. "You will not become like him. It's not in your nature."

He began to sob into her chest, his fingers clutching at the fabric at the back of her dress. She ran her hand through his hair, and when he finally pulled away from her, he reached for her face and pulled it toward his, hungrily kissing her.

"I should have told you the moment you asked," he said when he eventually broke away. "You are my wife."

August smiled weakly. "A wife you did not want."

"You're right," he said. August's chest tightened, and she worried what he might say next. "I never desired a wife, but I always wanted you. Even if the incident at the ball never happened, it was only a matter of time. Don't you see, August?"

She shook her head. He smiled, bringing his lips to hers once more, kissing her gently. "I love you, August," he said once he broke away a few moments later, his fingertips still wrapped around her chin. "I know it took me a while to say so, but I'm not so stubborn that I can't admit it now. It's as clear as day that I do, even if it scares me."

August grinned, tears now pricking her eyes as well. "You love me? Truly?"

Brooks nodded. "Truly. And do you still love me?"

She pulled him onto the same step as her, then wrapped her arms around his waist and pulled him close. Leaning her head against his firm chest, she closed her eyes. As she listened for his heartbeat, she realized this man now belonged to her—body and soul. August sighed deeply.

"Still? I am afraid I will always love you, Samuel Brooks, even if you hurt me. Is that all right?"

He kissed the top of her head. "It's more than all right, but I will never hurt you—not purposefully, anyway." She chuckled against his chest. "I promise."

LATER THAT NIGHT, while they laid in bed, Brooks turned to August. He sighed, and she looked at him, furrowing her brow with concern. "What is it?" she asked.

"I have not told you what happened to my sister Lucy yet."

August's eyes widened, and she shook her head. "You do not have to tell me tonight. Tell me when you are ready."

But Brooks had to tell her. If they were to be husband and wife, there could be no secrets between them. So he explained everything. August listened carefully and took him into her arms when he finished. "It's not your fault, you know," she said, shaking her head. "Or Swinton's. You should forgive him—and yourself."

Brooks grunted. "Why should you care if I forgive Swinton?"

"He was your friend, wasn't he? We all need a friend, Brooks."

He didn't answer. As they laid close together, Brooks took his palm and ran it over her bare stomach. He worried about what would happen if August fell pregnant. She ran her fingers through his hair, slightly laughing as she did. He looked at her, confused.

"You are already worrying about me, aren't you?" she asked. Brooks wasn't sure what bothered him more, the fact that she read his mind or that she was teasing him. He glared at her.

"It's a husband's right to worry about his wife."

She arched her brow. "Is that so? Well, I do not like to worry—not too much, anyway. I do not know what the future holds, and I do not think fretting over it will do us much good."

He swung his leg over her hip and pulled himself on top of her. "Is that so?" he asked, pressing a kiss to her neck. She nodded, closing her eyes and smiling as he trailed a line of kisses down her chest. "Do you know how I like to prevent myself from worrying?"

"How?" August asked. He found one rosy nipple, and she gasped as he circled the point with his tongue before latching onto it with his soft lips. He gently sucked as his hand drifted downward, deftly pleasuring her with his fingers.

He positioned himself just above her, bringing his mouth close to her ear. "I like to fuck you," he whispered, sliding himself inside her welcoming body. She moaned as he filled her, her intimate muscles squeezing his length with each thrust. He groaned, eventually pulling out of her wet heat.

"What are you doing?" she asked. But Brooks didn't answer, standing up beside the bed, pulling August by the hips toward him. She yelped, and Brooks chuckled to himself, positioning her so that she was facing away from him, her pretty bottom on full display. He kneaded her soft, round flesh, bringing his cock to her slick entrance and mounting her once more.

August arched her back and threw back her head, and he reached around to her front, taking her breasts into his hands and twisting her nipples until they were two erect points. Her breathing became erratic, and he knew she was close to finishing. He reached between her thighs, finding the sensitive bundle of nerves at the apex of her sex.

"You are so beautiful," he murmured in her ear. She whimpered his name as her intimate muscles rapidly clenched and unclenched his cock. He buried his face against her soft hair and neck as she came. "I love you, August. I love you so much."

He followed her with a climax of his own not long after. When they climbed back into bed together, they were slick with sweat. August giggled to herself. "You were right," she said, turning to him and smiling. "I don't think I am worrying about a single thing right now."

"And I'll make sure you never do," he said, kissing the corner of her upturned mouth before they drifted off to sleep together.

Epilogue

BROOKS AND SWINTON did eventually reconcile, and when Christmas came, Brooks and August piled into a post chaise headed for Hart House in Surrey. Mrs. Brooks joined them, much to August's chagrin. Now that she was three months pregnant, her mother-in-law constantly fretted over her, always asking if she was comfortable or needed anything.

"I wish she wouldn't worry about me so much," August told Brooks privately while stopping for a change of horses at a posting inn. "I am not as fragile as she thinks."

Her husband's mouth twitched, and she glared at him, knowing he was about to make an inappropriate joke. "Perhaps she does not know our technique for worrying less. Do you think I should tell her?"

August playfully hit him on the chest. "You are incorrigible," she said. But then she thoughtfully tilted her head to the side. "However, maybe you have a point. Shall we play matchmaker for your mother next season?"

Brooks arched his brow. "I like the way you think, Mrs. Brooks. Let's find my mother a wealthy man, one that will take her far away from Dover Street."

August giggled.

"I heard that."

August jumped at the sound of the female voice. She smiled at her mother-in-law over her husband's shoulder. "We were only teasing, Mama."

Mrs. Brooks shook her head in reproach, turning back toward the carriage. August and Brooks exchanged mischievous looks, then joined her, continuing their journey to Hart House. Swinton was there to greet them when they arrived, as were Lady Ramsbury and Rosamund, who remained in the dowager duchess's care.

The last August had heard, Lady Bolton had been living with family friends. As for Charles, he never extended an invitation to Rosamund to go to Linfield Hall for Christmas. Truthfully, no one heard much of Charles over the past few months. He seemed content to hole himself away at Linfield with only his shadow for company.

Lady Sarah, Mr. Talbot, and their dog Jasper arrived not long after them, and as they sat around the dinner table that evening, August ran her palm over her swelling belly. She smiled, looking around at the room and happily realizing her babe would have a family from the very beginning.

August and Brooks stayed in the same room as their honeymoon, except when he woke early the next day, he gently shook his wife awake this time. She slowly opened her eyes, blinking as her vision came into focus. "What is it?" she asked.

"Will you come on a walk with me? I want to show you something."

August looked out the window, finding it was still almost dark behind the curtains. She turned back toward her husband. "Now?"

Her husband nodded. August climbed out of bed and changed into a warm walking dress and pelisse. She followed

Brooks out into the hall, taking the narrow stairs to the service entrance at the back of the house together. They walked through the garden, where the freezing temperatures had already killed most of that year's flowers. August shivered, and Brooks pulled her close, guiding her through the gate that led to the meadow behind the house. The sun began to peek over the horizon.

"Once the sun rises, it'll be warmer," Brooks reassured her. She nodded, and they went to the end of the meadow, where the road into the nearest village was. They followed it, and August could just make out a stone church in the distance, surrounded by a copse of oak trees. The churchyard was closed off by a low stone wall.

August was surprised when Brooks walked toward the gate of the churchyard. He opened it, going inside. She quietly followed him down a line of gravestones until he stopped at one in particular.

LUCY SWINTON
WIFE,
DAUGHTER,
AND SISTER.
1792 – 1815

"The last time I was here was our honeymoon," Brooks told her. She reached for his hand, standing beside him and quietly looking at his sister's grave with him. "I woke early the first morning and walked to see her." Brooks looked at her, appearing remorseful. "I should have taken you with me."

August glanced upwards, smiling at him. "Do not fret, darling. You took me this time. That's all that matters." She ran her hand over her stomach, leaning her head against her husband's shoulder. "Lucy would be a pretty name for a baby girl, wouldn't it?"

Brooks nodded. They stood there in silence, the three of them and Lucy, while the rest of the world slept. "I wish I could have met her," she murmured against his coat sleeve. He turned and looked at her, hooking his finger underneath her chin and tilting her head to face him.

"How do you do it?" he asked, his blue eyes wildly searching hers. August knitted her brows together, confused.

"How do I do what?"

"Make me love you more every single day."

August laughed slightly. "Although you call me stubborn all the time, I do consider myself rather easy to love."

"Is that so?" he asked, bending his head so that his lips softly grazed hers. August pulled away, smiling.

"Not in front of your sister," she teased.

Brooks loudly laughed, and August nervously looked back at the church, afraid the vicar might hear them. "Then let me take you back to bed. I believe we still have an hour or two before breakfast."

August cast a sidelong glance toward Lucy's headstone. "I should like to speak to your sister alone first." Her husband arched his brow. "Could you go stand over there?" She pointed toward the gate of the churchyard. Brooks half smiled at her, thinking she was joking, but August narrowed her eyes. "I am serious."

Brooks sighed. "If you insist."

She watched Brooks walk toward the gate of the churchyard, then turned back to the headstone. She felt a little silly, but there were certain things she wanted to say aloud. "I'm sorry I read your diary," she said softly. "I only wanted..."

August pursed her lips, unsure of what she was even trying to do. She looked at Brooks, who smiled at her from across the yard, before turning back to face Lucy's headstone. "I read what you wrote. You always said that you worried about him, even when you were ill. I wanted to make sure you knew he's better now, and I will always look out for him. I promise."

She turned away, walking toward Brooks at the entrance of the churchyard. She brushed away an errant tear forming in her eye. "Is everything all right?" he asked, reaching for her hand. She happily took it.

"Everything is perfect."

And so it was.

Acknowledgments

I would like to thank everyone who helped this process along, especially Melinda and Crystal, as well as Leni Kauffman, who illustrated and designed *Lady August*'s fabulous cover. I would also like to thank my partner, Chris, as well as my family, friends, and my newfound fans from around the world, whose kind messages motivated me when I wanted to give up. Listening to Taylor Swift and Carly Rae Jepsen on repeat helped as well, though I doubt they'll ever read this. And in case you're wondering, yes, I named August after the best song off *Folklore*.

As it turns out, writing your second book is far more difficult than writing your first book, but I'm so glad *Lady August* is finally out in the world, ready for readers to enjoy it. Brooks and August are two of the most special characters I've ever written about, as they both contain little pieces of me and my life experience. I hope you love them as much as I do.

About the Author

Becky Michaels is a historical romance author and self-proclaimed Anglophile. After graduating from Boston University with a degree in English, she reluctantly decided to get a day job but never stopped writing—or dreaming. *THE LAND STEWARD'S DAUGHTER*, a Regency romance set in 1815 England, is her debut novel. Despite the cold winters and high rent, she still lives in the Boston area with her boyfriend and cat.

Also by Becky Michaels

The Land Steward's Daughter

Lightning Source UK Ltd.
Milton Keynes UK
UKHW011158300321
381250UK00003B/879

9 781735 140131